A matter of trust

In slow motion his head was bending toward hers, as though he were compelled by an outside force to kiss her.

She was so caught up in the physical sensations that she barely heard him mutter, "Damn, I hope you're not involved in this mess. I don't know if I could handle that."

His mouth was a hairsbreadth from hers when she gave him a hard shove in the chest. Springing to her feet, Rachel cried, "How can you try to kiss me when you don't even trust me! It's—it's deceitful!"

Looking dazed, Luke stood. "Deceitful? What are you talking about? You know I want you. And you know why I can't let myself totally trust you, no matter how badly I wish I could! Damn it, Rachel, try to understand."

Dear Reader,

When two people fall in love, the world is suddenly new and exciting, and it's that same excitement we bring to you in Silhouette Intimate Moments. These are stories with scope, with grandeur. The characters lead the lives we all dream of, and everything they do reflects the wonder of being in love.

Longer and more sensuous than most romances, Silhouette Intimate Moments novels take you away from everyday life and let you share the magic of love. Adventure, glamour, drama, even suspense—these are the passwords that let you into a world where love has a power beyond the ordinary, where the best authors in the field today create stories of love and commitment that will stay with you always.

In coming months look for novels by your favorite authors: Maura Seger, Parris Afton Bonds, Linda Howard and Nora Roberts, to name just a few. And whenever you buy books, look for all the Silhouette Intimate Moments, love stories *for* today's women *by* today's women.

Leslie J. Wainger
Senior Editor
Silhouette Books

Kay Bartlett
A Shiver of Rain

Silhouette Intimate Moments

Published by Silhouette Books New York

America's Publisher of Contemporary Romance

SILHOUETTE BOOKS
300 East 42nd St., New York, N.Y. 10017

ISBN: 0-373-07254-6

First Silhouette Books printing September 1988

Printed in the U.S.A.

KAY BARTLETT

has a B.A. in history and a master's degree in librari-
anship. She gave up being a public librarian to write
full-time, a dream that changed somewhat with the
arrival of her first daughter! Now she writes during
nap times and evenings, but she has managed twelve
books that way, including a Regency romance and five
novels for young adults. She lives with her husband
and two young daughters (plus three dogs and four
cats) in a rural area north of Seattle, Washington.

For story ideas she has drawn on her own background and interests. She has traveled widely, been a
ski racer and competitive swimmer, and enjoyed
mountain climbing and her volunteer work with troubled teenagers. Most of all, she loves to read, which is
why she became a writer in the first place!

Prologue

Lady, I'm not interested in your problems, but you'd better start getting interested in mine."

The man leaning in the open doorway of Rachel's office had probably once been stocky, but he was now running to fat. *Plump,* Rachel thought. *But not pleasantly.* Not at all. The expression in his eyes was enough to give her the willies.

"Because I'd do a lot for that money," he continued. "I'd rather not be rude enough to spell it out, but you get my drift, don't you? So why don't we leave it this way? I'm going to be a trusting fellow and assume you're telling me the truth. You don't know what Jack did with my money. But if you want to find it badly enough, I think you will. And you do want to, don't you?"

He hadn't raised his voice or changed its pitch, but for the first time Rachel felt a frisson of fear ripple down her spine. Until his last words, it hadn't occurred to her to be frightened. Sure, his appearance had startled her, and heaven knew his story was wild enough, but there'd been nothing menacing in his manner.

Now she was uneasily conscious of their isolation. It was after ten in the evening, and she was alone with him in the big old lodge. The guest rooms upstairs were shut for the winter; the kitchen employees had finished for the night and gone. The light in her small cubbyhole of an office was a fragile bubble in the black cavern of the rustic common room, which was a friendly place in the sunlight. But now shadows stirred in the unseen corners as a ghostly thread of chill air wafted from the enormous stone fireplace.

It struck Rachel that fear wasn't a wise emotion to reveal at the moment. So she pretended not to notice the change in atmosphere. Using a voice of careful reason, she said, "Please, listen. I *am* telling you the truth! Jack couldn't possibly be the man you're looking for! He ran this resort for years. If he had any extra money, there'd be some sign of it. So—"

His face twisted and he took a step forward. "He's not going to take it from me! I won't let him cheat me from the grave! I won't let *you* cheat me! I want my money!"

Rachel shrank back in the hard wooden office chair. So much for reason. "I'll look," she said quickly. "I promise. But . . . but you have to give me time."

For a petrifying moment she thought she'd waited too long to humor him. But at last he relaxed, the insane fury fading from his face. Then he smiled. Rachel wished he hadn't when she saw the effect of his pudgy cheeks pooching amiably below those cold eyes. "Good," he said with satisfaction.

"Ah . . ." She struggled for a casual, businesslike tone. "Why don't you check back with me?"

His chuckle raised goose bumps down her spine. "Oh, I'll be calling," he said. "And visiting. Regularly. See, I'm going to want progress reports. So don't waste time. And if you've got any bright ideas about the police, forget them. Even if they could find me, what could they do?'' He spread his hands. "Nothing. And they couldn't protect you forever, now could they? So just find it, okay?''

Fortunately, he didn't wait for an answer. As suddenly and silently as he'd appeared, he was gone.

Rachel started to her feet, then stopped. There was no way she could bring herself to step from the friendly light into the darkness. What if he was still standing out there somewhere, watching? Crouching, maybe, behind one of the massive couches. She listened for the sound of the door and didn't hear it. No, she'd sit down again and at least look as if she was finishing her paperwork. Then she could lock up and sidle the few steps along the wall to her own apartment. From there she'd call the sheriff. He'd been a friend of her dead husband's; he would know what to do. But right now she'd just pretend that the darkness wasn't out there, that there were no watching eyes.

Chapter 1

Rachel pushed open the plank door of the log cabin, which was one of the dozen that lined the bluff. Once within, she automatically noted the sand on the bare wooden floor, the empty beer cans overflowing the wastebasket, the tangled bedding and encrusted stove. Cleaning up after the guests was her least favorite job around the resort, but by this time of year, when the tourist season was ending, it no longer made sense for her to keep on so many employees. Since her own work was tailing off, too, she had time to do some of the dirty jobs.

Instead of going to work right away, however, she paused uneasily, listening to the silence. Only the familiar muted roar of the never-ending surf came to her ears. At least half of the thirty cabins were rented out this week, but the resort might as well have been deserted. No cars went by on the narrow lane that gave access to the cabins, nor could she hear any voices.

Crossing to the sliding glass door, Rachel looked past a wind-twisted fir that clung to the edge of the steep bluff. Beyond, the vast gray Pacific Ocean today echoed the chill gunmetal color of the sky. Paler mist played with the foaming crests of the waves. One solitary dark figure was out walking along the tide line, shoulders hunched and head down, too far away for Rachel to identify. The scene was enough to send a shiver through her.

But then she made an impatient sound. Darn it, she *liked* this late-fall season, when the beginning of the rains kept the tourists away and she could look forward to four months of peace and quiet. She refused to let the vague threats of one crank hang over her, making her see the bleakness instead of the beauty. If she wasn't stronger minded than that, she ought to be! Anyway, she was being particularly absurd right now. However gloomy the day, it was midafternoon, and there were bound to be guests in some of the cabins not far away. She knew for a fact that Brenda, her teenage helper, was cleaning a unit on the other side of the loop. If she wanted to indulge in an attack of nerves, she should save it for the middle of the night, when she was alone in the huge, ancient lodge. Then there might be good reason for it!

"Don't give yourself ideas!" she muttered. The sound of her voice took her by surprise, seeming almost to echo in the empty room. Rachel felt foolish, talking to herself. She couldn't resist a furtive glance over her shoulder to verify that she was still alone. That made her more impatient with herself. "That's enough!" she said loudly, defying her own fears as well as the silence.

Giving herself a brisk shake, she went determinedly to work, stripping the beds first and dumping the sheets and blankets in the bin on the maid's cart she'd left just outside the front door. As she began energetically to scrub the kitchenette that occupied one end of the main room, Rachel made herself plan the rest of her day. Business might be winding down, but she had plenty to do.

Still thinking, she went into the minute bathroom to collect the wastebasket liner and bent to pick up several crumpled tissues that lay discarded on the floor. She wondered with exasperation why people turned into such slobs when they were away from their own homes. Did they *like* the idea of other people crawling around behind them, picking up?

In the act of straightening, she suddenly froze. Had she heard the crunch of gravel outside? Before she could decide, the cart creaked and a footstep sounded in the doorway.

"Hello?" said a deep, male voice. "Is someone here?"

It wasn't *that* man again, she was sure. His voice had been peculiarly flat, the lack of resonance noticeable. Rachel's tension dissipated enough to allow her to step out of the bathroom. "Yes?" she responded with deceptive calm.

A stranger stood in a relaxed way just inside the cabin door, his hands in the pockets of his loose-fitting khaki pants. His soft brown hair was on the short side but ruffled, as though he frequently ran his fingers through it. Rangy and loose-limbed, he was a tall man who looked as though he would be incapable of moving quickly. His face was a little too bony, but an interesting mélange of angles and planes and shadows was dominated by narrowed gray-green eyes that studied her in return with interest. Rachel liked him on sight. She was also aware of a quiver in her stomach that told her liking might easily be the least of it. That surprised her.

Still, with more confidence she asked, "What can I do for you?"

"I'm looking for Rachel Brewer."

Pushing her curls back from her forehead with her free hand, she smiled. "I'm Rachel."

She'd no sooner spoken than his expression changed and, with it, her assessment of the stranger. For just an instant he looked disconcerted, as though she wasn't what he'd expected. But then his face hardened, became unreadable. He still appraised her but coldly and with distance now. Rachel stiffened, resisting the urge to step back a pace.

The smile that touched the man's lips, but not his eyes, was too perfunctory to be warming. He gave an equally cool nod. "My name is Warren. Luke Warren. I'm here on official business."

Rachel stared blankly at the metallic shield he extended toward her. What on earth could the U.S. Government want with her? Her mind took a panicky leap to last year's tax return, but she couldn't recall anything about it that would attract anyone's attention. Besides, didn't the IRS have their own agents?

Then her mind cleared. She'd called the sheriff about her frightening visitor with his strange story. Although the sheriff had been nothing but reassuring to her, he must have notified somebody. It gave her a funny feeling in her stomach to realize that the man was a serious enough criminal— or sufficiently crazy —to have the federal government interested in him.

"Are you here about that man?" she said straight out.

There was a flicker in his eyes, as though she'd surprised him. It was a moment before he answered, "Yes, indirectly. That is, if we're talking about the same man. Walt Krupinski?"

"Is that his name?" Rachel asked. "Walt Krupinski?" It sounded so ordinary. She tilted her head to one side as she tried in her mind to attach the name to that one particular face. She saw again those round cheeks, the high forehead and thinning brown hair. But most of all she pictured his eyes. She remembered the saying that eyes are the window to the soul. Well, his had been more like mirrors, cold and shiny and without depth.

With determination she swept the image from her mind. "I really don't know why you want to talk to me," she said. "I'm afraid I can't add anything to what I told the sheriff."

"The sheriff?"

Rachel's eyes narrowed. "You're not here because of the sheriff?"

As the tall man looked at her, his face was wiped clean of all expression until his eyes were as opaque as the ocean during gray winter days. In a stiff, deliberately formal voice he said, "I'm here to facilitate the recovery of the gold your husband was . . . uh, holding."

"Gold?" Rachel's throat closed and she retreated first one step, then another. "Not you, too!" Was she the only one who hadn't gone crazy? What in God's name was this all about?

He took in her reaction with clinical interest. "Ah. Then you have talked to Walt."

She hated him then for what he was doing to her, for the lack of kindness in his eyes. But she said tightly, "He did all the talking. Except that he didn't warn me to expect you."

"No." He actually smiled then, though it didn't in the slightest warm that granite countenance. How could she at first sight have thought his face was mobile and interesting?

"But you see," he continued, "Krupinski doesn't know that I followed him. He thinks we've lost interest in him."

Rachel knew deep in her heart that she didn't want to hear what this man had to say. But she gave up. "I don't understand," she said helplessly. She walked the few steps over to the unmade bed and sank down at its foot.

Luke Warren strolled farther into the room. Stopping a few feet away from her, he rested one elbow on the heavy old chest of drawers and leaned there, looking down at her. "What is it you don't understand?"

Her hand fluttered. "Everything. What do you want from me?"

"Your cooperation," he said without any particular emphasis. He sounded perfectly relaxed and casual.

Rachel waited.

"What did Walt tell you?" he asked.

Even before she answered, Rachel knew he wasn't going to believe her, or at least was going to withhold judgment. She'd never been looked at like that before, as though she were a suspect in a criminal lineup. She didn't like the feeling. But she was shaken enough not to tell him off, which she might have under other circumstances. Instead, she said truthfully, "Very little. First he asked for Jack, and when I told him Jack was dead, that he'd died almost a year ago in a car accident, he seemed mad. He said he wouldn't believe me, except he'd been watching the place and hadn't seen him. Then he started going on about this money, millions of dollars. He said he wanted his share, that Jack wasn't going to get by with keeping it all. That *I* wasn't going to get by with it. I tried to tell him that he had the wrong man, that I didn't know anything about that kind of money, but he wouldn't listen. He told me to find it. He said I'd *better* find it. And . . . and then he promised to be back."

Luke listened in silence. It was a good story, maybe even true. So far as it went. It sounded like Walt Krupinski, all right. The real question was, what had she said to him in return? Or had she played the innocent with Walt, too, hoping to pull a fast one? Or—in justice he had to consider the alternative—*was* she innocent? He had no way of knowing whether her husband had let her in on the secret. Hell, she looked properly confused, anxious . . . and so strikingly beautiful she'd put him off his stride for a minute. He hadn't expected that. In a way it just contributed to his suspicion of her. Why would a woman who looked like her marry a loser like Jack Brewer, unless there was money in it?

"Walt didn't have the wrong man," he said evenly. "I can tell you that much. Your husband was a free-lance pilot. We knew him as Bill Sand. The CIA hired him a few times, for jobs they didn't want to dirty their hands with. He worked for other interests, too. Mostly our people turned their heads."

She looked dazed for a moment, then, as quickly as a forest fire ignited, furious. "You're crazy!" she cried. "I was married to him! We lived here year round! Are you suggesting that I was in on it, too? Or maybe you think he sneaked off to someplace like Nicaragua in the middle of the night and was back by breakfast so I wouldn't suspect anything?"

If the situation hadn't been so difficult, Luke would have enjoyed watching her. With that tall, too thin model's body and those perfect cheekbones, why wasn't she gracing the cover of a high-fashion magazine? With her eyes flashing like that and indignant color in her cheeks, her looks were so vivid they would have leaped off the page. And why was he thinking about that? *Damn it,* he was getting distracted, and with her he couldn't afford to.

Working hard not to sound as though he was interrogating her, he asked, "How long were you married?"

He suspected she would have liked to spit in his eye, but instead she compressed her lips and finally answered grudgingly, "Two-and-a-half years."

He'd known the answer, as he knew an uncomfortable amount about Rachel Brewer and her dead husband, but he'd wanted her to hear her own words. Now he said quietly, "Precisely two years and nine months ago, Bill Sand disappeared after doing a job in Central America." He waited for her to take that in, then added, "When he disappeared, he took a pile of gold with him. A pile of gold that belongs to the U.S. Government."

"You're crazy," she said again, but it sounded weaker this time. "Jack has run Sahale for years." She looked around at the cabin as though its solid presence reassured her, added weight to her words. "All you have to do is ask the locals. He inherited the resort from his father."

Luke shoved his hands into his pockets. On one level he was suspicious as hell of her. On another he felt like a class-A heel. "We did ask around," he told her. "You're right. He ran the place for years. From April until elk season ended, in November. Then he shut it down and left town for four months. Said he was looking for the sun. Well, he found it. Bill Sand only popped up in the winter. Mostly in Central America, the Caribbean. Sometimes as far as South America, if there was a hot spot. Face it, Mrs. Brewer—your husband was moonlighting."

Her implacable gaze met his. "I don't believe you."

"You'd better start," he said almost gently. "Because it's the truth. And I've been assigned to get that money back if I have to tear this place apart. We were prepared to be patient, just to keep an eye on everyone connected with your husband. But only until Walt made his move. I'm not going to let him beat me to it."

He watched her get up abruptly and walk away from him, to stand staring out the glass doors at the ocean, which was stark today under the cold sky. Her back was slender and very straight, her head high. The only sign of emotion was the movement of her fingers, pushing nervously through her unruly dark hair.

Inside, Rachel was churning with outrage, grief and disbelief that this was happening. She tried to focus on the ocean, reaching for the peace it usually offered her. But she could see Luke's faint reflection in the glass, an insubstantial reality laid over the more vivid one beyond. And it was his presence that her nerves were attuned to, his deep soft voice that shook her. She watched as he pushed away from the bureau and came toward her.

Rachel whirled to face him before he could come too close. Her naked anger stopped him, as she'd intended it should. "Tell me," she said, her voice searing her throat. "Why is this gold buried in a hole somewhere, if my husband went to the trouble of stealing it? Why did Jack spend years scraping by on the rainy edge of the world when he could have been living it up on the French Riviera? Tell me that, since you're so damned sure about everything."

Her scathing sarcasm struck a nerve. "Maybe it was for the love of a good woman," Luke said softly, unforgivably.

They stared at each other for a taut instant. Then Luke looked away, continuing after a moment in a level voice, as though the last byplay hadn't happened. "I think he was lying low. If we ran him to earth, here he'd be, living his normal life. Once we'd given up, he could take off for the Riviera, or whatever he had in mind."

Rachel pressed her hands to her temples and shook her head. "This is a nightmare. You're asking me to believe, without a shred of evidence, that my husband was a mercenary and a crook! That we lived together for almost three years as husband and wife without him ever telling me about his past, or at least mentioning that our retirement was assured. No." She shook her head again. "I don't believe it. I won't!"

"We have evidence."

Her face felt stiff with anger, so that it was an effort to speak normally. "Do you have a picture?"

"Of Bill Sand? No. I wish I did."

"I want you to go away," she said. "And I want you to take Walt Krupinski with you."

"It's not going to be that easy, Mrs. Brewer." The words were said quietly, without any particular force, but it was impossible for her to take them lightly.

Rachel realized that somehow he had moved without her noticing, so that now he stood only a few feet in front of her. She felt hemmed in by his big frame, and she had no doubt that was how he intended her to feel. Perhaps he would simply stand aside, let her walk by if she chose, but she doubted it. He was trying to unnerve her, she thought. He wasn't succeeding, not in the way he intended. Nonetheless, she reached back and slid one of her hands along the cold glass behind her, groping for the lock.

Her expression must have given away her intention, or at least the creeping fear within her, which she didn't understand and which had nothing to do with him. Because his expression changed and he suddenly stepped back, as though consciously giving her breathing space. "Are you afraid of me?" he asked.

"Should I be?"

He frowned. "No. Did Krupinski threaten you?"

Rachel shivered, feeling as though she'd just been brushed by a cold breeze. "Not specifically," she said. "I mean, we didn't talk about how it feels to have your fingernails torn off. He said..." She stopped. "Would he *do* something like that?"

"Tear your fingernails off?" Luke's mouth tightened, and Rachel had the impression he was turning over possible answers in his mind. She felt sure that no matter what he believed about her, he would have liked to reassure her. But instead, sounding both reluctant and grim, he said, "I consider him a dangerous man. Unfortunately, there's not a damn thing I can do about it. He hasn't committed a crime that I can prove. But Rachel..." It was the first time he had used her name, she thought. "Stay away from him."

Rachel wrapped her arms around herself for comfort. "I'd love to."

After another frowning instant, Luke backed up and sat on the edge of the double bed. When he patted the spot beside him, Rachel hesitated.

"Come and sit down," he said, his voice sounding deliberately nonthreatening. "I'm not done, you know. Let's talk like reasonable adults."

"Reasonable adults?" she spat back at him. "If you were reasonable you wouldn't be here! You have the wrong man, and you're not listening to me!"

His dark brows arched in a particularly infuriating way. "But I can hardly take your word for it," he said in a voice he might have used to explain a very simple point to a three-year-old. "You were married to Jack Brewer. It's surely natural that I would regard your opinion with a certain amount of...caution."

"Caution?" As what he was really saying sank in, renewed outrage swelled in Rachel's breast until she could barely speak. "You mean, you think *I* have the money."

He rose to his feet as though needing to physically dominate her as well. "I have to consider that as a possibility," he agreed calmly.

"Go away," Rachel whispered, her voice hoarse. Even as she said it, she knew better. Luke Warren wouldn't be an easy man to dismiss. He wasn't going to disappear like some bad dream.

"No," he replied.

Rachel had nothing more to say. She stood there, rigid, feeling battered by his presence, by his accusations and his certainty. And it all made no sense. God, it made no sense!

Jack had had his faults; she couldn't lie to herself about that, even though he was dead now and she tried hard to remember only the good about him. And it was true that he had been a pilot in Vietnam, so he had certainly known how to fly. But the rest... No. He was too unimaginative, too unadventuresome, too ordinary. He'd never shown the least sign that he craved wealth. In his taciturn, even harsh way, Rachel thought he had been satisfied with his life. She found it impossible to conceive that in those last months Jack had been scheming to make liquid a stolen fortune. And for what purpose? He wouldn't have just walked away from Sahale. And he certainly wouldn't have left her. He'd *loved* her in his own, peculiar way.

Rachel suddenly realized that Luke was talking and had been for some time. "What?" she said. "I didn't hear."

He broke off. "Are you listening now?" His tone was one of careful patience. She nodded. "All right, then. What I said is that I'm going to stay here. It's time to go over this place with a fine-tooth comb. What I'd really like is to lay a little trap and catch Krupinski red-handed, but I'll settle for just finding the money."

Rachel reacted with alarm. "You can't! This is private property, and I won't let you! It's my life! It was Jack's, too, and I won't have you poking around in his grave!"

Her melodramatic tone sparked a flash of humor in Luke's eyes. So lightly she wasn't sure whether he meant it, he said, "Oh, I'll dig that up, too, if I have to."

"Damn you!" she said, tasting bitterness in her mouth.

This was a part of the job Luke had never liked. He liked it even less than usual today. If this woman wasn't as innocent as the dawn, she was a remarkable actress hiding her talent in a strange corner of the world. Or perhaps not so strange, he reminded himself. The missing gold offered an incentive not even Hollywood could match.

Nonetheless Luke backed down, letting her fury slide off him. If she honestly knew nothing about her husband's past, all of this must have come as a terrible shock to her.

"Rachel—Mrs. Brewer," he corrected himself, wondering why it was so hard to think of her as someone's widow. "I'm sorry. I'm not here to upset you. I shouldn't have said what I just did. But the fact is I can't just walk away. You asked me earlier what I wanted from you, and I told you. Cooperating with me is the best way you can show me you know nothing about this."

"What if I don't care what you think?" She was still bristling like a porcupine.

He wanted to soothe her, not confront her. But he didn't have a choice; this was his job. He did it the best he could. "Do you care what the community thinks?" he asked with calculation. "I can leave today and come back with a search warrant. Or you can let me look quietly. Nobody ever needs to know what Jack Brewer was."

"Are you threatening me?" she inquired. He couldn't help noticing that the hollows under her cheekbones looked deeper, her full mouth pinched and her eyes shadowed.

"No," he said steadily. "I'm telling you the truth. Damn it, you can look at it this way. If you're so all-fired sure your husband was innocent, prove it to me! Let me stay! If we can't find anything, anything at all, I'll have to go away, won't I? You can show me you're right."

She stared at him, and he could almost see the wheels in her head turning. Luke felt a little uncomfortable with himself. He *knew* Jack Brewer was guilty. She wasn't going to prove anything else to him. On the other hand, if she *thought* she could ... Well, sometimes any means were justified.

But it wasn't quite that easy. Because she still hadn't agreed. She just stood there, the suspicion in her eyes almost masking the distress that lay beneath. She needed a last nudge, and he gave it.

"Rachel, I'm not the only one you have to convince. Let's not forget Krupinski. I wish I could lock him up and throw away the key, but as things stand, I can't. And he worries me where you're concerned. If I'm here, that'll keep Walt away. And if we find the gold, he won't be interested in you anymore. If we don't, he'll give up, too. Let me protect you, Rachel."

He sounded so sincere. Rachel found herself wishing unreasonably that he really was, that this wasn't all a ploy to make her fall into line. But what difference did it make? She didn't have to like him or even respect him. He wouldn't be here long. She would put him in one of the cabins, pretend he was a guest and ignore his wanderings. That was all he was asking—no, *demanding*—of her. Clearly she had no choice but to agree. The idea was unpalatable, but it came to her then that she hadn't had a real choice from the moment he'd walked in the door.

"Very well."

Of course that wasn't the end of it. It was barely the beginning. Later, as she went through the motions of making dinner for herself, Rachel remembered.

Luke didn't want to be checked into a bluffside cabin and left to his own devices. "It would be better if I worked here," he suggested. "It might look funny if a guest is poking around too much."

Her muscles limp and her mind quiescent, she had felt as drained as if she'd just returned from climbing Mount Olympus. She had a hazy sense that there were questions she probably should have asked. She didn't even understand who Walt was, what he had to do with anything. But right now she didn't care.

"But I don't need any help," she argued weakly. "What would look funny to people is if I took you on right after I've let all the seasonal workers go."

"Couldn't you be training me for next year?"

He was like a fly buzzing around her head. Why couldn't he just be *satisfied*? Nonetheless, she considered the idea. She was vaguely relieved to think of a counter to it. "But you'd have to really work. I thought you were here to search."

"Surreptitiously," he reminded her. "If I can manage it. I don't mind helping you out."

Her first instinct was to refuse, to fight him tooth and nail again. A masquerade such as he was suggesting would mean even more involvement with him than she'd been imagining. But fighting would do her no good; she knew that. Besides... An appealing picture crept into her mind of herself giving him orders, with a snap of her fingers putting him to work at the worst jobs around the place—emptying the septic tank?

Even so, her agreement was more grudging than enthusiastic. "All right. I'll put you in the smallest cabin near the lodge. We'll pretend I'm training you to be my assistant. But I warn you, the work here is hard. Being the assistant, or even the boss, doesn't mean you don't dirty your hands."

"Are you threatening me?" he asked with a sudden gleam of mockery in his eyes.

She didn't smile. "Yes."

He crossed his arms as he moved his gaze lazily over her. It was a moment before he nodded. "I'll take the job, thanks. And I should warn you, I never let a tough boss drive me away."

Rachel shrugged to express her indifference. Indifference she wished she could really feel. "I may set new standards. In fact..." She grabbed the broom from where she'd earlier leaned it against the wall. Taking a step forward, she thrust the handle unceremoniously at him. "Why don't you finish up in here? You don't need to make the bed—I don't expect anybody for this cabin tonight. But otherwise it should be spotless. If you don't mind."

Inside, she trembled at her effrontery. For God's sake, the man was a federal agent on an investigation, and she was goading him, trying to assert some minuscule authority she knew darn well he'd never allow her, no matter what role they were to play.

She didn't even succeed in getting a rise out of him. All he did was shake his head and chuckle. "Mrs. Brewer, you have nerve. I'll give you that. But don't get too used to giving orders, okay? I don't always take them very well." With that he leaned the broom against the wall and started to walk toward the door.

Rachel's heartbeat accelerated with a rush, although whether from hope or anxiety she wasn't sure. Yet she managed to sound casual as she spoke, stopping him just before he disappeared. "Don't tell me you don't like your new job already."

Luke glanced over his shoulder with apparent surprise. "Like it? Why wouldn't I?"

She frowned. "Then where are you going?"

"To change clothes, of course. You don't expect me to clean house in my good ones, do you?" With that he was gone.

Rachel was left to grapple with an inexplicable reaction she could interpret only as relief. And that, she told herself, was downright stupid. Luke might protect her from Walt, as he'd promised. But the price he would ask in exchange was going to be too high. Today's capitulation was only the down payment. And for what? Protection from a man she might never hear from again? No, what she was paying for was a promise to shield her dead husband's good name. Rachel's mouth twisted a little as she thought about that. She'd really hadn't had a choice. That much at least she owed Jack.

Chapter 2

Her gaze fixed unseeingly out the window, Rachel lifted her mug to take a sip of the strong, unsweetened tea. With luck this second cup might galvanize her into action. The day was waiting out there, even if all she felt like doing was crawling back under her covers to make up for last night's sleeplessness.

She sat before the old oak table in the dining nook of her apartment, which was a wing of the old lodge. The view through the small-paned windows that wrapped the nook was one that nearly always inspired her. The Sahale, a creek that carried snow runoff from the Olympic Mountains, curved around the north end of the lodge. Once it passed under a weathered pier bridge that led to more of the cabins, it emptied into the Pacific Ocean. At low tide, like this morning, as it crossed the beach the Sahale spread into a wide, shimmering ribbon so shallow that children could splash their way across it. Strange swirls in the sand marked the creek's meeting with the grasping fingers of the ocean.

A dragon's spine of rocks was exposed by the low tide, attracting some eager children who peered into the tide pools. Beyond were the stacks, those mysterious islands of rock that had been eroded into majestic isolation by thousands of years of pounding waves. Clinging to the top of each were a few stunted trees. And dominating the beach and the stacks and the toylike people was the vast spread of ocean, a bowl of blue so brilliant it hurt Rachel's tired eyes. Not even the sparkling sunlight, rare in November, could awaken her enthusiasm today.

What in God's name was she going to do with Luke Warren? Despite yesterday's defiant gesture, she couldn't quite picture asking him to spend his days cleaning toilets. She wished she'd thought to ask what he *was* good at that would be of use to her.

Her hand jerked when a knock sounded on the door. Marching over to it, she swabbed irritably with a napkin at the spill that darkened the front of her red shirt.

Not at all to her surprise, Luke lounged in the doorway. What did surprise her and, more than that, unnerved her was that the night's sleep appeared to have effected a transformation on him. Gone was the stiff, hard-faced government agent, with his cuffs buttoned down and suspicion clouding his eyes. The most noticeable change was his clothes. Today he had on well-worn brown cords that hugged his hips and the long muscles of his thighs. On top he wore a faded, sagging black sweatshirt with the sleeves pushed up. The design on it made Rachel blink. The centerpiece was a grinning skull whose crossbones were twined with red roses. The psychedelic-style lettering said Grateful Dead. Rachel recognized the name of the San Francisco rock group. Beaten leather work boots completed the ensemble. She couldn't help noticing that in these more form-fitting clothes Luke wasn't as rangily built as she'd thought;

she doubted that he lifted weights, but there was nothing wrong with the muscle development in his chest and shoulders.

His eyes looked greener today than she'd remembered. It was a trick of the light, she told herself firmly. Refusing to even consider the good-humored spark in those eyes or the relaxed tilt to his sexy mouth, Rachel inquired repressively, "Is this how you always dress for your first day on a new job?"

"I like to blend in," he said with repugnant good cheer. He nodded at her front. "Did you forget to wear a bib?"

The feel of his mocking gaze on her made her even more irritable. "I got out of bed on the wrong side," she snapped. "What do you want?"

He came to attention with a jolt and whipped one hand up to his forehead in a salute. "Orders, ma'am."

"Oh, brother," she said. "Come in." She dragged herself back across the room and slumped in front of her teacup. "Make yourself some coffee if you want. Or there's tea."

"Thanks." A moment later she heard cupboard doors slamming and then the sound of humming. She didn't say anything until the teakettle whistled.

"What do you know how to do?" she asked abruptly.

A steaming mug of dark coffee in his hand, he pulled out one of the ladder-back chairs at the table and sat down. "That's a pretty open-ended question," he observed with amusement. "I can make instant coffee, for example. I can play a pretty mean round of golf. I can stay on a horse if push comes to shove. I can—"

Rachel interrupted. "Let's not play games. Try for useful talents, okay? If you can't do anything else, I'll have you cleaning up after guests." A thought came to her. "Maybe you want to poke around in the cabins."

Luke shook his head before taking a deep swallow of the coffee. "Jack wouldn't have put his stash anywhere a guest might stumble on it. And I'm not interested in your guests."

"Well, then?"

"I'm actually pretty handy. Plumbing, wiring—you name it. I built myself a house once."

"You did?" For the first time since she'd learned who he was, Rachel felt a spark of personal interest that went beyond the physical awareness she couldn't help. "Where?"

"A summer place in the Sierra Nevadas. I sold it a couple of years ago. I'd like to do that again someday."

She resisted an urge to ask him more. She couldn't afford to get intimate with him, on any level. "I'll remember your talents if the wiring or plumbing fouls up," she said. "In the meantime, I think I'll put you to work building a fence."

He nodded. "Sounds good."

Actually, it did. Rachel was pleased with her idea. There were several stretches along the edge of the bluff and along the path that wound down to the beach in front of the lodge that were edged with tumbling-down split-rail fences that had long needed replacing. But money and time were always short. Even in a few days or a week, Luke might be able to get quite a lot done.

Out of the corner of her eye she saw how comfortable he looked, with his long legs stretched out under the table. He was apparently enjoying his coffee and the view in equal measure. She was ashamed of herself when she asked waspishly, "Are you sure you aren't here for a free vacation?"

He quirked a brow at her. "My, my, we have a sunny disposition toay. Or are you always like this in the morning?"

"With you, always." She pushed her chair back from the table. "Let's get on with it."

The humor in his eyes vanished. He set down his coffee cup with a decisive click. "Yes, let's," he agreed crisply, standing, too.

"The tools are—"

Luke made an impatient gesture. "We don't need tools yet. Unless you have an idea?"

"An idea?" Rachel stared at him blankly. "I thought the fence—"

"Forget the fence. Where would Jack have hidden the money?"

He still looked relaxed, but his eyes held hers in a way she couldn't evade. She was reminded too suddenly of everything his presence meant.

"Don't ask *me*," she said. "Finding it is your job."

"And yours is to cooperate," he reminded her, his voice deceptively gentle. "Remember? You're going to prove to me that it isn't here. So where should I look first?"

Tension stretched tightly between them. Rachel gave a brittle, angry laugh. "You're being illogical, Mr. Warren. If I believe it's not here, how am I going to tell you where it is?"

He smiled, too, but without altering the hard lines of his face or the watchful look in his eyes. "Be illogically logical, Mrs. Brewer," he suggested. "*If* your husband had had the money, where would he have been most likely to hide it?"

"Since he didn't have it," she retorted stubbornly, "there isn't any likely place."

The next question was like a thin knife between her ribs. "Then let's put it this way. Where would *you* hide it? Assuming you were trying, of course."

Rachel looked with intense dislike at this tall, cold-eyed man, who she was beginning to think was no better than Walt, even if technically he was on the side of right and justice. "*I* have nothing to hide," she said, letting the words drop like chunks of ice. "You're the expert on greed and deceit, aren't you? So get to work."

He reacted unexpectedly. "Damn it, Rachel! Help me."

His appeal melted away her anger, leaving her with a muddle of conflicting emotions that included perplexity. She didn't understand Luke Warren. Who was he really? Was he so untrusting of other people that he couldn't respond normally to anyone? But then why did he sometimes reach out to her so honestly? Probably, she thought, he'd learned this tactic, like all his others, in an FBI classroom.

She shook her head, breaking their eye contact. "I don't even know how big that much gold is."

He was silent for a moment, regarding her. Then, as though he'd made a decision, he said, "We don't think it's gold anymore. We know Bill Sand flew directly to Europe from the job where he took the gold. We're assuming he converted it there to something less bulky, something easier to smuggle and hide. But obviously it would still have to be something that could be converted again without too much effort."

A feeling of unreality crept over Rachel. Here they stood in the apartment she'd shared with Jack, having an amazingly matter-of-fact discussion about something totally absurd.

As though of its own volition, her head began to shake again. "You're asking the wrong person. I can't even think of anything that's worth that much money! Go consult Elizabeth Taylor or somebody like that—not me."

"Rachel..." Luke bit off whatever he'd been going to say, stiffening at the muffled sound of a car engine from outside. Rachel half expected to see him flatten himself against a wall and reach for a gun. Except she could see all too clearly that he wore no shoulder holster.

"Are you expecting someone?" he asked sharply.

"This *is* a resort," she reminded him. "Guests come at any time. Cars go in and out all day."

The dangerous look in his eyes faded. His mouth actually twitched into a smile. "Oh. Yeah."

"So I had better go see who this is," Rachel said, starting for the door. "I don't know if my receptionist is here yet."

Luke was practically stepping on her heels as she crossed the lodge's common room, with its massive fireplace.

Rachel saw that her receptionist was already behind the counter, but since she was on the telephone, Rachel decided to go ahead and check out the car. Lois nodded in response to her casual wave, but her brown eyes were fixed with curiosity on Luke. Rachel realized that on the way back in she'd have to introduce Luke as her new assistant. She grimaced. It wouldn't make any more sense to her employees than it did to her. She wasn't looking forward to having to explain.

Through the windows, which allowed in a flood of daylight and offered a view of much of the resort, Rachel saw a dark blue sedan parked on the gravel in front of the lodge. A tall, uniformed man was climbing out.

"Oh, the sheriff," she said, smiling with relief. "He must be here to see me. I'm sure you'll want to—"

Luke's hard grip on her wrist made her jump. She hadn't realized he was so close. When she looked up into his eyes, his cold expression sent a shiver through her. Sometimes he seemed so human that she was shocked by this reminder of how predatory and suspicious he really was.

His voice was unyielding. "No police, Rachel. You're not going to tell your friend the sheriff a word about me. You haven't heard again from Walt. You've put the whole thing out of your mind. Understand?"

She couldn't look away, but, both indignant and a little afraid, she tugged at his grasp. "No, I don't. Aren't you both good guys?"

Luke glanced down at his hand, and she saw his mouth twitch as though with surprise. He instantly released her and stepped back, a frown between his brows. "I didn't mean to come on so heavy, Rachel. I'm sorry." His gaze slid to the window, then back to her face. He said urgently, "There isn't time to explain now. Please, just cooperate. Go talk to him."

"You mean, go lie to him."

Muscles twitched in his jaw. "If you have to. Remember, we have a deal. You help—this whole affair is kept quiet. If you don't, my tactics will have to change."

The threat was plain. Rachel stared at Luke for another instant. Then, remembering Lois, she looked beyond him. The older woman was involved in the phone conversation and had her head bent over the reservation book. She hadn't noticed anything. Rachel was a little relieved, but she also felt very alone. Without meeting Luke's eyes again, she whirled away, tugging open the heavy outside door. "George!" she called in what she hoped was a voice of welcome. Or was it a call for help?

"Rachel. Good to see you." The tall, heftily built man moved toward her. He was smiling, but she thought he appeared observant, as well.

He was as homely as ever. His short, rough mat of sandy hair looked as though it had been groomed by a mountain goat; his raw-boned, lightly freckled face, with its crooked nose, was so familiar. Seeing him like this, with her nerves taut, she experienced a flood of memories. He'd often had dinner with Jack and herself, or stopped by just for coffee. Yet despite his frequent visits, Rachel had never looked on George Olson as a friend. In fact, during her short marriage she'd had the opinion that the sheriff didn't like her very much. In addition, there was some quality about him with which she hadn't felt at ease. Nonetheless, this past year she'd appreciated his continuing habit of coming by for coffee, his ready advice, and she'd been very glad she'd had him to turn to the other night, after Walt's visit. She still couldn't really warm to him, but he'd been so nice that now she felt both angry and guilty at the idea of having to deceive him.

"How are you?" she said as naturally as she could. She wondered if she dared invite him in for a cup of coffee, or whether that, too, was a no-no. She didn't have to look to know that Luke was watching from behind the glass, his piercing eyes taking in every nuance of their expressions.

The sheriff seemed to sense her discomfiture, because his smile faded and his gaze grew more assessing. "I really stopped by to make sure you hadn't heard anything more from that oddball."

Hastily she said, "No. No, I haven't. I, uh, didn't really expect to. *You* sounded sure he wouldn't be back."

His pale brows rose as he considered her. "Reasonably sure," he said. "The whole story was crazy, but not the kind of crazy that would make me think he was out for the fun of scaring you. No, I'd bet my last dollar your visitor had the wrong place, the wrong man."

"Yes, that's what I think, too," she said with unusual fervency. *Damn it,* why wasn't Luke Warren out here, listening to this? Probably because he didn't *want* to hear a reputable authority who'd known Jack dismiss his theory as hogwash! She forced a smile. "We both knew Jack too well to think otherwise."

The sheriff nodded in comfortable agreement tinged with sorrow. "We'd been friends a lot of years. Jack never had any money to speak of. This can't have anything to do with him.''

"No, of course not." For the life of her, Rachel couldn't think of anything else to say. Finally she cleared her throat. "But the man scared me a little, I have to admit." This time her smile was more relaxed. "Thanks for being so reassuring, George. I appreciate it *and* your stopping by here today."

"Trying to get rid of me?" he asked with heavy humor.

"Of course not! Although I, uh, do have a full day today, George."

"At this time of year?" he asked in surprise.

She was a lousy liar, she knew. Maybe now it was more a case of not really *wanting* to lie. The temptation was unbearable to spill the whole story and worry later about what Luke would say and do. George was another policeman! What reasonable objection could Luke have? Or did he plan to explain at all?

Trying to look casual, telling herself defiantly that he would have to accept a fait accompli, Rachel shifted so that she had her back completely to the lodge. She'd have to talk quickly. "George..."

Even from a distance, Luke recognized right away what she was up to. The relief and profound pleasure on her face when she'd greeted the sheriff had put him on his guard.

Swearing under his breath, he quickly opened the front door and started across the porch, deliberately letting the screen slam behind him. With a sweeping glance he automatically took in the otherwise empty parking lot, the unbroken green of the forest on the other side of the highway, a woman emptying a dishpan of water outside one of the cabins. Then he focused on the pair he was approaching.

Damn it, right now he'd just as soon not meet the county sheriff, of all people. The lack of honesty could later be awkward, if he had reason to need the locals. But Rachel was giving him no choice. Luke wondered if the visitor was more to her than the representative of law and order. The idea was a disturbing one.

The sound of the door slamming had caused Rachel to start. Luke noted with interest the guilty look she shot over her shoulder. Her lack of subtlety made it likely that she really was a poor liar and therefore had meant every angry, passionate word she had spoken the day before. Still, he couldn't dismiss the possibility that she didn't really want to tell the sheriff anything, but wanted Luke to *think* she did.

Both the sheriff and Rachel had turned to watch him saunter toward them. Hands in his pockets, Luke appraised the other man. He was a big, beefy guy, with pale hair and freckled, peeling skin. By the time Luke had taken the last couple of steps, his feet crunching on the gravel, the uniformed man's eyes had narrowed and his stance had altered, projecting to Luke assertiveness, or even aggression. That put Luke even more on edge than he'd already been. How much had Rachel had time to say?

Luke glanced at Rachel, and saw that her teeth had closed on her soft lower lip. Her big dark eyes sparkled unnaturally. Probably with tears of frustration, he thought sardonically, acknowledging his own uncomfortable spasm of guilt.

"I thought maybe you could show me where the tools are, Rachel. If I'm not interrupting."

"Heavens, no. You wouldn't want to do that, would you?" Her tone dripped sarcasm.

The sheriff's eyes narrowed even more as he shifted his gaze from Luke to Rachel.

"Sorry," Luke said with a shrug. Her tone worried him. It made him want a stronger hold on her than he had. If he could feel what she was thinking before she said it, he'd be a step ahead. There wasn't time for him to examine his motives for wanting to touch Rachel. Throwing caution aside, he decided to go with his instinct. He offered the sheriff a big, insincere smile and ambled closer to Rachel. As though he had a perfect right to do so, he laid a hand on her upper arm. He was surprised at how much he liked the feel of it.

Jovially he asked her, "Aren't you going to introduce me?"

Through the nerve endings in his fingers he felt the reaction course through her. Her slender body was taut, and if she chose she could pull right away from his touch. She grew rigid under his hand, not stepping away but not yielding to his proprietary gesture, either. Trying to convey a warning, Luke met her gaze, expecting anger. It was there in her eyes, along with something else. Alarm, and a shivering awareness of him that provoked a rush of dangerous exultation in Luke. Damn, he couldn't afford to show his own reaction!

When his smile didn't falter and his eyes remained hard, rebellion flared on her face, and for a moment he thought he'd pushed her too hard. He wondered, too, if she'd sensed the mixed motives that had driven him to deliberately test both the other man and her. But she couldn't have, because after a charged instant she lowered her gaze.

"Luke," she said colorlessly, "this is George Olson. George—Luke Warren, my new . . . assistant."

Regretting the loss of contact, Luke took his hand from Rachel's arm and held it out. "Nice to meet you," he said with a friendly nod, intending to ease the atmosphere.

It didn't work. The sheriff, flexing his big shoulders, just stared at Luke's hand for a moment. The handshake, when it came, was perfunctory. He turned right back to Rachel, frowning. "I didn't know you were thinking of hiring anyone. Why, you just let half a dozen people go!"

"Well, it was kind of spur of the moment, when I met Luke.... George, you know it hasn't been easy since Jack died. I worked awfully hard last year, and I'd like to have a more relaxed pace next year. I thought I could train Luke this winter."

Hell! Luke thought. Her friend here didn't have to be a genius to see the resentment just under the surface. The sheriff's expression already mixed perplexity with growing suspicion. Part of that would probably disappear if Luke went about his supposed business and left the two of them alone again.

But he couldn't risk it. Pretending to be impervious to the dangerous undercurrents, Luke put in easily, "This winter I'm going to get to some of those things that Rachel tells me have been on her mind for a long time. The edge of that bluff really needs a new fence. It's an accident waiting to happen. I'm surprised her husband didn't do something about it years ago."

The sheriff nodded. "It needs doing, all right. But it isn't more than two weeks' work." In a rather obvious gesture, he rested one huge hand loosely on the butt of his gun and looked straight at Rachel. "There isn't a problem here, is there? You seem a little nervous. If there's something you want to say, you can step right into this car with me. I'm here to help if there is."

She hesitated, frozen. At last she dropped her gaze and flushed guiltily. "No," she said in a low voice. "Really there isn't."

"This fella here—" he nodded obliquely at Luke "—doesn't have anything to do with that matter we talked about on the telephone?"

If she'd looked guilty before, now she looked stricken, Luke thought. "No. No, of course not. I . . . I don't expect to hear anything more from . . ."

Walt. Her lips were already forming the name, a name she wasn't supposed to know. Before she could utter it, Luke interrupted ruthlessly, using his voice to drown out the gentler timbre of hers. "What's this all about? Is there something I should know? Some problem?"

The sheriff cast him a look of obvious dislike. Rachel's expression of puzzlement changed to one of comprehension. Her quickly indrawn breath was almost a gasp.

"No! No, I'll tell you about it later, Luke." She swallowed hard and tried to smile at the sheriff, her lips trembling. "I don't expect to hear from that—that man again. I feel safer with Luke here, anyway. Please, don't worry about me."

Well, it was a good try, Luke thought. He knew he was probably being overly cautious. He would have given up ten minutes ago if it weren't for one thing: the unknown quality of the relationship between these two. It might not be a romantic one, but it still made him nervous.

By this time the stony suspicion in the sheriff's eyes was mixed with doubt. The picture was undoubtedly clouded for him by the thread of sexual tension between Luke and Rachel.

Whatever his reasoning, he evidently felt he'd pushed as hard as he could, because he did no more than nod curtly, give Luke a stare that told him he hadn't seen the last of him, and say, "I can't help worrying, Rachel. Call if you need me. Anytime. In fact, I'll be expecting it. If I don't hear from you, I'll drop by in a day or so." He didn't wait for a response. Without another glance at Luke he turned his back and walked to his car.

As Luke watched the unmarked car drive away, he was kicking himself. He'd handled that about as badly as he could have. He'd managed to antagonize the head of the local law enforcement agency—although he wasn't sure why the man had reacted the way he had. He'd kept Rachel from talking—but only until she could get to a telephone by herself. And, of course, he'd once again upset her, and he badly needed her cooperation.

In his own defense, he had to admit that some of it wasn't his fault. But some of it was. Sure, the appearance of being her lover would make a nice addition to a cover that was patently too thin. If he'd stopped to think, he would have known she wouldn't sweetly go along with it. Just because he'd wanted her to, for more than one reason, wasn't good enough.

Rachel's thoughts weren't any happier. She couldn't remember ever having felt lonelier than she had as that car disappeared up the highway. George was familiar, safe, a reminder of sanity and normalcy. Now he was gone, leaving her to the mercy of the mysterious stranger who stood silently beside her. His mere presence made her edgy—no, more than that. Panicky. She knew, even though she tried not to think about it, that her overreaction had too much to do with her involuntary physical response to him. The lightest touch of his hand and she felt a jolt of pure electricity. She didn't know now whether it had been cool reasoning or the effortless force of his physical domination that had made her say what he wanted. She didn't like having to wonder. She'd be a fool if she ever showed this man her vulnerability.

When she pulled her gaze from the now empty highway, she made herself take the offensive to hide her fear. "What was all that about?" she asked belligerently.

"That's called damage control," he retorted. "How good a friend of yours *is* he?"

"That's none of your business!"

Luke set his jaw. His tone was low and harsh as he said, "No, Rachel. You still don't get it, do you? You were going to tell him all, weren't you? That makes him my business!"

She started to deny it, then changed her mind. She refused to descend to his level. Lifting her chin, she said, "Yes, I was. And I wish I had! Do you have any idea how isolated I feel?" Her voice was passionate. "I don't know you. You show me a badge and expect me to obey your every word without question, even when it doesn't make sense. You're asking me to trust you without any reason. Tell me why I should!"

He considered her for a minute, then made a wry face. Shoving his hands in his pants pockets, he said, "I haven't given you much reason to, have I? But it's tough when I can't trust you, either." He appeared to be waiting for an answer. When she remained silent, Luke sighed. "I don't want you to be frightened. About the sheriff... We haven't had very good luck in confiding our operations to local departments. Half the time we're investigating some well-respected citizen, and we've had covers blown too often by a well-meaning cop passing on a word to a friend who couldn't *possibly* be guilty. Maybe I seem unreasonable to you, Rachel, but remember, I didn't know he was a friend of yours."

"Would that have made any difference?" she demanded, not wanting him to see that his careful explanation had dissolved some of her anger.

Again he grimaced. "I'll be honest with you—"

"That's a change," she muttered.

He gave her a look that told her he'd heard, but otherwise ignored her interjection. "I'm afraid it wouldn't have made any difference. In fact..." He broke off.

Speaking into the charged silence, she finished slowly, "It makes you trust him even less."

His gaze was direct. "Do you blame me?"

When he appealed to her like that, it was harder for her to fight him. Her defenses were undermined by the softening of her feelings. But she could understand his logic, even if in her case—and Jack's—it was wildly off base. "I suppose not," she conceded, her tone grudging. "But I don't like it."

There was a short silence as they stood there and looked at each other. Wariness lay between them, but also the tenuous beginnings of a more equal relationship. Rachel might have been glad of that if it hadn't been for the indefinable tension that lay beneath the surface. Fretfully she pulled her attention away from him and focused on the toe of her tennis shoe, with which she was scraping bare a circle in the gravel. He'd given her an answer; she owed him one in return. She couldn't bear the thought of being in debt to him, even for something as simple as this.

"George isn't really a friend of mine," she said abruptly. "He and Jack were close. He'd certainly resent it if he knew why you were here. Walt he dismissed as crazy, but you..." She shrugged. "He'd be furious if he thought the federal government actually suspected Jack of something so outrageous."

She couldn't tell what Luke was thinking. All he said was "He might have to find out eventually. I hope not." Then his voice changed, became gruffer. "There's nothing between you and him, then?"

"Between George and me?" Rachel repeated, incredulous. "No! Of course not! Where on earth did you get that idea? We never even got along very well!" She didn't stop to analyze her determination to make him understand. "The only reason I called him instead of 911 is that I was afraid some bored deputy wouldn't take me seriously. I thought... Well, I guess it was instinctive. I *knew* him."

Luke nodded, and Rachel suddenly became aware that they were still standing in the middle of the parking lot. A ranger's truck passed on the highway, and a young couple with a toddler on the man's shoulders were making their way toward the beach, only yards from where they stood. Two of the ubiquitous seagulls wheeled overhead, their harsh calls blending with the rhythmic sound of the ocean.

Again Rachel was overpoweringly struck by how attractive Luke was. She wasn't sure what quality it was that she found so compelling. Maybe it was the unusual capacity he had for stillness. Here she was, fidgeting, looking everywhere but at him, and he simply waited, his pose one of utter relaxation and his expression neutral. Or perhaps it was his face, a collection of features she couldn't exactly call handsome. He had a high, broad forehead and a thin nose that missed being aristocratic by the slight crook in it. Slavic cheekbones vied with a strong jaw for dominance of his face.

Reflecting his change of mood, or perhaps just the angle of the sun, his eyes appeared greener again as he studied her in return. Rachel wished his expression weren't so impassive. Perhaps he'd had so much practice hiding his thoughts, he was incapable of exposing them.

When he spoke, he caught her by surprise, as much with the gentleness in his voice as by his words. "I *am* sorry. I should have handled that differently."

She couldn't say it was all right, because of course it wasn't. But she ducked her head in awkward acknowledgment, then resignedly started toward the lodge. Even to her own ears she sounded weary when she said, "I suppose we're back where we started."

He fell into step beside her. "I'm afraid so. But for now, why don't you show me what you have in mind for the fence?" His gesture encompassed the increasing activity around them. "If I'm going to work here, I'd better look the part. But Rachel..." He stopped at the foot of the porch stairs, his gaze compelling, his tone forceful as he spoke. "I want you to think. You knew your husband best. Where should I start searching?"

She waited for another surge of anger but didn't feel one. She couldn't resent him as much now as she had an hour ago. She wanted to—she *needed* to—but she couldn't. So all she did was nod. "All right."

"And, Rachel, one other thing. No phone calls, okay?"

She paused in the act of climbing the steps but didn't turn her head. "I'm not making any promises."

"I didn't expect one," he said softly.

Chapter 3

By the dim light of the bare attic bulb overhead, Rachel peered into the cardboard box. Finally she reached in and stirred the contents around. "It's all phone bills," she said in amazement. "Ancient ones! Why on earth would Jack have saved these so long?"

Luke was flipping through piles of old papers in another carton, and he answered without even glancing up. "Income taxes. Most of his calls were probably deducted as business expenses. Didn't you know that?"

"Of course I did!" Rachel said impatiently. "But *years* worth of them?"

"The IRS can back-audit you. So don't throw anything away yet." There was silence for a moment as Luke read an old invoice culled from his box. Then he sighed and tossed it back. "Well," he amended, "maybe a few things."

"Yeah, like these phone bills. They're ten years old, for heaven's sake. Surely not even the IRS—"

"No," Luke admitted. "Save them for now, though. If I get desperate, I'll go through them. There might be some interesting calls recorded there."

"Not on the resort phone," she told him unhesitatingly. "Jack never used it for personal calls. And it doesn't look as though he saved the bills for our line."

Luke gestured vaguely, his attention on a sheaf of papers. "Save them anyway. I can get your billing if I need it."

The evasive note in his voice made Rachel suspect he'd already examined the telephone company record on her number. She decided not to make an issue out of it, however; what was one more indignity amid so many?

Rachel blew upward, cooling her forehead and ruffling her bangs. Without enthusiasm she surveyed the next box in the rows that lined the cramped, hot attic space that occupied the peak under the lodge's roof. "This one says it's guest registers," she announced. "1969 to 1973. Can I skip it?"

"No." His answer was implacable.

She groaned and straightened her back, stretching her cramped legs. "Why not? For crying out loud, Jack was a pack rat! If we look in every box up here, we'll develop permanent curvature of the spine! And I can think of better things to do with *my* time. I have a business to run, you know."

Luke appeared unmoved. "This is more important right now. Don't forget—you chose to help me. And—" he nodded at the box at her feet "—quit being so trusting. Do you judge books by their covers, too?"

"Yes," Rachel said from between clenched teeth. "As a matter of fact I do. It's a pretty accurate way to pick out what I want to read. And, for your information, those of us who aren't cops get by very nicely, trusting people." Thinking of the stolen linen and bad checks that were a common-

place occurrence at the resort, she added, "Within reason."
Still, her point was valid, she knew. She said more strongly,
"Most of them deserve it!"

Luke Warren showed no sign of being affected by her re-
pressive tone. He just grinned. "Ah, but those of us who are
cops, as you so vulgarly put it, know how many people don't
deserve trust. We reserve it for special occasions. And I
don't think—" he looked significantly at the box labeled
Guest Registers "—that this is one of those occasions. Your
dear husband was obviously sneaky as hell."

Rachel stiffened, retorting icily, "My dear husband was
honest to the point of rudeness. And please don't forget that
he *was* my husband! I'm cooperating with you because I
have no choice, but I don't have to listen to insults."

Luke just grunted at her angry rebuke. They worked in
silence for a few minutes, while Rachel stewed as she flipped
blindly through the big, leather-bound registers. Luke's very
presence, this whole quest, was the ultimate insult to her
dead husband. And yet as she sat here, poking through his
past, that didn't bother her as much as Luke's one petty,
flippant remark. She couldn't brook criticism of Jack, no
matter how far off base it was.

Rachel wasn't proud of herself for this. She knew quite
well why she was so determined not to hear any derogation
of Jack. Guilt wasn't a rational emotion. And she couldn't
escape feeling guilty for the relief that had swept over her
when she'd been told of Jack's death. But that had nothing
to do with Luke, or her response to him, she told herself
quickly. He'd deserved every pompous, pugnacious word
and more.

Rachel felt hungry and tired and cross. Dinner time had
come and gone during the three hours she'd been closeted
up here with Luke. This was the second evening in a row
they'd spent sifting through the attic's contents. She could

only shudder at what her employees must think she was doing with him behind closed doors. They'd kept their mouths shut when she'd introduced him around, though their astonishment and speculation had been apparent.

She thought about her more immediate problem. Was she crazy to be helping Luke to this extent? She'd told him she had no choice, but of course that wasn't true. She doubted he even wanted her help, since he didn't trust her. In fact, she realized now that *he* was the one who'd had no choice. Short of throwing her in jail, he couldn't keep her from Jack's papers. He'd probably figured that this way he could keep an eye on her, and indeed, she often looked up to find him watching her.

Why hadn't she just stayed out of his way? It would have been so much easier.

Rachel gave a tiny sigh. Maintaining distance, staying uninvolved—she'd never been able to do that. She had to dig in, to prove *personally* that the government was wrong.

She'd rationalized that she could hurry Luke on his way if she volunteered to actively search. The faster every scrap of paper Jack had left was examined, the sooner this would all be over. Perhaps, too, she'd thought to protect Jack. She was appalled by the idea of a total stranger poking through his belongings. Now she wondered if she wasn't violating his memory just as brutally by helping.

She was still brooding when Luke startled her by breaking the silence. In a reflective voice he said, "That's the part I don't understand."

"What?" Rachel blinked and looked at him.

Luke was only a few feet from her, sitting on one box and examining the contents of another, but he'd abandoned his scrutiny for the moment. His elbows rested on his jean-clad knees and, with furrowed brow, he was studying her.

"Have I turned green?" Rachel asked uneasily.

"Why did you marry Jack?" he asked.

"That's none of your damned business!"

He wasn't fazed. "Everything about you is my business. Especially everything about you and Jack. Besides...I'm curious. You don't seem to go with what I know about him."

"Has it ever occurred to you," she suggested pointedly, "that might be because you don't really know anything about *him*?"

"No," he said.

Exasperated, Rachel rolled her eyes. "Anyway, aren't you getting distracted from more important matters? You could direct your curiosity to the no doubt fascinating collection of memorabilia in that box."

Luke grimaced, then forced a smile. "I'll tell you what," he said grandly. "Why don't we knock off for tonight. We can finish up here tomorrow...well, continue with it, anyway."

Rachel eyed him with dislike. "I have a wonderful idea," she said. "Why don't you continue tomorrow. I'll look somewhere else. I have to close up some of the cabins for the winter, anyway. Maybe if we split up our efforts..." *Oh, to be out from under his eye!* she thought. *To no longer have to guard her expression or blink back the tears...*

Luke chuckled. "Nice try. But if you want to help, this is how you can do it. It'll go faster with two of us. Besides, I've already told you I consider the cabins extremely unlikely hiding places. Unless they have attics..."

She shook her head, her hostility defused. "I suppose in theory something could be underneath, where the pipes are, but it gets cold, and we sometimes find animals living there."

He sighed. "I'd better look, anyway. But, damn, this would be easier if we could find some clue as to *what* we're looking for! As it is, it's a needle in a haystack."

"And the needle isn't even there."

His mouth quirked in acknowledgment, but he chose not to argue. Instead, he said briskly, "Now, how about some dinner?"

Rachel's eyes widened in disbelief. He must know the restaurant would be closed by this hour. Was he expecting her to cook for him? "If you think—" she began, her voice rising.

"Do you have a wok? If you're stocked with a few basics, I can stir-fry us something. I took a Chinese cooking class not long ago." He rose to his feet and stretched until his bones cracked and his knuckles almost brushed the rafter, then held out a hand to Rachel.

She stared up at him, astonished. A Chinese cooking class? Government agents took their recreation on the firing range, or working on their black belts in karate, not in the kitchen. Her mind balked at picturing him in an apron, armed with a wooden spoon. The twinkle in Luke's eyes as he waited told her that he knew precisely what she was thinking.

Rachel snapped her jaw shut. What the heck. She hadn't planned anything for dinner, and she was starved. She laid her hand in his.

Luke pulled her up with an ease that was somewhat unnerving, and he didn't seem in any hurry to let her go, either, while she would have been just as happy to have the length of the room between them. As she nervously tugged her hand free and stepped back, however, she could see that he hadn't shared her doubts about consorting with the enemy, or at least if he had was concealing them successfully. His smile was suspiciously casual.

Then he came up with the punch line. "While we're eating, you can tell me how you met Jack."

He had the persistence of a four-year-old, if a little more patience. And as with a child, Rachel suspected it might be more trouble fighting than it was worth. Besides, what little she had to hide was personal, nothing that would interest him. She discovered that she wanted to tell him about Jack, about the undiluted ordinariness of their marriage. If Luke listened with anything approaching an open mind, she might be able to convince him that she had never heard of his damn gold and he wasn't going to find it here.

But she didn't want to give the appearance of buckling too easily. So she shrugged. "We'll see."

By Rachel's choice, they ate in the informal atmosphere of the kitchen. She had lovingly remodeled the room herself, sanding and refinishing the fir floor, painting the old glass-fronted cabinets and hanging the wallpaper. She'd even chosen the antique oak trestle table for just this spot in the nook of the bay window.

By the time the meal was over, Rachel was feeling a much greater degree of charity for Luke. He was a wonderful cook, which she found astonishing, considering his profession. She was glad he hadn't spoiled the meal by pressing her to talk about the past. Instead, he'd asked about the area, and she told him about the great amount of rainfall the west side of the Olympic Mountains received and about the crashing storms that flung against the coast, leaving driftwood and debris in their wake.

"You really should go up the Hoh or the Queets River valleys and look at the true rain forest before you leave," she suggested. "This is the only alpine one in the world."

He murmured something noncommittal and pushed his plate away. Rachel sensed that he'd lost interest in their chitchat. He nodded his thanks for the coffee she poured him, then cradled the cup in his hands and looked steadily at her.

Rachel realized that she'd been hoping he had forgotten his question. She gave him a wry smile. "Yes? Do you want something?"

The humor in his answering grin was infectious. "Don't make me beg!" he pleaded.

Rachel had to laugh, shaking her head. When he treated her like a friend, it was hard not to respond like one, even though she tried to convince herself that his charm was calculated. "Okay, you win. Where shall I start?"

Luke stretched out long legs under the table and crossed his arms comfortably. "How did you and Jack meet?"

"I was a senior in college. At Seattle University. Some friends suggested coming over to Sahale for spring break, and a group of us did."

"Love at first sight?"

She couldn't detect any sarcasm in his voice, although she knew it had to be there. "Something like that," she replied with care. "He checked us in—"

"And checked you out?" This time his tone was definitely mocking.

Rachel studied him. "Does the idea offend you?"

His mouth compressed. "Why should it?"

"I don't know." She waited.

Under the dusty work shirt he wore, Luke's shoulders jerked. "Let's just say I've taken a dislike to your husband. If you're suggesting that I keep it to myself, you're right. I'll try."

His frank admission disarmed her. What was he implying? Surely it wasn't normal for an experienced federal agent to develop strong feelings about people he encountered in his work. Particularly long-dead ones. Did it have something to do with her? No. She'd known him only two days!

She was reaching, for what she didn't like to think. "Did he ask you right away to marry him?" he prompted her.

Rachel shook her head. "We spent time together that week, and at the end he offered me a job for the summer. Like any college student, I needed one, so of course I accepted. I wanted to see him again, anyway."

"Why? What was he like?"

Rachel saw that Luke was genuinely curious. She wondered if he really wanted to know what Jack had been like, or if he was more interested in her perception of him. She shrugged, for some reason not minding a question that should have seemed unbearably intrusive.

"Not really romantic," she said, then turned her head away, trying to look out the window at the dark ocean. Already she had trouble picturing Jack, and he'd been gone less than a year. When she was concentrating on Luke, with his fascinating, mobile face and eyes that were so full of life, she couldn't see Jack at all. But focusing on the night outside, she managed to dredge up an image of her husband as he'd appeared to her that summer. She remembered the sunshine and the waves foaming at their feet as she and Jack walked on the beach. All the workers at the resort had shared a real camaraderie, making Rachel feel comfortable, as though they were a big family and she belonged. In retrospect she knew that that deceptive feeling had become inextricably entwined with her emotions for Jack and had contributed to her decision to marry him. She, who had grown up with a brittle, essentially unloving mother and without a father, had thought she'd found a home.

Rachel pulled her thoughts back to the present and said aloud, "Jack was big and blocky, with huge hands and a slow way of moving and talking. He was handsome, too, and strong. He didn't talk much. At the time I thought he was a little shy with the guests. I was . . . flattered that he hadn't been shy with me. Not that we talked a lot, either. Jack just didn't.''

"So the strong, silent type appealed to you." Luke sounded thoughtful. His voice tugged her attention back to him.

"I guess it did," Rachel said a little sadly. "Growing up, I didn't have a father. I always read a lot, and that was how I came up with my image of the perfect man. I married him when I met him."

"You've changed your mind?" With his gaze he seemed to probe her thoughts.

Rachel forced a smile that she felt twist on her lips. "I've just grown up, that's all. Maybe I don't have any ideal anymore.''

"Because he's dead?"

Rachel almost laughed. If only Luke knew! But she contented herself with another smile that reflected her true feelings no more than the first one, and said only, "Because I've grown up."

He studied her in silence for a moment, his expression enigmatic. When she sat, unmoving, under his scrutiny, outwardly unperturbed, a muscle in his cheek twitched. At last he leaned back in his chair. She hadn't realized that he'd abandoned his after-dinner slouch and sat up at all. Maybe the conversation wasn't a comfortable one for him, either.

"Not a perfect marriage, eh?" he remarked.

"Is there such a thing?" she asked.

"I wouldn't know," he said. "Does it bother you to talk about Jack?"

Rachel made an impatient gesture. "No. He's been dead a long time. What do you want to know?"

"Why it wasn't perfect." Now Luke looked completely relaxed, leaning back again lazily, his eyes hooded. Beneath the heavy lids, however, those eyes were watchful, intent.

Rachel took a swallow of coffee and shrugged. "Part of the trouble was that to move here I gave up something that meant a lot to me. I was supposed to start law school that fall. Being a lawyer was my dream. But from here that was impossible."

Suddenly there was pity on his face, and empathy for her that was discomforting. "I'm a lawyer, you know."

"You are?" Rachel couldn't hide her astonishment. She'd heard that FBI agents had law degrees, but she had had no reason to connect that fact with Luke.

"Not practicing, of course," he clarified. "But I finished law school, passed my bar in California. Is it so difficult to believe?"

"No," she said. "Not about you personally. I just can't understand why anyone would go through law school and then not use the degree."

"I am in law enforcement," he pointed out.

"But could you do your job without the law degree?" she asked bluntly.

He hesitated before answering. "Yes. And sometimes I regret that I'm not using it. When I was in college I had plans to be the kind who battles tirelessly for the poor."

Rachel heard and understood the self-mockery in his voice. It felt so good, to talk for a minute to someone who might understand in turn how she'd felt. "If you were like me, you were going to do the battling without ever expecting a reward," she confided. "Except something tells me I, at least, was envisioning lots of admiration."

"Naturally," he said with a sudden grin that lightened his expression remarkably. "But then, we were only twenty-two."

"Yes." She was silent for an interval, then sighed. "Anyway, my class at the University of Washington started without me. And summer ended. I like winters here now, but that first one was tough. All the college kids leave. There are only four or five permanent employees, and I didn't have a thing in common with any of them. It rained all the time. We're having a stretch of good weather right now, but for most of the winter there isn't even a beach to walk on. We're so isolated here it's hard to make friends."

She waved a hand. "Who is there to be friends with, anyway?" She'd meant the question to be rhetorical, and he waited as she sighed again. "It should have given Jack and me the perfect chance to get to know each other. I suppose it did, in a way. But I was in for some surprises, and I imagine he was, too. I discovered that silent meant uncommunicative and that the fun I'd been having had been with other people, not him. He probably decided I was flighty and a chatterbox. Anyway, we had quite a few adjustments to make."

Rachel fell silent, having said more about her marriage than she'd intended. She found Luke unexpectedly easy to talk to. He had the ability to change himself to suit the occasion. She'd seen him overpoweringly forceful, then there'd been flashes of surprising vulnerability and, at other times, a lopsided grin so charming that it twisted something painfully in her chest. And now he sat quietly listening, his personality seemingly damped down, so that he gave the impression of being colorless, unobtrusive. It was a useful talent, she mused.

"Have you ever been married?" she asked in abrupt challenge. Since Rachel had bared her soul to him, she felt entitled to a little reciprocation—and it had suddenly, unpleasantly, occurred to her that he might well have a wife dutifully waiting at home.

He grimaced at her question. "Yeah. Years ago."

"You're divorced?" When he nodded, she probed, "Is it anything you regret?"

Luke shook his head. "It was too long ago. Even then..." His mouth took on a wry twist. "We got married too young. I thought she was beautiful. She thought I was exciting. In the end, she didn't like my job and I wished she weren't quite so beautiful. Or at least that she'd forget she was. Like—" his eyes suddenly held a disturbing expression "—I have a feeling you do."

Although she felt wary, Rachel managed a flippant "Is that a compliment?"

"Maybe. You know you're beautiful."

She had never been told she was quite so flatly. She also wasn't accustomed to thinking of herself that way. As a teenager she'd been gawky and unsure, and still found herself wanting to peer into a mirror whenever she received a compliment. Luke's was more than flattering, however; it was exhilarating.

Tamping down her response, she answered honestly, "No, I don't think so. My mother had the right word. She used to say my face had 'character.'" Rachel didn't add that her mother's tone had implied her daughter should be thankful for small favors.

For a long moment Luke studied her as though she were a painting, and she forced herself to sit still under his gaze.

"To say your face has character is probably more accurate," he agreed finally. "Your looks wouldn't appeal to every man."

She clamped her mouth shut to stop herself from asking the obvious question.

Devilish amusement shone in Luke's eyes. *The cursed man can read my mind,* she thought, irritated.

"Of course," he assured her kindly, "*I* think you're quite attractive." Rachel could see that he was having a hard time not laughing.

She set her cup down on the table. It was time—no, past time!—for her to reerect the barriers to this relationship. What had she been thinking, to have allowed herself to banter and even flirt with him? "I'm flattered," she said coolly, then stood up, pushing her chair back. "Thank you for cooking dinner. I'll see you in the morning."

Luke cocked a brow at her. Laughter still lurked in his eyes. "Was that meant to be a subtle request for my departure?"

"Yes."

He smiled again, now with a different look in his eyes. "Oh, I'll be on my way. You won't have to boot me out by the seat of my pants. At least, not if you tell me what I want to know."

Wary now, she asked, "And what's that?"

"How you knew about the gold. What Jack told you. What kind of agreement the two of you had."

Rachel stiffened. When she spoke, her words were clipped and angry. "I will not permit you to hound me! I've answered your questions truthfully. I've cooperated above and beyond what you asked. That's enough!"

Looking at the proud defiance on her face, Luke hated himself for doing his job. It wasn't the first time he'd felt this way lately, but for some reason he didn't fully understand, this woman was bringing that restlessness and doubt to a head. He didn't know how much longer he could keep enough distance from her to maintain any kind of objectivity. He also wasn't sure how much longer he could keep his hands off her. *But damn,* he'd feel like a fool if he let his unbidden response to her beauty and courage make him a patsy. Shock tactics sometimes worked. Tonight was the right time for them, although he'd only just realized it. He hadn't set her up deliberately.

Now he went on as though she hadn't spoken, his tone contemplative. "My guess is that Jack got carried away by his lust for you. Maybe he bragged about the money. Maybe he showed it to you. Although I doubt that. Anyway, it was enough enticement for you. I'm sure part of the agreement was that he change his will right away. But tell me, were you going to split the money when he converted it? Or was it part of the deal that you had to stay with him to come into your share?"

"You're crazy!" she exclaimed bitterly. "I told you why I married him!"

"You also told me that all wasn't roses and candlelight," he reminded her, hating himself. "So why did you stay with him?"

Her face paled. Apparently he'd struck close to the bone, which intrigued him at the same time as it shook him. He didn't *want* this little scenario to be true. But he had to push now.

Her answer was a cry of despair. "How many times do I have to tell you! I don't know where the money is!"

Luke leaned back in his chair and clasped his hands behind his head. He knew he would appear relaxed, though it wasn't more than skin-deep. "Oh, I believe you," he assured her. "I'm convinced you don't know where it is. I think Jack pulled a fast one on you, too. I think he died and left you in the dark about the money."

Her hand was shaking as she reached up in agitation to push curls back from her face. "You don't believe me, then. You haven't even listened to me! I don't understand what more I can do!"

The hopelessness on her face wrenched at him in a way her anger hadn't. Luke couldn't push any more. Instead, he heard himself explaining, in what she had to understand was a half apology, "I know people." He shrugged. "That's how I make my living. And let me tell you, no one walks away from millions of bucks. No one."

For some reason that brought life back to her face. She gave a small, brittle laugh. "I'd trade all those millions in a second for the law degree you're letting gather dust in a drawer. So what does that tell you about me?"

He didn't comment. He'd upset her, but the trail he had pursued had gotten cold. Luke was beginning to wonder if whatever nerve he'd struck had nothing to do with the money. Or was that wishful thinking?

Her long slim hands now gripped the back of the chair. "Why are you doing this to me?" she asked. "If you believe I don't know where the money is, what possible use am I to you?"

"Oh, you're plenty of use to me." Luke unclasped his hands and straightened in the chair. He couldn't let her see how moved he was by her plea, how much he ached to stand up and draw her into his arms to comfort her. Not that he kidded himself it would stop there. "You knew Jack better than anyone," he said. "You know how he thought. If anyone can find the damn money, you can."

Rachel just shook her head. "You're right. I knew him. And I'll tell you how he thought. *He didn't take risks.* Period. He didn't go over the speed limit when he was driving. He wouldn't walk on the beach in the winter when the tide was coming in. He used to drive guests crazy by standing there, laboriously reading their checks, as though that would tell him anything. And you should have seen him chew his food. After all, if he hurried he might have choked on it. He drove me nuts!"

Luke opened his mouth to tell her that Bill Sand had precisely that reputation as an extraordinarily, even fanatically
careful operator. But she didn't give him a chance.

"And you're trying to convince me that this is the man
who was a mercenary pilot! Who committed a daring heist
of millions of dollars worth of gold! Well, think again."

Luke felt pity even as he shrugged off her tirade. "Jack
volunteered to be a helicopter pilot in Vietnam," he reminded her. "Maybe you should remember that."

He watched her struggle to explain. "That was an anomaly, an impulse, a—"

"If he surrendered to one impulse, why not another?"

The question was unanswerable. Why not, indeed? For
the first time, Rachel truly faced it. Could Jack have done—
have *been*—the unthinkable? Had she been searching to
prove her husband's innocence not to Luke but to herself?

"And if he did—" Luke's voice picked up where her
thoughts had left off "—what would he have done with it?"
He was leaning forward now, his gaze unwavering, his tone
intense. "Where would he have hidden the money?"

Rachel stared at him for a moment, then bit her lip and
turned away, hugging herself with her arms. She felt disoriented, uncertain, as though the ground had trembled under
her feet. She couldn't let herself believe this!

"I don't know," she whispered.

She heard the chair legs scrape on the floor as Luke rose
to his feet behind her. He spoke more gently. "Think about
it, Rachel. That's all I ask."

Still with her back to him, she nodded. She drew a deep
breath and began to pull herself together. Tiredness was all
that was wrong with her, that and a dangerous susceptibil-
ity to the magnetism of Luke's personality. She couldn't let
him sway her, even momentarily. It wasn't fair to Jack or,
perhaps more important, to herself. What Luke was asking

would require that she accept that her judgment of people was hopelessly flawed. She refused to do that. She had to hold on to her faith in herself.

When his hands closed on her slender shoulders, she quivered as though she'd been struck. And yet his touch was exquisitely gentle as he turned her slowly to face him.

"Rachel..." But he seemed to forget what he'd been going to say. His gaze searched her face, as though he hoped to be able to see her soul. Rachel stood wide-eyed and helpless under the intensity of his look and the weight of his big hands. She wasn't surprised by the slow change in his expression. When his gaze came to rest with unmistakable hunger on her mouth, and his fingers tightened on her shoulders, she shivered. Standing here so passively was foreign to her, but so was the excitement that was being kindled in her by the desire in his eyes, which was mixed with tenderness, compassion and an anger she didn't think was directed toward her.

It seemed inevitable when his head bent, so slowly that with one part of her mind Rachel knew he was giving her time to withdraw. Honey-thick warmth spread through her limbs, holding her immobile. She didn't want to like him, didn't trust him, resented his presence, yet from the beginning she'd had this heated response to him that had fueled her other feelings. It was insane for her to let him do this, but she had to know what his lips felt like. So she tilted her head back just a little, and when his mouth closed on hers, she made her lips soft and receptive.

The feeling was explosive, yet at first the kiss was tentative. Rachel sensed the struggle in him, the holding back. When she let out a breath against his mouth with a little whimper and lifted her hands to lay them against his chest, his mouth hardened momentarily. Passion shimmered between them. Her body began to yield even as her mind fought to remind her of what he really thought of her. Still she dissolved as his hand slid up to tangle in her hair and cup the back of her head. She couldn't think, could only feel the compelling force of his mouth and his hands.

It ended almost before it had begun. Luke released her and stepped back with an abruptness that echoed the anger in his eyes. More than that, she could see distaste for himself, and that hurt. So she drew herself up proudly and met his gaze with defiance. Emotion twisted across his face, and he swiftly turned away.

When he spoke his voice was low and gritty. "I'll see you in the morning."

She didn't answer, just watched him leave. The instant she'd clicked the lock shut behind him, she sagged against the door, resting her forehead on the cool wood. It was going to be a long night, she thought.

The strident ring brought Rachel fumbling up from darkness. The next ring set her to wrestling with her covers, blindly and clumsily, as she groped for the phone on the bedside table. Instinctive fear tightened her stomach; nobody called with good news in the middle of the night.

She snatched up the receiver. Her voice was high-pitched. "Hello?"

"That was quick," the man on the other end said approvingly. "I hope you weren't awake because of bad dreams." He didn't sound as though he meant it.

"Who is this?" Rachel asked sharply.

"Don't tell me you've forgotten already. And here I've been telling myself that we'd come to an understanding."

She was wide-awake now, her nerves taut. "I remember."

"Good."

"How could I?"

"I'm glad I made an impression on you." There was a smile in his voice that made Rachel's skin crawl. Then Walt's tone changed. "Well, have you found it yet?"

"No."

After a tiny pause he said coldly, "That disappoints me, Rachel. And I hate to be disappointed."

Rachel was sitting up in bed, but now she swung her feet to the floor. With her free hand she switched on the small brass reading lamp that stood beside the telephone. She needed the sanity of light.

She didn't allow a trace of her lingering fear to sound in her voice. She couldn't afford to. "Do you know that it's two o'clock in the morning?"

"Let's not chitchat, okay? Who's the guy building the fences?"

He'd been watching her. A shiver of reaction ran down her spine. Rachel's fingers felt ice-cold around the receiver. "He's . . . he's my new assistant. I needed help."

"This wasn't a good time, Rachel. I don't like it that you have someone new. I guess I'm going to have to pay another little visit. Maybe I can persuade your boyfriend to leave. . . ." And his voice hardened as he said, "One way or another."

A hand tightened around Rachel's heart.

"Expect me," he said, then she heard a click that was followed by silence.

After a minute Rachel slowly hung up the telephone with a hand that shook. Could Walt possibly have meant what she feared he had? What should she do? Warn Luke? But what good would that do? He was already expecting Walt, who would have visited sooner or later, no matter what. And there was no way on earth she was going to leave the fragile safety of her apartment to make her way through the darkness to Luke's cabin. Even while Walt had been on the phone it had occurred to her that he could be calling from downstairs in the lodge. It wouldn't be hard for him to break in.

She realized she was sitting absolutely still, listening. Which was absurd. Walt had probably called from a hotel room miles away. Anyway, he wasn't going to hurt her. He wanted her alive and well, searching for him.

With a shiver, Rachel pulled her feet back into bed and tucked them under the quilt for warmth. She turned out the lamp, though she really didn't want to. She hadn't closed the curtains, and through the window she could see the moon and the luminous ocean. Against that paler background, at the edge of the nocturnal picture, stood the dark bulk of the first cabin, the one she had put Luke in. She strained her eyes to see movement around it. She wondered if there was any use in her watching. What could she do? Run out into the darkness, swinging that old softball bat she'd had beside the bed since Walt's first visit? But she couldn't tear her eyes away.

The darkness was already subtly altering with the arrival of dawn before she slid down onto her pillow and slept once more.

The shriek of the alarm clock brought her bolt upright in bed, heart pounding as she looked wildly around. It took her only an instant to realize that the sky was a crystalline blue and to identify the source of the annoying sound. After slapping the alarm off, Rachel groaned and sank back onto her pillow, pulling the covers over her head.

Two cups of coffee later, still bleary-eyed, she clumped down the wooden back steps into the yard. The sun was just appearing behind her over the forested foothills of the Olympic Mountains, but its rays offered no warmth. The air had a crispness that made her shiver as she struggled into an oversize Irish knit sweater.

Remembering that she hadn't even brushed her hair, Rachel hesitated, then gave a shrug and shuffled on. What did she care? Most of the guests didn't even know who she was. If Luke noticed her hair, she'd tell him she was imitating Medusa, hoping the sight of her wildly waving locks would paralyze him and Walt.

Rachel quickened her steps as she neared his cabin, anxious to hear what he thought about Walt's phone call. She'd tell him, then walk around for her usual morning inspection of the resort.

She was only a few feet from the door when Luke strolled out to meet her. Dressed in work boots and jeans, with a heavy sweater adding bulk to his shoulders, he should have looked pedestrian, a laborer on his way to the job. But with his hands thrust into his pockets and a slight swagger to his walk, he might easily have had a sword strapped to his waist or a laser pistol thrust into his boot top. As though last night had never happened, he was surveying her with a devilish gleam in his eyes. Perhaps that was what gave him the air of an adventurer. Whatever it was, Rachel thought irritably, she didn't like it.

All the same, she should have gone back to brush her hair. She was just opening her mouth to offer a disgruntled goodmorning when it happened.

First came a cracking sound so loud she thought a tree might have splintered. Openmouthed, she started to turn to look, when another crack, followed by a thud against the side of the cabin, froze her. *Gunfire!* her mind screamed even as her body refused to move. The next instant she was clobbered from behind with a force that emptied her of air in one whoosh and sent her sprawling facedown in the grass.

Chapter 4

Disoriented, shocked, Rachel struggled to understand what was happening. Why couldn't she breathe? The next instant she realized it was because Luke was lying on top of her, his weight crushing her into the hard, close-cropped lawn. A big hand on the back of her head thrust her face down.

"Wha—?"

"Don't move!" he whispered.

Rachel gurgled a protest. The rough grass scraped against her cheek as she turned her mouth a fraction to one side.

Another crack sounded and she felt Luke's body jerk. "Damn it!" he muttered, then, "I changed my mind. Let's move. Quick."

Rachel was entirely in agreement. "How?" she mumbled.

Still another crack sent dirt and a tuft of grass spurting past Rachel's face.

"Run!" Luke snapped, his mouth close to her ear. "Go!"

Since he was already moving, Rachel wasn't required to comment. She was too busy, anyway, since she was doing her best to break the world record for the ten-yard dash. She flung herself the last few feet and landed rolling on the bare floor of Luke's cabin. Luke was right behind her.

"The door!" he exclaimed, rising to a crouch. He jammed his shoulder against it and swung the heavy plank door shut. "Now," he said harshly, "it's time for a little reconnaisance. You stay here."

Rachel didn't argue. She was sitting on the floor, trying to decide whether she should lock herself in the bathroom or crawl under the bed. She hadn't gotten any further than staring down at the grass stains and dirt on the front of her jeans when Luke returned to her side. When he paused there, squatting on his heels, she blinked and looked up at him.

This was yet another side to the man. His face was hard, his mouth compressed in a grim line. Dirt and a reddening scrape streaked one angular cheekbone, and his nostrils were flared. But in his light eyes she could see both chill determination and tender solicitude.

"You okay?" he asked, his voice very soft.

Rachel only nodded, not trying to speak. She was beginning to feel so trembly she wasn't sure she could stand, either.

Their gazes held for a penetrating moment, and then he leaned over and pressed his lips to hers. It was a quick, searing kiss, over almost before it began. Nonetheless, Rachel's stomach tensed in reaction and another shot of adrenaline sped her already racing pulse. She turned her head to watch as Luke grabbed a small, deadly-looking pistol from the drawer of the nightstand, then, his body bent over so he wouldn't be visible from the windows, made his way to the back door. Without another word to her or glance over his shoulder, he slid through the opening and disappeared.

Rachel abandoned the idea of hiding. Crawling to a side window, she raised herself enough to peer through. She could see two of the cabins across the narrow gravel lane. As she anxiously watched, Luke flitted between them, moving across the grass with an unnerving, sinuous grace that she hadn't guessed he possessed. With both hands he gripped the nasty snub-nosed gun, its barrel pointing up. His sharp gaze caught sight of her almost imperceptible movement, but he didn't acknowledge her with even a momentary hesitation. Almost in a blink of an eye, he'd vanished from sight again.

She didn't quite dare peek out the front. Sliding to the floor, she huddled in a ball, listening hard. Even through the thick walls of the cabin she could hear the distant, muted rush of the waves, but that was all. There were no more gunshots, no shouts. She tried to think where the fire had come from. The noise had come from behind her, and the dirt the shot had propelled past her face had gone almost directly toward the cabin. The gunman had to be hiding in the thickly forested area beyond the lodge, just behind the few cabins on the other side of the Sahale. Rachel wondered if Luke had realized that. Did he intend to cross the bridge? She felt a jolt of fear at the image of him unbearably exposed for those critical seconds. Before she knew it she was moving again, crawling toward the front door.

She opened it a crack and waited with her heart pounding as she stared at the shaft of sunlight. At last, taking a deep breath, she nudged the door far enough open with her foot to allow her to put her head around the frame. She snatched a look that couldn't have lasted more than a microsecond, but the picture stayed with her: Luke, strolling down the gravel lane toward the cabin, gun nowhere in evidence.

She yanked open the door, standing in the opening as with mounting anger she watched his casual approach. Only when he neared her did she see that his expression was still taut, his steps were fast and his eyes anxious.

"Why aren't you being more careful?" Rachel exploded. "Did you find him? You didn't cross the bridge, did you?"

"Hey." He touched her arm. "Calm down. He's gone. I showed myself to see if he was still waiting. When there was no shot, I ran up to the highway and across that bridge, but I was too late. From around the bend I could hear an engine accelerating, but it was going the other way. Later I'll see if I can find exactly where he was standing."

"Oh, God." Rachel closed her eyes and tried to collect herself. "He called last night. I was on my way here to tell you."

"He?" Luke frowned. "Who? . . . You mean Walt?"

"Of course I mean Walt!" Rachel exclaimed. "Who else do you think was shooting at us?"

"Actually, I'm not so sure." Luke reached up to tentatively feel the scrape on his cheek. "Those shots were aimed at me. Why the hell would Walt want to shoot me? He knows me by sight. That means he'll also know that if he kills me, ten agents will take my place. There's no point to it."

Rachel shook her head urgently. "He didn't know it was you. He just asked who it was working on the fences. He's watching us, but I don't know where from. Not close enough to identify you."

Luke looked thoughtful. "He couldn't be across the highway. It's too heavily wooded. And if he hung around too close he'd be taking a chance of being spotted or having his license number reported. Maybe he's just been driving by once in a while."

"Whatever." Rachel didn't care. "He didn't know it was you and he tried to shoot you. He said on the phone he'd get rid of you."

"Did he? But there must have been sights on that rifle. He'd have known who I was the minute he looked through the 'scope. No. I still don't like it." There was silence for a moment as he stared, frowning, toward the highway.

"Maybe he just wanted to buy some time," she suggested.

"What for?" Luke asked reasonably.

Rachel couldn't think of an explanation. Walt Krupinski didn't know where the money was. So what good would it do him to buy twenty-four hours or so of anonymity by shooting Luke? It made more sense that he hadn't known who Luke was and had just been trying to scare him off.

Or else... A chilly feeling of apprehension took root in Rachel's chest. "Who else *is* there?" she said. "There are things you aren't telling me, aren't there? Who is Walt, really? And who else is there?"

She didn't even turn her head as a car pulled in off the highway. Narrow-eyed, Luke did. But then he looked back at her, expressionless. "Walt was Jack's partner. Just like he told you. There was another partner, but he died only a few weeks after the heist in some crazy border skirmish in Honduras. Someplace he shouldn't have been. But he definitely died. So there isn't anyone else. Not unless Jack shared the knowledge later."

Rachel wasn't convinced or happy with his answer. Nobody had ever shot at her before, and she intended that it would never happen again.

"That's it," she said coldly. "You're leaving. No more cooperation from me. It was bad enough before, but this is intolerable! I will not allow you to put me in danger so you can play your little games!''

He spoke mildly. ''The shots were aimed at me.''

Her hands hurt, so tightly were they squeezed into fists. ''Do you think he cared if he hit me? Do you?''

''Rachel—''

''Don't 'Rachel' me! I've had enough!'' Out of the corner of her eye she saw that a man was stepping out of the car in front of the lodge. She was also aware that several cabin doors had opened, although no one had yet worked up the courage to appear. ''What the hell am I going to tell my guests?'' she demanded. ''That you're a government agent, here to add fun and thrills to their vacations? Or should I just tell them not to worry, that the gunman was shooting at you, not them?''

Luke reached out and took her arm. ''Rachel—''

She slapped his hand away. Fury had her in its grip. ''Quit it! Don't tell me to calm down! Just go pack your stuff, then go arrest Walt! And both of you, get out of my life!'' She turned and stalked toward the lodge.

With long strides Luke caught up with her. He grabbed her arm and wheeled her around to face him. His cool veneer had shattered, leaving his face tense with anger that reflected hers and a bleak frustration that thinned his mouth. ''Understand something, Rachel,'' he bit out. ''If your problems would end by my walking out, I'd do it. I'd do it in a second. For you.''

She swallowed, not totally understanding the powerful emotions that blazed in his eyes. The only reference she had was the terrible fear she'd felt when he'd been out there alone with the gunman.

''But I can't arrest Walt,'' he went on. ''I have no evidence. This is America, remember? I'll try to get it. I promise. But in the meantime, if I leave, you'll be in danger. Damn it, maybe you don't like me, but at least I won't hurt you."

Rachel wasn't so sure. Maybe that was why she'd been fighting him every step of the way. He could hurt her worse than Walt, without even trying.

Luke released her arm and stepped back. His voice was still tight, but its tone was more moderate. "And this may not have been Walt. You won't be safe until the money is out of here. Help me, Rachel."

Her mouth began to tremble as she stared up at him. Without answering, she turned jerkily away. Raising her voice, she called, "Folks, it's safe to come out now." As several timidly did, she added loudly, "I'm going to call the police, but I think it was just a poacher who probably didn't know the resort was here. My assistant heard the car leaving up the highway, so it really is safe now. But if any of you saw anything, please stick around so you can talk to the deputy when he gets here."

"Nicely handled," Luke murmured out of the corner of his mouth.

Rachel didn't even look at him. She walked quickly toward the dark green sedan and the man leaning against the hood. He was short and slender, she noted automatically, not quite effeminate but not the rough-and-tumble type either. Dressed in pressed flannel shirt and jeans, with unusually pale skin and dark, styled hair, he looked out of place against the evergreen backdrop. An urbanite who thought he wanted to see the great wilderness but who probably would end up eating every meal in the coffee shop and seeking out the nearest bar at night, Rachel diagnosed. He appeared vaguely familiar to her, as though he'd been a guest here before.

She was greeting him with a mechanical smile, explaining that they'd just had a little problem but they'd find him a cabin, when her gaze was drawn to the back seat of his car. A fully assembled rifle lay there, carelessly in the open.

She looked again at the enigmatic dark gaze. His thin, straight brows quirked slightly, as though he were amused. The timing was right, she thought. All he would have had to do was turn around a mile up the highway and come right back. What better cover could he have, in case they'd called in time to set up a road block? And now he would be here to finish what he'd begun.

She had been silent too long, but he stood there and waited without remarking, those very dark eyes reflecting no emotion except for that hint of amusement.

Rachel cleared her throat. "Ah... Sorry, but I couldn't help noticing your gun."

"I'm here for the elk hunting."

It was a good explanation. She couldn't argue. Early November was elk season on the slopes of the Olympic Mountains. Several of the guests had arrived for that reason.

"Yes, well, I just wanted to mention that guns aren't allowed in the park. Probably you knew that." He nodded, still waiting. "If you came from the north, you must have passed through national parkland. Technically you could have been fined for having it on hand like that and not disassembled."

"Oh, really?" He sounded mildly surprised. "I'll be more careful on the trip back."

"*Did* you come from the north?" Luke asked casually, his voice coming from just behind Rachel. She started. Luke could move on cat feet when he wanted. She'd had no idea he was there.

"Yes," the man answered. "Through Forks."

"By any chance did you pass a car just a few minutes before you got here?"

He appeared to think. "Quite a few, I'm afraid. I really didn't notice any individually."

Luke shrugged. Rachel forced a smile. "The registration desk is just inside. Lois will take care of you there."

She watched him walk away, his steps short and precise. No, she thought. It was crazy! He was a total stranger. What possible reason would he have to be taking potshots at them? None! She was getting paranoid. Walt was the one she had to worry about. Walt and the tall man who stood by her side, squinting against the sun as he stared after the new guest.

Walt picked a lousy time to show up. From Luke's point of view the day was already an all-around flop. He didn't enjoy being shot at, and he was particularly angry because of Rachel's proximity. He'd told her the truth when he'd said he thought the shots were aimed at him. But how could he be one hundred percent sure?

The deputy who had been summoned by Rachel's call wasn't much help, although Luke hadn't expected him to be. In the guise of Rachel's assistant, Luke had walked along with the deputy as he'd searched for the gunman's covert. They hadn't found any cartridges, but trampled undergrowth and a branch broken off a low-growing vine maple had alerted Luke and the officer to the spot. Unfortunately, there was no clear footprint, and the turnout beside the highway was graveled, which ruled out the possibility of their getting some tire tracks. They dug the bullet out of the cabin wall, but since it was a common caliber, it told them only that it had come from a hunting rifle—one like the Winchester that had been on the back seat of that oddball's car. As the deputy pointed out, though, half the population around here had a rifle of the right type. Unless they had a suspect, and therefore a gun to look at, the bullet wasn't any more use than a clod of dirt. Unfortunately, the deputy was right. The whole exercise had been a waste of time.

Now Luke and Rachel, along with several curious guests, stood listening to him explain his theory in a slightly condescending tone.

"Had to be a poacher with no idea the resort was here."

Luke couldn't imagine how the nitwit could have come to that conclusion, considering the bird's-eye view of the whole place one got from the covert. It didn't wash. From Rachel's tightly controlled expression, he could tell it didn't in her opinion, either. But both listened to the deputy in silence.

"Remember, ma'am, your husband had to call us last year when a few wild shots actually hit the lodge."

Luke's straying attention snapped back. But he watched as Rachel, after a glance at the crowd that had collected about them, visibly forced an unconvincing smile. "I'm a little concerned because the shots today didn't seem wild. Some of them came inches from Luke and me. They were repeated over several minutes."

The deputy just shrugged. "Ma'am, I don't know what to say. There's no motive here. Why would someone shoot at you?"

Rachel's expression became even grimmer, but she didn't say anything. Nor did she look at Luke, but he had a feeling she could hardly wait to sink her teeth into him.

"And unless he comes back," the deputy continued, "there isn't a thing we can do."

His statement was unanswerable, Luke knew. Summoned after the fact, with no obvious clues left, and not let in on the whole truth, the police really were helpless.

A couple of the guests who'd been eavesdropping began muttering together, and Luke overheard a few whispered words that included something about not being safe and about getting their money back. Rachel curled her hands into fists. Watching her, Luke hurt.

And that was when he became aware of the man standing in the background, just by the corner of the small grocery store that stood across the parking lot from the lodge. Thinning hair, a little plump, cold eyes taking in the scene with no sign of emotion: Walt Krupinski.

Seeing the look on Luke's face and the direction of his gaze, Rachel turned. Her gasp was audible but went unnoticed by the young policeman. In the same instant Luke started to move, and the deputy turned to him with a cordial smile, holding out his hand.

"Thanks for your help today, Mr. Warren. Sorry we couldn't do more, but I'm sure you'll be keeping an eye out for any trouble."

Luke had no choice but to take the hand and shake it, but he was seething with impatience. "Excuse me," he said evenly, letting the deputy's hand go as quickly as possible and backing out of the group. Damn! Krupinski had disappeared around the corner of the store. Luke knew the other man had recognized him.

Dismissing thoughts of the policeman, Luke broke into a run. He covered the twenty-five yards in seconds, but even before he rounded the corner, Luke knew he'd be too late. This time he caught a glimpse of the back of the car, a bluish-gray sedan. But the spinning wheels had left a cloud of dust, and a convenient bend in the highway had the vehicle out of sight before Luke could read the license plate. By the time he retrieved his own car, Walt would be long gone.

Tense with frustration, he walked back to where he had left Rachel. It had been inevitable that Walt would recognize him when they encountered each other, but Luke had wanted that meeting to be at a time and place of his own choosing. He was out of luck now. Walt was forewarned. If he'd been a danger to Rachel before, he was a greater one now. As long as he'd thought he was the only player in the game, he could have afforded to be patient. But no longer.

That wasn't an idea Luke liked at all. He sought out Rachel and found her. The guests were dispersing, and the deputy's car was disappearing up the highway. She stood in the middle of the parking lot, arms crossed and face rigid.

He was still ten yards from her when she said tightly, "No Walt, I see."

"He had too much of a head start."

"Wonderful!" The single word was scathing. Her eyes raked over him before she said frigidly, "If you'll excuse me, I have work to do." With that she turned and marched away. Frowning, Luke stopped and watched her go. So. Just like that, whatever gains he'd made with her in the past three days had been obliterated. But even though it hurt, her anger wasn't what disturbed him most. It was knowing that she was afraid. And, worse yet, that she had reason to be.

The five cabins across the creek from the rest of the resort were the first to be closed for the winter. Rachel was able to turn off the water for all five, then proceeded to drain the pipes and make an inventory of what needed to be done over the next months. This was when curtains were washed, floors were stripped and revarnished, mattresses replaced. Since it was solitary and active the work suited her present mood, yet also gave her something to think about besides the corrosive anger and fear that bubbled in the back of her mind.

She was making notes on the condition of the bathroom in number 32 when a sound behind her brought her spinning around. Through the open door of the tiny bathroom she saw Luke standing in the main room.

"Oh!" she gasped. "You just took ten years off my life!"

"I'm sorry." He looked contrite. "I wanted to talk to you. I thought you'd see me coming."

"Well, I didn't! And I don't want to talk right now."

"Why not?"

Rachel rubbed the knuckles of one hand against her forehead and closed her eyes, grasping for an inner core of serenity that didn't seem to be there. "Because I'm upset," she said. "In case you hadn't noticed."

"You have reason to be," Luke observed. He strolled farther into the room and sat on the edge of the bed, giving it a trial bounce. "Lousy mattress."

Rachel rolled her eyes. "I know."

"Okay." He looked directly at her. His eyes held honesty and a wry compassion that another time might have dissipated her anger. But she wasn't going to make the mistake of trusting him today. She felt used, unclean, and didn't doubt that if he thought a show of sympathy would bring her back on his team, he'd come up with it.

"What are you mad about?" he asked. "Do you think I haven't been honest enough with you?"

"Honest?" She stared at him in infuriated astonishment. "*Honest?* You don't know what the word means!"

A muscle twitched in his cheek, but he said gently, "You haven't asked for explanations. I haven't lied to you."

Her lips curled. "The soul of integrity, are you? How can you stand to do a job like this?"

His brows went up. "Maybe you'd better tell me what you're talking about."

"Oh, everything!" Her muscles were coiled so tightly she needed to move or she'd explode. She tossed her notebook and pencil onto the dresser and crossed the room to stare out the open door at the immense vista of ocean. "You have a law degree. You could do so much good with it! Think of the people who need help. Don't you ever wish you could do something meaningful for someone, make somebody's life better?''

Luke's face was impassive, but the warmth in his eyes had been replaced by a wintry gray chill. He watched her from his place on the bed as though waiting her out.

She turned her back on the ocean and gestured tautly. "But look at you. No eloquence in court, no guidance for the lost and hopeless. No, you play dirty little games with dirty people. The innocent ones you put in danger without the slightest qualm!"

He interjected quietly, "That, at least, isn't true."

Unwilling to stop her tirade, Rachel ignored him. "Like this week's worthy cause. You're trying to recover money that was no doubt being spent on something underhanded. What was it, funding some guerrillas so they could raze another poor village?" Luke's face tightened still further, telling her that her guess wasn't far off. "You're going to find that money, aren't you? Not because it'll go to education or to HUD, so they can provide more housing for the needy. No, that money will no doubt fund another batch of guerrillas." She made a small, disgusted sound and swung away again. "Doesn't it ever keep you awake nights?"

There was dead silence behind her. In the tense moments that followed, Rachel suddenly realized that she might have gone too far.

But she'd meant every word. The way Luke made a living was abhorrent to her, which was why she was appalled to be so attracted to him. How could she be drawn to a man who lived and walked naturally in a world of shadows and deceit, where good intentions were a lie and bad ones the only honesty? But still she began to cringe as the silence dragged on.

At last she heard his voice, low and harsh. "Yes, it sometimes keeps me awake. Does it satisfy you to know that, Mrs. Brewer?"

She swallowed hard and turned to look at him. He was standing, his hands shoved deep in his pockets and his shoulders hunched a little, as though he'd pulled himself inward. His face, on which she'd expected to see pain, held a look of boredom.

"We'll talk later," he said shortly. "Go back to work, Rachel."

"Luke—"

"Later." Without another word he walked past her, his arm brushing hers, and headed down the lane toward the bridge. Rachel didn't know whether to cry or scream.

"Aaargh!" she yelled in frustration.

She wasted an hour staring at curtains without noticing whether they were soiled, studying sinks without seeing the rust stains. Finally, annoyed with herself, she stuffed the pencil and notepad into the back pocket of her jeans and went looking for Luke. She hated feeling guilty. If only she hadn't made her attack so personal!

He wasn't building fences or, unless he was ignoring her knock, in his cabin. She didn't find him in the lodge either, but his rental car was still parked beside his cabin. On the verge of giving up, Rachel walked over to the edge of the bluff and looked down at the wide sweep of beach. She could see a family roasting hot dogs over a small fire. Others were wandering toward the path or already making their way up the crude stairs, probably with lunch in mind. The sun was high overhead, although it offered so little warmth today that Rachel still wore her heavy sweater.

At least half a mile down the beach, a figure caught her eye. Someone was staring out to sea, sitting on a bleached log that rested just above the tide line. Tiny though the figure was, Rachel was irrationally certain it was Luke. She hurried down the stairs and began to struggle across the soft sand, which sifted into her tennis shoes. At last she stopped, took them off, stuffed her socks into the toes and tied the laces so she could dangle the shoes around her neck. When she reached the harder, damp sand, walking was easier.

Luke sat, elbows on his knees, chin resting on his cupped hands, as he stared meditatively out at the blue vastness. He didn't look up at Rachel, who hesitated, then sat beside him on the gritty, weathered log.

The call of a seagull floated down from above. Rachel waited, digging her toes through the sand's crunchy surface to the soft texture beneath. She watched a band of tiny speckled sandpipers dash after the retreating water, peck frantically at the sand and then dash as quickly back before the incoming wave.

When Luke first began to speak, she could scarcely hear his voice. Since he still hadn't acknowledged her presence, it was as though he were talking to himself.

"There's something about the ocean, isn't there? It shows us how petty we are. Those waves were coming before man struggled to his feet, and they'll still be coming after we're a long-faded memory."

Rachel studied him obliquely. The philosophical bent surprised her, as did the defeat in his voice. He was involved in a reverie that left her as an audience whose applause wouldn't matter.

"Sitting here long enough could bring peace to your soul. Or maybe torment, if you can't bear to be made small. I actually like the feeling. I've sure felt small often enough with less reason." His chuckle was a whisper of sound. "And it's so clean here. The water and the sky and the birds, unchanging, inexorable and honest. What you see is what you get."

Rachel thought of the gray, creeping damp days and wasn't so sure. But not for anything would she have interrupted.

When he resumed, he'd shifted gears, though he spoke in the same musing way. "I remember the exact moment I decided to go to law school. I took an undergraduate class in civil law, just an intro kind of thing. We were studying a case, and I suggested an alternative argument the lawyers might have tried. My professor congratulated me and said that later, with another case, my argument had been tried and had succeeded before the Supreme Court." The corners of Luke's mouth curled up, though his face held no real amusement. "At the time I saw vistas open up before me, beautiful logic entwining with my own noble motives. Now I see youthful ego puffed up by one good guess. But what the hell. I probably did have a bent for law."

Rachel didn't know what to say, didn't know if Luke even wanted a response. Leaning down, he picked up two handfuls of sand and let it slip between his fingers. He appeared to be concentrating utterly on the mindless activity as he scooped up more sand, let it fall and scooped up still more. Rachel found herself equally mesmerized, as much by his hands as by what they were doing. They seemed to express all the contradictions of his personality. He had broad, strong palms, and the fingers were blunt-tipped. Yet those same fingers were long and slender, like those of a pianist, with a delicacy of movement that made her wonder how it would feel to have him touch her bare skin.

She was startled when she realized he had begun to talk again and she had been only half listening.

"I used to sneer at my fellow students who specialized in corporate law." This time Luke abruptly tossed a handful of sand; the pale shower startled some nearby sandpipers, who scattered momentarily before returning to their routine. "They laughed at me, thought I was a do-gooder." For the first time he looked at Rachel, his gaze ironic. "Does that surprise you?"

She nibbled on her lower lip and didn't respond.

"Would you like to know why I joined the agency, what happened to all my noble impulses?"

After a moment she nodded.

It was as though she'd pushed a button, the wrong one, because he said impatiently, "Ah, who knows. It was an impulse. I had visions of manipulating great events."

When he fell silent, she asked bravely, "And do you?"

He looked at her again—without quite seeing her, she thought. His voice had become dreamy again, but with a rougher texture of anger or pain in it. "Oh, I manipulate, all right. But great events? More often sordid, pathetic ones. Like this whole damn affair. Because you're right. There's no honor or moral rectitude to be upheld here. What do we have? Two thieves, a government that won't admit publicly that the money was stolen, because it can't confess to where those funds were going, and yours truly, bent on intimidating the widow to the best of my ability. Your role in this farce is the only one with any justice or dignity to it."

Rachel didn't understand his bout of harsh analysis. She couldn't help wondering if there was a chance he was deliberately seeking her pity. Had she become too cynical?

Whatever drove him, though, she doubted that sympathy was what he needed. So she said bracingly, "My role has justice or dignity only if I'm innocent. Are you so sure I am?"

He stared at her, startled. Then his mouth curled in a smile of genuine amusement. "Perhaps," he said in a tone that combined humor with something she couldn't fully analyze, "I'm indulging in wishful thinking."

"I'm surprised," Rachel said tartly. "I didn't know you were on my side."

The laughter in his eyes stilled. "You can be sure I'll protect you, with my life if I have to."

The matter-of-fact way he said it was at odds with the disturbing look in his eyes. Rachel had to blink several times before she could wrench her gaze away.

Staring down at her sandy feet she said awkwardly, "I—I haven't thanked you for this morning. You put your own body between me and the gunman. I did notice, even if I haven't been gracious enough to say anything. Thank you."

"All in a day's work," he returned lightly, his gaze shuttered now.

Rachel wasn't sure what she meant to do when she reached out to lay a hand on Luke's arm. An apology was on the tip of her tongue. But the result startled her. He swung his head toward her, his expression blazing into life, desire and sadness and humor glowing in his eyes and shaping his mouth into a curve that had a wary crook.

"I wish I'd met you at another time, in another place," he murmured. His soft, husky voice caressed her. "I'm finding it damned hard not to make love to you."

Rachel wasn't sure how she would have responded to that even if she could have thought clearly. She couldn't pretend there weren't a thousand obstacles between them, even if, like him, she wished it might be otherwise.

She was astonished to hear her own voice, sounding crisp and slightly mocking. "Faint heart ne'er won...."

Luke snatched her against him, his arm an iron band, his fingers gripping her chin to lift her face. Before she could react, he closed his mouth on hers with determination and passion. His lips were curiously tender as well, so that she melted into his embrace, sliding one hand up around his neck while the other hand clutched at his heavy sweater. His essence, of after-shave and sweat and maleness, blended with the scent of the sea. His heart thudded against her palm, while her other hand savored the sensitive skin of his neck and the soft brush of hair, which were a delicious contrast to the rasp of his hard cheek against hers and the demand of his mouth.

Her lips parted when he nipped at them, seeking access. She was becoming mindless and pliable, desperate for more of his touch, more of his heat. If he'd asked, she would have slid down onto the sand with him so that she could feel even more of him against her. She had never known that desire could leap so acutely to life or that it could be so sweet even while it consumed her independence, her very identity. It was he who slowly pulled back, moving his mouth more gently against hers, sliding his hand down her neck, hesitating over the curve of her breast before closing it on her shoulder to set her away from him a bit.

She looked helplessly into his eyes, at the triumph and regret that curved his mouth. Regret was paramount in his quietly spoken words. "Another time and place would have been better."

Rachel pulled herself together, regained her pride. "Much better," she agreed, forcing herself to pick up the tennis shoes she'd dumped on the sand and to stand on legs that didn't quite want to hold her. The ocean breeze, from which his bulk had protected her, tangled her hair and sent a shiver through her.

On impulse she said gruffly, "I'll take you out to lunch. After all, it doesn't cost me a cent."

His grin was both wicked and tender. "Haven't had a better offer in a long time," he said. "Maybe we can *talk* there." The subtle emphasis on "talk" made her glance at him, to see that his smile had grown faintly rueful. Reluctantly Rachel smiled, too, and slid her hand through the proffered crook of his arm. Her tennis shoes bumped on her chest as she and Luke walked back the way they'd come.

Chapter 5

Rachel reached into the box and took out the next piece of paper, which appeared to be an invoice. She skimmed the typescript, mumbling, "Cartons of toilet paper, a gross. Paper towels, toilet seat covers..." She sighed and tossed it onto the growing pile intended for the garbage. Who cared about toilet paper?

This latest box, which thus far contained orders from suppliers and some related correspondence, was typical of what she'd spent her last week poring over. She had yet to find anything of interest. It was beginning to seem odd, how little personal imprint Jack had left, particularly when she considered the sheer quantity of paperwork he'd saved.

She rubbed her tired eyes with her fists, then looked out the window. Drizzle had collected in tiny droplets on the glass, and the ocean beyond was gray, with a damp, lowering mist that made the sky seem heavy. Rachel was glad to have an excuse to stay in, although she was sick of her present task. Attired in a yellow slicker she'd provided, Luke was out doggedly digging holes for fence posts.

They had finished checking the contents of the attic and were now taking turns reading through the boxes of paperwork Jack had left in the closets. The fact that Luke had left her alone to search was a measure of how their relationship had changed—or, at least, so Rachel wanted to believe.

Thus far the search had been unproductive. Rachel was working with determination, more desperate than ever to find something—anything—that would make Luke Warren leave. He hadn't touched her in the past week, but she could sometimes see it in his eyes that his restraint was costing him. The tension between them was stretched so thin that Rachel could scarcely stand to be in the same room with him.

And yet, paradoxically, she didn't think she'd ever enjoyed anyone's company so much. Luke was funny, well-read, thoughtful, a good listener who liked to share what he was thinking. The day before, when they'd discussed the resort's insurance, which had come due, Rachel had realized with shock how often she'd been turning to him for advice. Luke was becoming indispensable to her, and she couldn't let that happen. She couldn't let herself forget his darker side.

The silence in the room was beginning to seem stifling. Rachel shut her eyes and let the prickling atmosphere close around her. She didn't believe in ghosts, but she almost wished Jack would appear.

"Jack," she said tentatively into the stillness. "Can you hear me?" She waited, then fumbled on, "If you weren't Bill Sand, let me find something to prove it. Please."

No ghostly voice whispered in her ear; no piece of paper floated mysteriously out of a box to land in front of her. Feeling mildly foolish, Rachel opened her eyes.

A strangled cry burst out of her. A man's face, his nose nearly pressed to the glass, appeared through the rain-washed window. He was standing no more than three feet from her.

Rachel realized immediately that the face was shadowed and the effect was distorted by the dark green hood that shielded his head from the rain. In the next moment she recognized the thin, saturnine countenance. Peering in her window was the guest who'd arrived the day of the shooting.

Drawing a sharp breath, she pushed back her chair and indignantly rose to her feet. The man retreated from the window instantly, as though startled by her movement. He gestured, mouthing what she could see was an apology, and vanished toward the front of the lodge.

Rachel stood still, her heart pounding in her ears, and stared out the window. The lawn was empty again. But she no longer felt cozy in her small, bright enclave. The silence had thickened, and now she was desperate for human voices.

She tried talking sternly to herself. It was absurd that she had reacted with such melodrama. Guests frequently wandered this way, not realizing that the wing housed private quarters. She'd just been startled, that was all, and then unnerved when she realized who this wandering guest was. He gave her the creeps, and not only because of the circumstances of his arrival. Recently she'd begun to feel as though he were shadowing her. When she would walk through the lobby, there he'd be, smiling at her from a big overstuffed chair. She'd actually chickened out of a walk on the beach one afternoon because she'd been conscious of his presence behind her.

She was so on edge lately! Another time, she might not even have noticed him. Or she might have assumed he was attracted to her but not quite sure how to approach her. Heaven knew she might be imagining things altogether! It had been rainy for the entire week, and the poor man might simply be hanging around the lodge because he was at loose ends. If only he didn't have that little smile in his eyes all the time, that creepy hint of mockery that belied his every pleasant word. If only he didn't scare her so.

She jumped again when a knock sounded on her door. Her pulse racing, she strove to sound normal. "Who is it?"

"Luke."

With a rush of relief she let him in. But the moment he stepped past her, dripping on the floor and bringing a shiver of cold air with him, Rachel's nerves began to tighten in a different way. He was so large, effortlessly dominating the room as he struggled out of the wet slicker and slung it on the rack beside the door. His wet hair was plastered to his head, and droplets ran down his nose and jaw.

"Find anything?" he asked as he pulled off the yellow rain pants he wore over his corduroys. "Damn, I'm chilled to the bone," he muttered.

Rachel retreated to a safe distance. "Take your boots off," she suggested. "They're wet."

"No kidding." He hung the pants on the rack and bent over to unlace his boots. "I feel like I've been breathing in water."

Her mood lightened a little. "You practically have. And, no, I haven't found anything. Unless you're interested in toilet seat covers."

Luke glanced up with a grin. "No, I think I can live without knowing any more than I do."

"Luke..." Rachel stopped, wishing for a second that she hadn't begun. It wasn't as though that guest, whose name she had discovered was Henry Kirk, had really *bothered* her.

But maybe Luke could check on him without the man's ever knowing.

At her troubled tone, Luke brought his head up quickly. "Is something wrong?"

"No... Not exactly."

With two thuds he dropped his wet boots beside the door and padded toward her in his damp socks. "What is it?" he asked in a voice that wouldn't be denied.

Rachel shifted uncomfortably. "Do you remember that guest who arrived just after we were shot at? The one with the rifle on his back seat?"

He nodded.

"Well... Oh, this is going to sound crazy." She pushed her fingers distractedly through her hair and turned to walk into the kitchen, needing something to do while she talked. Luke followed, watching her from the doorway of the small galley kitchen. His shoulders nearly filled the opening. Rachel held the teakettle under the faucet and spoke over the sound of the running water.

"I'd swear the guy is following me around. Just a few minutes ago I was working at the desk, and I looked up and he was staring in the window at me. It scared the daylights out of me."

"Maybe he was trying to check out the menu in the dining room. It *is* almost dinnertime."

"I know there's probably some reasonable explanation," Rachel agreed, though her tone didn't hold much conviction. "But he makes me nervous. I feel as if he's looking over my shoulder all the time. And didn't you wonder about him when he arrived?"

"Yes, of course." Luke looked at her with a small frown. "But who the hell could he be? I decided that his appearing then *had* to be a coincidence."

"He seemed familiar to me," Rachel told him reluctantly. "I figured he'd stayed here before. A lot of the guests, I see only in passing. I don't really *remember* them later. And his name doesn't mean anything to me."

Luke's frown deepened. "But there might be another reason for his familiarity to you. Could you have seen Jack with him?"

"I—I don't know." Rachel gestured helplessly. "I just don't remember. I can't even swear I've actually seen the guy before! It's possible he reminds me of someone else. All I had was an impression. Do you know what I mean?"

"I know, all right." His grim expression told her he was taking her story far more seriously than she'd anticipated. She waited while he thought. Finally he said, "I'll have a background check run on him. What did you say his name was?" When she told him he seemed to file it away. "Can you get me whatever other information he gave when he registered?"

"Yes, of course."

"Good." He nodded with satisfaction. "I ought to be able to turn up something on him."

As she turned to pour hot water into the mugs, Rachel tendered her guest a silent apology. She'd probably just ensured that the poor man would have an FBI file before the week was out. She had always resented the notion of the government being able to collect such private information without an individual's knowledge. Here not only had she contributed to such an invasion; she was grateful for it!

"Thank you," she said quietly to Luke, handing him the mug. She was painfully conscious that she had turned to him once again. This time doing so was logical, at least, but she wished it didn't feel so natural.

Their gazes met and clung. He narrowed his eyes for a beat, then nodded brusquely. "It's my job." He wheeled and walked away.

Rachel made a production of stirring honey into her tea to give her erratic pulse a chance to recover. At last she followed him into the living room, where he'd settled into a bentwood rocker. That was when she noticed the wet footprints that crossed the wooden floor.

She set down her mug on an end table. "You're still soaking!" she exclaimed. She detoured into the bathroom, then tossed him a towel.

"Thanks." He rubbed his head dry, then gave it a shake so that his hair settled in casual, damp disarray. His nose wrinkled, he peeled off his wet socks and chucked them over to join his boots.

Then he grinned at Rachel. "Sorry. I don't usually undress in a lady's living room."

"Only in her bedroom?" Rachel regretted the teasing but slightly barbed words the moment they were out. They didn't contribute to the careful formality she and Luke had been trying to maintain this past week. On the other hand, she thought waspishly, his bare feet and tousled hair didn't help much in that area, either. He was beginning to act as if he lived there.

Luke didn't move; for a minute she wasn't sure he breathed. She could feel his sudden tension. He spoke quietly. "You know I'm willing anytime."

Warmth spread on Rachel's cheeks as she evaded his gaze. Stiffly she said, "Let's stick to the matter at hand, shall we?"

Luke's tone mocked them both. "For a minute I thought that *was* the matter at hand. My mistake."

Rachel took refuge in an incautious gulp of the hot tea, which burned her mouth. "Damn," she muttered, then

made the mistake of looking at Luke. In his eyes she saw
regret and something deeper, a hunger that struck an answering chord in her, but in another moment he had wiped
his face clean of expression.

As they regarded each other warily, the silence once more
grew constrained. Rachel broke it, determined to tear down
the dark curtain of intimacy that hung between them.

Abruptly she said, "You never told me why you're so sure
it's not gold you're looking for."

His expression altered, as she'd anticipated.

"You never asked," he pointed out.

She hadn't wanted to know, she realized. It had seemed
to her that asking for details would be a concession that
there might be truth in the whole accusation. One way of
distancing herself had been ensuring that she just didn't
know enough to be haunted by pictures of a battered, prop-
driven plane being loaded furtively in the dark with wooden
crates. Or of it taking off down a narrow, bumpy runway
just as dawn began to illuminate the tangled treetops of the
jungle. For some reason that was how she'd imagined the
heist despite herself; but she wasn't kept awake nights by the
scene, because it wasn't real. She had no idea how the gold
had been stolen.

"I want to know now," she said. "Let's just say I'm curious."

She refused to consider the possibility that her curiosity
might spring from doubt. She'd had to acknowledge that
Luke was right about Jack's absences from Sahale; in all
that paperwork there were unexplained gaps. Jack's absences might never have happened, and yet there they were.
These past few days Rachel had been searching as much as
anything for evidence of where he had gone. All it would
take was a ticket stub, a letter, anything, so that she could

prove he'd innocently wintered in Arizona or somewhere equally innocuous.

"Okay," Luke had agreed, making his tone nonjudgmental. He was relieved that Rachel had started asking questions. She hadn't yet accepted the truth, but at least her certainty had begun to erode. He'd been dreading the possibility of having to present her with proof of how wrong she had been about her husband. If when that happened it came as less of a shock to her, she'd also be less likely to hold Luke to blame.

His mouth twitched wryly as he realized what that thought said about his priorities. He'd broken a cardinal rule by letting himself get emotionally involved; in his doing so, whatever control he'd had of the situation had evaporated. He'd never wanted so badly to believe in another human being. And for a man who lived so much of his life in the midst of danger and lies, the prospect of losing control was terrifying.

It wasn't just that he hungered for her physically, although the initial attraction he'd felt for Rachel had grown into desire that had lodged as a constant ache in his belly and came sharply to life at unexpected moments. Just thinking about it and looking at her now as she waited on the couch, her hands folded in her lap and her expression a mix of wariness and inquiry, made that desire jolt through Luke.

He wasn't sure what it was about her that had so thoroughly gotten to him. All he knew was that she was everything he'd ever wanted or dreamed of finding in a woman, and because of that he'd let himself trust her beyond common sense. The thought that he could possibly be wrong about her had become so nightmarish he didn't let himself linger on it. He was falling in love with her, a woman he should be regarding as a suspect; a woman he sometimes feared was still in love with the husband he was investigating. Worst of all, she was a woman he had no damn business making love to until this was all over. Then, he knew quite well, she might not have him.

She began to stir uneasily under the silence. He realized he hadn't yet explained why he was so sure the money wasn't in gold. So, as matter-of-factly as possible, he told her about Bill Sand's detour to northern Italy right after the heist, about the brief stopover, which indicated that whatever he'd done had been arranged ahead of time. Watching for any hint of her thoughts, Luke told Rachel about the report that had crossed his desk the previous December. Bill Sand had contacted at least one powerful black-market dealer about selling something that was valuable but was, unfortunately, not identified in that first, tentative feeler. Apparently he'd considered the time ripe to make his move. He'd died before he could carry it any further.

Rachel listened warily, but without protest. Luke speculated on whether she was wondering, as he was, what part Jack had intended her to play in his new life.

But she said thoughtfully, her brow crinkling, "When you say dealer, you're talking about art, aren't you? I guess I'd been picturing a jewel or something."

"It could be anything valuable and portable," Luke said. "Art's a possibility." He liked the fact that she hadn't lingered over thoughts of her husband.

"What about a painting?" she asked.

Luke reflected that she seemed unaware of the leap she'd taken in talking as though her husband *had* hidden the stolen wealth.

Rachel continued. "Jack collected the work of local artists. Well, you can see that." She gestured at the walls, on which hung a number of framed pieces, primarily watercolors.

Luke's gaze followed hers to the largest painting, which hung over the fireplace. Done in storm-washed grays, it was a huge oil of the bridge right out in front. Barely visible in the background was the lodge. Luke had to admit that the piece powerfully conveyed an eerie mood, though he found disturbing the impression of darkness moving behind that curtain of rain. Jack had apparently liked and perhaps even enjoyed the painting, Luke mused. Otherwise, why its prominent position?

Luke was aware that Rachel had pulled her attention back to him. Her eyes were suddenly shadowed. Had the painting brought back memories? Or was it that she felt like a traitor, looking around for something she had been so determined wasn't here?

She went on with difficulty. "I'm familiar with some of the artists, of course, since we sell their work, but I'm really no expert. Jack liked some pretty abstract ones. There could be a Picasso or something like that mixed in and I'd probably never notice."

Luke hated to squelch what was her first real idea, but he had to shake his head decisively. "That's already been checked. The answer isn't that obvious."

"Already checked? But how could it be?" she asked in astonishment. "You haven't been in the apartment alone long enough to look at all the paintings!"

His mouth tightened. "Rachel . . . I have to tell you that a cursory search of the place was done when we first tracked Jack down and found he'd died. Surely you didn't think we just walked away."

"Search?" she repeated as though that were the only word she'd heard. A rush of anger swept across her face, and she leaped to her feet. "Then it was *you* . . . !"

Totally perplexed by the outrage in her voice and eyes, Luke lifted his hands in an instinctive gesture of innocence.

"No! That's not my department. A couple of operatives who are good at that kind of thing were sent."

"Good?" Rachel balled her hands into fists at her sides. "Do you have any idea what chaos they left? This place was destroyed! I had to buy new curtains, have the furniture reupholstered, get a new desk.... They even tore the refrigerator apart! Haven't you wondered why Jack's papers are such a mess? It's because they were all dumped onto the floor! Is that what you call 'good'?"

"Now, wait a minute." He, too, rose to his feet. "I think we have some crossed wires here. When our people search, you don't know they've been there. What you're describing is not our style."

"Maybe you should inquire as to whether some of your colleagues have changed their style!" Rachel said, furious.

He reached out to grip her upper arms. "I'm sorry our job sometimes requires us to be so underhanded. I know it doesn't feel good to hear that somebody went through your things. But trust me—our agents are *not* responsible for the mess you're telling me about. Their orders were to look around and make notes of anything obvious, not to tear your furniture apart!"

"Not...?" He heard the beginnings of uncertainty in her voice.

"Not," Luke said definitely. With gentle hands he pushed her back onto the leather couch. He sat beside her, close enough to see the faintest tremble in her lower lip. "Tell me about it," he commanded her. "When did this happen? Did you call the police?"

Rachel nodded. "They figured it was an interrupted burglary. I was away that day."

"That day?"

"It was two weeks after Jack's funeral. A Wednesday, I think."

"Then it was after our, uh, look."

Rachel said sourly, "It's too bad all of you didn't run into each other."

Luke conceded her point with a wry grin. "Yes, it is. That would have been . . . illuminating."

"All it would have meant is that I'd have had to clean blood off the floor, too," she remarked wryly.

"Oh, we'd have helped."

Rachel rolled her eyes. "Thanks."

Frowning, Luke focused on something she'd said. "To backtrack a little . . . Did you say everything was destroyed? How about the paintings? Were there any you had to throw out?"

Rachel shook her head quickly. Luke knew she understood what he was thinking. "No, the paintings weren't touched, except for being knocked crooked. Whoever it was seemed to be looking for hiding places. The back of the couch was slashed. Every drawer in the place was thrown on to the floor. It was that kind of thing. Malicious, but . . . with intent, if you know what I mean. The police said the culprit was probably looking for jewelry and things like that and the destruction was just for fun. But I had the impression the intruder was hurried and angry. He wanted something specific he didn't find. At the time that didn't make any sense."

"But now it does." Luke relaxed against the couch and laid his arms on the back, trying to block out his awareness of Rachel's thigh touching his, the brush of her curls on his sleeve. He needed to think clearly. Although her story pointed at Krupinski, there was a flaw in that notion. He stared at the wall across the room, trying to pinpoint what was wrong.

Still, he was conscious of Rachel's tension and knew its source, which further distracted him. He could tell she was as aware of him as he was of her.

"Or does it make sense?" Luke said softly.

"What are you talking about?" she asked, her eyes showing her bewilderment.

"We had Krupinski under twenty-four-hour-a-day observation during those weeks. How the hell could he have slipped away for long enough to get out here and search your place? Either somebody fouled up badly or we have a new actor in this little drama."

Luke felt Rachel's body relax as she became interested in what he'd said. "Maybe it really was a burglar," she suggested.

"I'd like to think so," Luke said, not believing it. He added, "Your story makes me uneasy."

Rachel nodded, unsure what else to say. She felt uneasy, too, but that was partly because she'd suddenly become conscious again of how close Luke was.

With a jolt she became aware that she was staring up into his eyes. Worse yet, *he* was returning her scrutiny with interest. The groove to one side of his mouth became more pronounced as his lips curled. In his eyes, sensual intensity replaced the spark of humor. Rachel realized she had provoked trouble.

She began to scoot forward, saying brightly, "I have a casserole in the oven. Would you, uh, like to stay for dinner? Or do you have plans?"

"Plans?" He stopped her escape by sliding one hand under her dark curls to lightly clasp the back of her neck. A shock wave ran through her. So individual was the imprint of his, it was as though no hand had ever touched her there before.

"I have no plans," he said huskily. "But I can't deny that you keep giving me ideas."

She wanted to quarrel with that suggestion, but the slow circles his thumb was drawing on her sensitive skin made it difficult. Besides, this time maybe she was at fault. If she'd stood up briskly, instead of sitting here mooning at him, she might be safe in the kitchen now, not flirting with a dangerous temptation.

"I had no such intention," she managed to say.

"I know." His voice was as velvety as his touch. "But where you're concerned, I get those ideas easily. Tell me, do you reciprocate?"

She swallowed her answer. It was all she could do to keep both hands firmly clasped on her lap. She longed to explore the smooth skin of his neck, to spread her fingers on his chest over the vibration of his heartbeat, to...

In slow motion he was bending his head toward hers, as though compelled by an outside force to kiss her. She knew she ought to turn away, but the voice of cool reason had become too tiny and too distant.

She was so caught up in the physical sensations that she barely heard him mutter, "Damn, I hope you're not involved in this. I don't know if I could handle that."

The words replayed in her head, nonsensical at first. Confused, she thought of course she was involved! But then, with painful suddenness, his meaning came clear.

His mouth was a hairbreadth from hers when she gave him a hard shove. He rocked back, his hand falling from her neck, his surprised expression almost ludicrous. Springing to her feet, Rachel cried, "How can you try to kiss me when you don't even trust me!"

Looking dazed, Luke stood. As Rachel took a quick step back, he reached one hand out in appeal. "What are you talking about? You know I want you. And you know why I can't let myself totally trust you, no matter how badly I wish I could! Damn it, Rachel, try to understand.''

She didn't want to. Love, even infatuation, wasn't supposed to be so complicated. "No, I can't," she said sadly, her flare of anger gone. "And this will never be behind us. Trust has to be more basic than you're making it sound." She turned away and started for the kitchen.

Luke's voice stopped her. "Don't kid yourself, Rachel. Someday we'll have this little stewpot your husband created cleaned out. And then I'll be back. You know that, don't you?''

Rachel felt nauseated, so powerful and tangled were her emotions. "No," she said, her back still to him. "I don't know anything anymore. I just wish you'd leave me alone."

Once again the silence was heavy and dark. Then Luke spoke quietly. "I've been trying, Rachel, and I'll keep trying. But ... it isn't easy.''

It wasn't easy for her, either. Why did she have to be so shatteringly attracted to this man, who wouldn't waver in his pursuit of a goal that he knew would hurt her? He was a man whose job it was to be secretive, whose work was sordid and dangerous, a man who had no doubt done things that would horrify her. He was someone whom no woman in her right mind would open her heart to.

Only, the man she knew didn't fit that description. He was vulnerable to the painful barbs she had launched. He was tender with her, gentle despite his strength, humorous. She knew there were things he wasn't telling her, but what he did say, she would have sworn was honest. She was so confused. Was he two different people, the chameleon she'd once likened him to? Or had he deliberately constructed a front, a personality calculated to gain her cooperation? If there was a chance she'd made such a mistake once, then why not again? But she wanted to think differently. She wanted to believe that Luke was letting her see his real self.

When the telephone rang, she was grateful for the interruption. Without looking at Luke, she said abruptly, "You can stay for dinner if you want." With that she left the room.

She was probably crazy, she thought, heading for the phone that hung near the kitchen doorway. She ought to kick Luke out by the seat of his pants, as he'd put it once. But as angry and confused as she was with him, she was also reluctant to be alone. She wasn't sure whether she feared the man who'd peered in her window or her own emotions. Either way, the evening would be very long without anyone to talk to. Over the dinner table, with food and maybe some wine, she and Luke could keep the conversation light. Surely it would be all right. Most of the time Luke was good company. In fact, her liking him so much was one of the things that made the attraction so hard to fight.

As she reached for the receiver on the fourth ring, she wondered with sudden dismay if the sheriff would be on the other end. She'd called him the day after his visit. Since then, he had telephoned at least every other day. In a way she found it awkward. They didn't have much to say to each other. But his calls were also reassuring, a lifeline to the outside. Tonight, though, she didn't feel capable of dealing with his not-so-subtle probing.

With relief she heard the voice of her cook, who had a routine question to which she was able to give a routine answer. Rachel was almost disappointed not to be needed; she could have used the distraction. The lasagna she'd put in the oven earlier was beginning to smell very good, however, and she'd hate to have it ruined, as happened to her dinners all too often.

After hanging up, Rachel hesitated. Reluctantly she decided that before she made a salad or set the table, she'd better see if Luke was still there. She realized she was apprehensive. She was no longer sure what she wanted. In a way it would be a relief if he were gone. She'd been kidding herself to hope that they could somehow magically revert, in the space of about five minutes, to any kind of easy relationship. They'd bared too many raw emotions in the last half hour.

He was there, standing in the living room with his back to her as he perused titles in a glass-fronted bookcase. Although she'd stepped quietly, he said without turning around, "That wasn't a call to duty, I hope."

"No," she said without elaborating.

Luke turned to face her. "Can I set the table for you?" he asked. Some strain was visible around his eyes, but otherwise his emotions were veiled. Rachel relaxed just a little.

"Thanks," she said. "I'll make a salad while you're doing that."

She was able to relax further as they began to eat. They had a stimulating discussion, during which Rachel discovered to her surprise that Luke's views weren't so far from her own. Only his cynicism contrasted with her deeply felt belief in the possibility of good triumphing. When that topic ran down, it was Luke who kept the conversation undemanding, telling humorous stories about a few bungled jobs he'd been involved in.

"Is it always money you're chasing around after?" She was finding she couldn't even imagine what his life was like.

"Um...not always." He took a sip of the red wine. "We have our fingers in a lot of pies."

"How did your fingers get stuck in this one?" Rachel asked with reluctant interest. She was becoming more and more curious and tried to convince herself that was natural. After all, how could she possibly be expected to understand how she herself had become caught up in this mess unless she knew what the background was? Still, she had a suspicion she was making a mistake.

She listened with both distaste and fascination as Luke explained that his department had taken over once all the parties came back to the States.

"The CIA sometimes minds their p's and q's," he said wryly, going on to tell her that Walt was regular army. One reason he hadn't appeared long before was that he'd had to finish up his enlistment. "That was part of the plan the three of them had agreed on, of course," Luke added. "Bill could disappear, which he did regularly, anyway. The other two would go about their normal business. Once the heat was off, they'd divvy up the goodies. What apparently wasn't part of the plan was that Bill didn't leave his forwarding address. That's what Krupinski is so fired up about."

At her urging, Luke told her about the third partner. "Chuck Willis was a CIA stringer. Kind of a nasty character, from what I can gather. He was an MP in Vietnam, later got involved with the Agency. A few months after the gold disappeared, he popped up in Honduras, where he got in the way of a stray grenade. One of ours, ironically."

Luke wondered suddenly if he'd said more than Rachel wanted to hear. Her face was pale, her eyes rather blank. But she needed to know, he thought. She wasn't a woman who would ever hide from reality just because it was unpalatable. All the same, this particular reality could be taken in small doses.

He wasn't surprised when, after the silence had lingered just a fraction too long, she changed the subject abruptly. "What are you planning to do after dinner?"

Luke wanted to tease her, to bring a smile to her lips. But something in her expression made him keep his distance. "Get on with the job," he said with a shrug.

She said, "I need to work in the gift shop this evening. "I've gotten behind on reordering. I don't even know what's been selling. But tomorrow—" she hesitated "—if it's okay with you, I thought maybe I'd start reading Jack's diaries."

Luke froze with the wineglass halfway to his lips. "His . . . what?"

Chapter 6

"Jack's diaries," Rachel said in surprise. "Didn't you see them out there in the bookcase?"

Luke swore under his breath. "Why didn't you tell me there was such a thing? We've been wasting our time these last ten days!"

"No, no," Rachel said quickly. "You don't understand. They're not personal at all. That's why I left them until last. I really shouldn't even call them diaries. Notebooks, maybe. All he did was keep track of weather and business details, like when suppliers delivered. He says things like, 'Raining today. Order from Capitol Linen didn't show.' I never understood why he kept them at all."

"Show me," Luke said tersely.

Without arguing, Rachel fetched one from the bookcase. She flipped it open at random and laid it down before Luke. He read in silence, turning several pages. At last he closed it and handed it back to her.

Almost apologetically, she said, "When you first arrived I did look, to see what he wrote about his absences."

"And?"

"Nothing. There's an entry one day, and the next one is five months later. No explanation at all."

"Doesn't that strike you as strange?" Luke asked. His gaze was intent on her face.

"Very," Rachel admitted. "But . . . well, he was kind of a strange man."

Luke seemed to be waiting, but she said no more. She had been confused enough about her marriage before Luke's advent. Now she found it impossible to even try to sort those feelings out. She'd come to realize that before she could make peace with her memory of Jack, she had to know once and for all who he had been.

She didn't know if she'd be ready to talk about Jack even if her relationship with Luke had been different. As it was, she felt as though she'd be putting a weapon into Luke's hands if she told him any more about the difficult, often unlikable man she'd married. Nor could she bear to see the look in Luke's eyes if he knew she had actually rejoiced in a man's death because it had freed her.

Luke had been watching her over his glass of wine. He seemed to sense that it wasn't the time to push, because he said out of the clear blue sky, "You're something of a radical, aren't you?"

"Radical?" Rachel blinked as her mind shifted gears. "Oh, you mean because of this morning." Her smile was faint and a little wry. "Yes, I suppose I am. But . . . I really owe you an apology for that."

His brows rose. "Are you trying to tell me you didn't mean every word?"

"Of course I did. But I wasn't being fair. I don't know that much about you or what your job involves. I was letting my prejudices talk, and also, I think, my own sense of guilt.''

"That's a strong word.'' She couldn't read his expression.

"I spend a lot of time feeling guilty," Rachel admitted. "I look around at everything I could be accomplishing— *should* be—if I'd earned that law degree. But what did I do instead? I got married. Now I'm running a resort. Sometimes it's challenging, sometimes I even enjoy it, but I can't convince myself that the work is very important.''

"Most people's work isn't, you know.''

Rachel sighed. "I know. I didn't say my feelings made sense.'' As though to end the conversation, she began clearing the table. Luke silently joined her in carrying dishes out to the kitchen.

As she ran water into the sink, however, he commented quietly, "You don't owe anybody anything, Rachel. Guilt is a destructive emotion. It's a way people have of manipulating each other. Think about who is doing it to you.''

He didn't sound as though he expected an answer, and she didn't offer one. Later, however, as Rachel began checking the stock in the gift shop, she thought about everything she'd said to Luke and about his last remark. Why had she never before realized consciously how often she felt guilty?

She was quite sure it had something to do with her mother, who had excelled in making Rachel feel that way for the least little thing. One that popped up in her memory was a time she'd ruined a blouse by spilling grape juice down her front. Her mother, who had made the blouse, acted as though Rachel had done it on purpose just to have an excuse not to have to wear it. It was true that she really hadn't liked the blouse very much. But the spill had been an accident. Afterward, Rachel had felt bewildered and guilty about the incident and begun to wonder if she *had* ruined the blouse on purpose.

"What a dumb little thing to remember," she murmured aloud.

Perhaps not so dumb, she thought as other, similar incidents began to tug at the corners of her memory. Maybe it was important that she remember. She only wished that it hadn't taken Luke to open those floodgates.

Rachel had no chance the next day to start reading the diaries. Several minor calamities filled her time, and she was annoyed at herself for being so preoccupied with Luke and his quest.

In midafternoon, she was informed that a guest had slipped on the steps to the beach and had broken a leg. Somehow she was not surprised to find that it was Luke who was splinting the leg after he'd called for an ambulance. His air of matter-of-fact competence was obviously reassuring to the woman, whose face was white with shock.

Rachel saw the ambulance off with a promise to follow it.

"Thanks," she said briefly to Luke as she reached for her car keys.

"Shall I come with you?" he asked.

"No, you'll be more help here. Heaven knows there's nothing I can do at the hospital but stand around and look concerned."

"Your insurance should be adequate, you know. So don't worry about that," he said.

"Yes, I know. Still, the poor woman! And on her vacation!" Rachel sighed. "I wish these things wouldn't happen."

To her surprise, Luke reached out one large hand and gently tipped her face up. Looking down into hers, his eyes were warm and sympathetic. "Relax," he said softly. "To-morrow can't help but be better."

Rachel thought about Jack's diaries and Walt and the unknown gunman. She had to laugh. "You're either an outrageous liar or quite an optimist."

Luke bent to brush a feather-light kiss across her lips. Rachel could feel his smile against her mouth.

He dropped his hand to his side and stepped back. His voice held an affectionate, mocking undertone when he said, "Guess which."

Rachel didn't even try, but as she pulled out onto the highway she realized that her mood had improved considerably.

The effect didn't last, however, particularly since the only evidence of Luke she saw that evening was a scrawled note telling her that he'd taken some of Jack's papers to his cabin.

Nor did the next day improve. The weather was dreary, gray and drippy, and several people called to cancel reservations. Rachel saw Luke in the morning, but he was noncommittal and curiously distant. She thought perhaps he regretted yesterday's show of warmth, however brief it had been. After their brush with danger the evening before, any instant of closeness probably raised a warning flag in his mind. Even she could see that the potent attraction between them must be as big a problem for him as it was for her. Making love to someone who figured in an undercover investigation—or, worse yet, was a suspect—had to be taboo for federal agents.

Doing her best to dismiss Luke from her mind, in the early afternoon she set Brenda, the young maid, to work taking down the draperies in closed cabins, and washing, hemming and mending them. Just when Rachel had succeeded in forgetting him, Luke appeared in the doorway.

"I need to go into town, Rachel. Can I pick up anything for you?"

He wasn't making any pretense of asking permission, she noticed.

She shook her head in answer to his question, wondering what his errand was. At least once a week he'd disappear for several hours. She hadn't yet seen him use the resort telephone, so she supposed he reported to his superior from a pay phone.

Luke didn't linger. As soon as he had her answer he said, "Fine," and as promptly vanished from the doorway.

Rachel toyed with the idea of spending the afternoon looking at Jack's notebooks. Curiosity about them had begun to tickle at her mind since she'd announced her intention to read them. She knew that they were boring; she'd occasionally glanced over her husband's shoulder when he made an entry. Nonetheless, surely he'd recorded at least *some* personal thoughts or events of significance to him. She wondered, for example, what he'd written the day he met her. Until now she had adamantly not wanted to know. She had even considered burning them, so she would never be tempted to find out. But the cloth-bound volumes had seemed to belong in their neat row on the bottom shelf of the glass-fronted bookcase, so she had left them.

Reluctantly, she decided that she should spend the afternoon working on accounts. She'd fallen way behind, and the job was laborious enough even when she stayed on top of it. Today was ideal. The weather was so dismal that only a few of the cabins were occupied, and as a result the chances were good that she could work uninterrupted.

Two hours later, thinking longingly of a cup of tea, Rachel looked up from the open ledger on her desk. She was startled to see the sheriff leaning against the door frame as though he'd been there for a while, watching her.

For an instant there was a fleeting expression in his eyes that disturbed her, though she couldn't pin down why. He smiled, and she decided his thoughts had been elsewhere as he waited for her to look up. Heaven knew what his morning had been like already. For all she knew, he might have spent it looking at a dead body.

"I don't want to bother you if you're busy," he said.

Rachel was delighted to have an excuse to close the ledger book. She felt warmer toward George today, perhaps because of the distance Luke had opened. "I'd love to be bothered!" she assured him. "Can I talk you into a cup of coffee? Or are you here on business?"

George shook his head. "Just passing by. We had a little trouble down by the reservation. I couldn't resist turning in here for a break on my way back to the station."

"Well, I'm ready for one, too," Rachel announced, then stood and led the way into the coffee shop.

Straddling stools at the counter, she and George exchanged chitchat as they sipped hot drinks. Finally she walked him out to his car. The drizzle had eased, so they strolled over to the edge of the bluff and looked out at the ocean. The gulls wheeling and turning above them were the only sign of life.

After a long moment of silence, the sheriff said reflectively, "Hell of a place."

Rachel nodded and automatically ran her hand along the new fence Luke had been building. It looked nice, she thought. What was probably more important, it was the ideal height for leaning on, and very sturdy. Luke was a real perfectionist, a craftsman.

When they turned away from the bluff, she was for a moment startled to see the sheriff's unmarked car in one of the parking slots right near where they stood, only a short distance from the first cabins but several hundred yards from the lodge. Glancing in the window, Rachel saw the debris of a brown-bag lunch on the front seat, and realized that probably George had sat there, eating a late lunch and gazing out at the ocean, before he'd come in to see her. Now he opened the car door, and she could hear the crackle of voices on the radio as dispatchers and deputies exchanged information.

The sheriff ignored the radio as he leaned on the open door and looked seriously at Rachel. "You're getting by okay out here alone?"

"Hardly alone! But yes, of course." She managed a small, rueful laugh as she thought back over the past year of trial and error. "I'm not sure I'm cut out to run a resort, but... I'm managing."

"Amazingly well, from what I hear." He shook his head. "It was a damn shame, Jack dying that way."

"Yes, it was," Rachel said quietly, despising herself for her hypocrisy. No, that wasn't quite fair. Of course she'd grieved for Jack. But she could never let herself forget that first, inextricable mixture of shock and relief. Until life had opened again for her, in that one, stunning instant, she hadn't known she'd felt so trapped. Now she wished that she had worked up the courage to divorce him before the accident.

Rachel glanced around. The resort was so empty today, she thought, so bleak. She was about to turn back to the sheriff, when something slightly out of place caught her attention and she frowned. Had she seen a movement through the window of Luke's cabin? His car wasn't in its slot, she realized, starting to dismiss her jarring reaction. The next moment, she saw that the door of his cabin stood a few inches ajar.

"George..." Rachel clutched at the sheriff's sleeve. Looking puzzled, he turned to follow the direction of her gaze. She was dimly aware of the continuing crackle of the radio from the interior of the car. Before Rachel could take a step forward, Luke's door opened farther and a man appeared in the opening.

For a moment Walt Krupinski appeared as shocked as Rachel felt. But then his eyes narrowed and a peculiar, menacing expression transformed his face. Rachel could feel his anger, see it in his eyes. She tightened her fingers on George's arm.

Suddenly she realized that the sheriff had no idea why she was acting so peculiar. He probably assumed that the man standing in the doorway was a guest. She opened her mouth again to explain, but she felt him stiffen under her hand as a burst came from his car's radio. He snapped, "Rachel, I've got to be off. That's my call. You take care."

"George, don't go! Please! That's—"

He was already in the car, slamming the door. He gunned the motor and accelerated backward in a big swing, then the car leaped forward, toward the highway.

Rachel took a nervous step back and bumped into the fence. She saw that Walt wasn't looking at her, at least for the moment. He was staring after the sheriff's car, his eyes slits in his pudgy face.

Taking advantage of his distraction, Rachel eased her way another step, then two, along the fence. She couldn't believe how isolated she felt here, in the open, with a dozen cabins and the lodge in sight. Where was that strange guest who liked to haunt her footsteps? Rachel thought about opening her mouth to scream, then wondered if anyone would hear. Besides, what if Walt had a gun?

Her question was answered immediately. Walt did have a gun, and it was pointed now at her. Only a distance of about ten yards separated them. Rachel swallowed and stared at the black, snub-nosed weapon.

"Rachel, I want to have a little talk with you. Why don't you come on in?" His voice was flat and sounded curiously dead.

Rachel decided to try for bravado. "Why don't *you* put that gun away?"

He smiled. "I like it—it gives me confidence. I like to use it, too."

She hesitated for another second, then reluctantly began to walk toward him on shaking legs. "All right, I'm coming," she said, her voice amazingly steady. "I don't mind talking to you, Walt. I just wish we could do it without the gun between us."

He simply broadened his smile, making the contrast with his cold, expressionless eyes more unpleasant for Rachel. When she reached him, Walt stepped aside to let her pass. She cringed away from him as they brushed.

Luke's bed was unmade, and some faded jeans lay across it. She could see the indentation his head had made in the pillow. A book lay open, spine up, on the bedside stand.

She stopped in the middle of the room and turned to see that Walt had followed her in and was closing the door behind him. As the latch clicked, her muscles twitched in an involuntary spasm. In an effort to control her body's reaction, she clenched her jaw and curled her fists, holding herself utterly rigid.

Walt's smile had disappeared, she saw, although the dispassionate way he looked her over wasn't much better. After a moment's apparent reflection, he tucked the gun into a holster hidden inside his dark blue windbreaker.

Rachel didn't relax at all. Walt outweighed her considerably and had the ruthless instincts that would take advantage of any opening. She knew he would be willing to hurt her, and she wasn't sure she could do the same to him. Her best chance was to conciliate him and, above all, not to show her fear, which she instinctively knew he would enjoy.

"I suppose you want a report," she said as matter-of-factly as she could manage.

He inclined his head. "For starters."

That was ominous, she thought. "Searching would be easier if you could tell me more about what I'm looking for."

She knew immediately that she'd made a mistake in saying that. Walt hated the lack of knowledge that meant he needed her, and his face hardened.

"What I know," he said through gritted teeth, "is that your husband tried to pull a fast one on me. He's not here anymore, but you are. I'm going to have satisfaction of one kind or another. I'd rather go home rich." He paused, and her hands grew clammy. "I think. But if I can't have that, I'll have blood. Do you understand?"

Rachel nodded, frozen with fear. She'd never before seen real hate.

"Then tell me what that damned fed is doing here. If you called—"

She found her voice. "No! No, I—I didn't. I swear! He just showed up, right after you. He said he followed you."

"Followed me?" Walt uttered a vicious curse, then said as though to himself, "But they have nothing on me. There isn't anything they can do."

Rachel wondered if in his lexicon holding her at gunpoint was "nothing," but she wasn't about to argue.

"I'll get the money and disappear. I can do it." He seemed to be mumbling to himself, his eyes not really seeing her.

Rachel shifted her weight surreptitiously, slid one foot back, then the other. If she could get close enough to the rear door...

Unfortunately he'd reached a point in his monologue that included her. He focused his cold gaze on her. "I'm running out of patience. I might have shared if you'd handed it over right away, but I'm beginning to think another kind of persuasion might work better."

Rachel fumbled another step backward. Walt was smiling again, his eyes like a snake's. He walked forward, the gun mercifully staying hidden.

Rachel bolted. The narrow door was only a few feet away, and her hand was on the latch when Walt caught her. Events blurred and slowed as with a hard grip on her shoulder he swung her around and smashed the back of his hand into her face. Her head rocked sideways and her vision misted over, then she tasted blood. She tried to push at him, to knock his arm away, but then he backhanded her again, his knuckles grinding into her cheekbone. Her knees began to buckle, but he caught her before she could fall. For a minute she hung, unresisting, in his grip, until new pain roused her. He had bent her arm behind her back and slowly twisted it until a gurgling scream burst from her lips.

Rachel had never imagined what it would be like to be tortured. She was so shocked she couldn't think, could only react. Time had both slowed down and compressed, as though this had gone on forever and yet was happening with dazzling speed.

One minute he was twisting her arm until she could hear it creak as the pain sent electric impulses into her brain. The next, he flung her to the floor. Rachel landed heavily on her shoulder. She was dimly aware of another man, but before she could get a grip on herself, she heard the crack of a fist striking flesh. She thought fuzzily of scrambling out of the way, but it was too late. A body landed on her, flattening her painfully against the hard floor.

When she realized with repugnance that it was Walt, Rachel began to struggle. She could taste fresh blood as she turned her head to look up. Luke loomed above her, his face a mask of fury. His legs were braced apart as he waited for Walt to make the next move. Rachel noticed the blood on his knuckles, the reddening on one cheekbone. She had never known a man could look so angry, so powerful.

As Walt pushed himself off her, she rolled away. In the split second that followed, he levered himself to his feet and slipped his hand under his jacket.

"Luke!" Rachel cried. "He has a gun!"

The moment Walt's hand emerged, Luke's foot shot up in a karate kick that connected squarely, sending the gun flying across the room and onto the bed. Walt grunted with pain and launched himself at Luke, who hadn't yet regained his balance. A blow to the stomach had Luke bent over, exhaling in agony. Rachel crawled toward the bed, determined not to let Walt have the gun again.

He looked at it and at Rachel. Her hand was inches from closing on the butt. His appearance was dreadful, his color pasty, the side of his face already swelling and darkening. He drew his lips back from his teeth in a feral snarl.

"I'll be back, bitch!"

Even as Luke painfully straightened, Walt disappeared out the door. Luke started after him, holding his stomach, but then he looked back at Rachel. She saw the indecision that tore at him. Then, after one last look at the open door, he came across the room in long strides and knelt by Rachel where she sagged against the bed.

"Ah, damn," he murmured, reaching out to tilt her face up so that he could examine it. The heat in his eyes was still there, but his touch was exquisitely gentle.

"I'm—I'm really not hurt," she told him. "You can go after him. I'll be all right."

He gave his head an impatient shake. "It's too late. Anyway, you're more important."

"But he'll get away!" Rachel protested.

For a moment Luke seemed to ignore her words. With his fingertips he tenderly explored the side of Rachel's swollen cheek. But when he answered at last, his voice was knife-edged. "I'll catch up with him eventually. Don't worry."

Rachel searched his face and saw the truth. For the first time, she was grateful for what Luke was. She had never needed or wanted vengeance before, but now she did, she realized.

Then she wiped thoughts of Walt out of her mind and took Luke's big hand in hers, holding it so she could see his knuckles. She wondered if he had broken a bone.

"We're a pretty pair," she said wryly.

"I'd better get you to a hospital."

"I'm really all right," she said, knowing with surprise that it was true.

"There's blood in your mouth," he observed.

"There is?" Rachel thought back. "I must have bitten my tongue. I know I did when Walt crashed down on top of me. I guess I can't exactly blame him for that."

Her effort at lightness failed. Luke stood abruptly and strode into the bathroom. She heard water running, and a moment later he came back, hands full. Rachel had by this time made it to the bed. Seated there, she could see her reflection in the mirror that hung above the bureau across the room. She looked like hell but was amazed to discover that all her injuries were superficial.

Once she'd rinsed the blood out of her mouth with the glass of water Luke presented, and patted her sore face with the wet washcloth, she felt almost human.

She met his anxious gaze with a shaky smile. "Luke... Thank you. You seem to be making a habit of rescuing me."

She was more than grateful; she was touched. He was such a cool, collected man, one who seemed able to humorously shrug off everything. Then she saw the anger that still simmered in his eyes, and something twisted oddly and sweetly in her chest, because she knew it was for her sake. On a primitive level she reveled in the knowledge that she had roused so much emotion in him. Rationally she knew his job had demanded that he pursue Walt. As a woman, though, she couldn't help exulting because Luke had not been able to leave her.

Some of her thoughts must have shown on her face, because his expression slowly changed. The heated anger in his eyes was transformed into a hungry desire. Slowly and very deliberately he reached over and picked up the gun, which still lay on the bed. He walked over to the bureau, set down the glass and towel and carefully laid the gun beside them. He walked back to the bed with a taut grace, leashed tension evident in every line of his body. His gaze was predatory and unwavering, and determination hardened his jaw.

Rachel waited with quickened breath and racing heartbeat. She was a civilized woman, for God's sake, she chided herself. It was insane to be aroused by a show of purely masculine power. On the other hand, the adrenaline surging through her body had brought to fever pitch the desire that had lurked there since she'd set eyes on Luke. All she knew was that she wanted him. Now.

She sucked in her breath when he swept her up and let them both fall across the bed. The mattress gave beneath their weight, but Rachel scarcely noticed, because Luke's mouth was already on hers, hard, passionate and demanding. She parted her lips before the force of his hunger and twined her arms around his neck to pull him closer.

Desire exploded between them, electrifying, shocking. Even as he tasted her mouth, he had his hand beneath

Rachel's shirt and was pulling impatiently at her bra. She didn't care when she heard the distinct pop of a button hitting the floor. All she wanted was for her skin to be bare for his seeking, exploring touch, to delight in the feel of her breasts against his hair-roughened chest.

She heard the gritty sound of satisfaction he made when her bra followed her shirt onto the floor. Lifting her heavy lids, she saw the smoky passion in his eyes as he bent his head to caress the soft curves of her breasts with his mouth. She arched her neck and moaned in the back of her throat as his tongue enticed her nipple and his teeth grazed it lightly. Then, as her own impatience took over, she wrenched at the buttons of his shirt and bared his tanned shoulders and chest. She stroked the smooth skin of his arms and shoulders, then slid her hands around for the pleasure of feeling the well-defined muscles in his back ripple and shift under her touch.

But neither she nor Luke had the self-control to indulge in the exploration, in the tentative touches and sweet sampling of each other's bodies that usually presage lovemaking. With her every nerve Rachel was aware of his arousal, and her hips pressed up against his seemingly with a will of their own. With his knee he separated her legs, and even as he returned his mouth hungrily to hers he fumbled at the fastenings of her jeans. When at last the two of them had to separate to kick off their heavy jeans and shoes, there was a kind of desperation on Luke's face that fueled her. His breathing was swift; hers came in tiny gasps. Nothing mattered but their closeness, the heat where they touched and the chill where they didn't. Rachel almost groaned with pleasure at the sight of him naked, long and lean and taut, and she saw by the flare in his gaze that he was just as excited by her body.

For a moment Luke looked almost reverent, and with excruciating slowness he moved his hand up the slender line of her thigh to her hips and stomach. She looked down and saw Luke's long, muscular leg where it lay across hers, but still he leaned on one elbow, looking his fill. At last his gaze met hers. The gleam in his eyes, possessive and passionate, was all that any woman could want, and it melted any last reserve in her.

His voice, rough with desire yet tender, was just as affecting. "You're incredibly beautiful, Rachel. I knew you would be. I've been haunted by imagining how this would be."

But before his words could invoke any kind of reality, his mouth descended again to hers, and Rachel's bones seemed to dissolve. With lips and hands and teeth he brought her to a fever pitch of aching urgency. A maelstrom of need, dizzying in its intensity, had caught her, and she strained upward as he parted her thighs. When he thrust into her, tiny whimpers escaped her, and she clutched frantically at his damp, muscled back. Luke's face, strained and yet exhilarated, was almost unrecognizable above hers, his teeth showing in a triumphant, silent cry. A sweet spiral began to coil in Rachel, tighter and hotter, until she could have screamed with the exquisite agony of it. When it exploded, she called out his name as fire ran through her veins, leaving sweet tremors in its wake. She felt his body convulse at nearly the same instant, and she saw the raw pleasure on his face.

Time stretched and shivered like watered silk rippling in a draft of air. She and Luke lay on their sides, pressed together, the top of her head tucked under his chin. There was warmth and lingering sweetness in the atmosphere. She felt as though she were floating on air, delicious tingles making her conscious of even her toes and the tips of her fingers.

But, inevitably, reality began to creep in on her. Rachel became aware of the covers bunched uncomfortably under her waist, of how chilly the room really was. She could feel the vibration of Luke's heartbeat against her cheek, and as the seconds ticked past, his pulse slowed, telling her he'd regained control of his own emotions.

As had she. Rachel wasn't sure she could bring herself to look into Luke's face. She'd been wanton, utterly uninhibited. She was ashamed of her wildly sexual response to a frightening event. Where did it leave her now? Her relationship with Luke had been fiery enough before, igniting dangerously with only a look or incautious word. Now the memory of their passion and of that explosive and incredibly pleasurable finale would lie between every glance they exchanged. *I must have been insane,* she thought desperately.

Luke must have felt her almost imperceptible withdrawal, because the arm that lay across her tensed, and she could see the deep breath that expanded his chest. A sudden impulse made Rachel long to tilt her head forward and press a kiss on his chest, maybe rub her cheek sensuously against the fine, light hair that gilded it. Instead, she abruptly rolled away, lying for a moment on her back, staring up at the ceiling. Her head still rested on his arm, but otherwise their bodies didn't touch.

Then, bracing herself, she turned to look at him. Immediately she wished she hadn't. The expression in his eyes shattered her to the core. What they had done was insane, yes. But, God help her, she wouldn't have taken back this time even if it had been within her power.

But he didn't look as though he felt the same. He had regretted their kisses—she'd known that—but this was cutting at him in a way that hurt her to see. He wanted to undo what they had shared. His lips were compressed into a thin line. His eyes were clouded and dark.

But then he focused on her face, and something in her expression caused his to alter instantly. "Rachel—"

"No!" Emphatically she cut off whatever he'd been going to say. It could only hurt her worse. "Let's not talk about it."

He reached out for her. "Rachel," he said again, more softly. "We have to—"

"No!" She twisted away from his hand as though his touch would burn her. She rolled off the bed, snatched up her clothes from where they lay on the floor and began to scramble into them. "What's done is done," she said quickly, not looking at him. "We'll just spoil it by talking about it. Let's forget it, okay?"

"Forget it?" The harsh timbre to his voice brought her eyes up, momentarily stilled her movements. Luke's face looked gaunt with frustration. He said, "I don't think we'll be forgetting it, Rachel. So don't even try."

She swallowed hard. It was a moment before she could wrench her gaze away and resume dressing. At last, in silence and without touching her, he did the same.

Chapter 7

As he hurriedly pulled his clothes on, Luke kept a watchful eye on Rachel. Something had upset her; that was obvious. The trouble was, he didn't know what.

He was disgusted with himself for letting Krupinski walk away. What had stopped him? One look at Rachel, on her knees, clinging to the bed for support. One look, and he hadn't been able to leave her, hadn't been able to do his job.

Deep inside, Luke knew it was just as well he hadn't gone after Krupinski. Luke had never wanted to shoot anybody before, but the moment he had walked into the cabin and seen that bastard hurting Rachel, he had felt a cold rage he hadn't thought himself capable of. He had no longer wanted to arrest Krupinski, to see him behind bars. He had wanted to kill him.

But he hadn't done that. No, instead he'd made passionate love to the one woman of all others he had no right to touch. His job would go up in smoke if anybody in the department ever knew, though he no longer gave a damn about that. What mattered was Rachel. She needed to be able to depend on him to protect her. She needed to be able to trust him. How could she do either now? He'd taken advantage of her vulnerability after the attack and of her gratitude toward him for the rescue. He had hurt her, just when he most wanted not to.

What he would be expected to do, of course, was back out and ask for a replacement. This afternoon was a good example of why. He'd let his emotions get in the way. But just as he hadn't been able to walk out of the cabin an hour ago, now he couldn't walk away from Sahale. He didn't know another agent he'd trust to protect her. And while he'd frustrated this attack, he had seen the look Walt had leveled at Rachel right before he fled. Walt would be back.

And Walt wasn't the only danger. Luke had come to rely on a sixth sense, and it was telling him that someone else was involved. Luke didn't have the evidence to convince anyone else. But he knew. That made him more anxious about Rachel's safety. He'd seen her as the linchpin, and so would anyone else looking for that damned gold.

He couldn't be her lover and have any respect for himself. If anything was to come of their relationship, it had to be when they were on free and equal terms.

And there were other, just as compelling arguments that kept him silent. Someday Rachel might hate him because he'd exposed her husband's secrets. Even if by some miracle she hadn't loved the man, what Luke was doing would still undermine her faith in her own judgment. He couldn't expect her to be grateful for that.

What he had to do this very minute was wrench open a deep gulf between them. Then he had to find the strength to keep his hands off her.

If only he could forget that for a few minutes he had been happier than ever before in his life. He had never known a man could want a woman so badly, on so many levels, that the pain of that wanting became part of himself.

Luke gritted his teeth against a renewed surge of desire and turned around. Rachel was at the door, her hand on the knob.

He made his voice hard and commanding, worlds away from what he felt. "Rachel, wait."

She paused without turning, her back straight.

"There are a few practical matters we ought to talk about."

"Like?" The single word was uncompromising.

"Like what you're going to tell people about your face."

She was still for a moment, and then her hand crept up to touch her swollen cheek, as though she had forgotten about it. Finally her shoulders slumped a little, and she swung around to face Luke. She made a small, defeated gesture. "I don't know what I'll say. That I fell, I suppose."

"Where?" he asked ruthlessly.

Her chin came up at his tone. "On the stairs from the beach."

"Why didn't anybody see you?"

"There wasn't anybody around this afternoon." She paused, adding pointedly, "Nobody at all."

Silence followed her statement as he looked thoughtfully at her, trying to interpret the chill in her tone. At last he said, "Are you trying to say something?"

"Yes." Her nostrils flared. "Where were you when I needed you?"

Luke paced across the room, his eyes never leaving her. "I was under the impression that I appeared rather expeditiously."

Rachel reached up to touch her face again in an unconscious gesture. "A few minutes earlier would have been nice."

In a vivid flash, as though it were happening again, Luke saw Walt's hand connecting with Rachel's cheek. Cold fury exploded in his chest, and his jaw hardened. "I'm sorry for that, Rachel. Sorrier than you can imagine. Krupinski *will* pay for hurting you."

The sting in Rachel's cheek, the ache in her shoulder, were minor compared to the pain Luke had dealt with one look. She didn't want him to make Krupinski pay. She wanted him to draw her into his arms, tell her he loved her, kiss her and caress her and let her see warmth in his eyes. Because he wasn't doing any of those things, she wanted to hurt him as he was hurting her.

"When you can take the time to catch up with him," she jeered. She hated herself instantly for the petty bad humor that had made her lash out.

The gray of Luke's eyes turned to ice, and she could almost feel the cold. But backing down might have meant crumpling into tears, so with a show of elaborate nonchalance she leaned against the wall and crossed her arms, waiting.

He looked even more intimidating than usual as he continued to prowl back and forth, and yet, achingly, she could see the man she'd just made love with.

Frost crackled at the edges of his voice when he said, "Now that I have something definite on Krupinski, I'll have an APB put out on him. From the Department, without my name on it. We won't have to worry about him for long. As to where I was this afternoon . . . that's really none of your business, is it?"

Her gaze fell, and she said nothing.

"I did plan to tell you about the report given me on your very interesting guest," he informed her.

Rachel looked up quickly.

It was Luke's turn to mock her with a twisted smile. "Curious, are you?"

"You know I am," she said, pressing her lips together.

He shrugged, as though impatient with himself. "I didn't find out anything useful, unless you'd like to know how promptly he pays his bills."

"Not really." Rachel felt an unpleasant pang again at the thought of the wolves she'd set loose on the poor man. "What . . . what does he do for a living?"

"That's not altogether clear," Luke said grimly. "He's either changed jobs often or changed his mind about what sounds good. Insurance salesman, real estate, assistant manager of an all-night grocery store . . . Oh, hell. The income he reports fits in. There's no real reason to doubt him. I just wish he'd turned out to be somebody we could really pin down, like a nice, respectable doctor."

"He's too . . . odd to have been that."

Luke regarded her intently. "He really gives you the creeps, doesn't he?"

"I guess he does," she admitted. "Although it's partly circumstances. I might not even have noticed him another time. And if I had to choose between him and Walt . . ." Her hands fluttered revealingly. "I have to admit, I actually wished the guy had been hovering around this afternoon."

"Yeah. I wish he'd been, too." There was silence for a moment as they considered each other warily. Finally Luke said, "How did Krupinski catch you alone, anyway?"

She shrugged. "It wasn't hard to do. This place is so spread out, with most of the cabins empty. . . . I have to do my work, you know."

"So he was lying in wait for you?"

She frowned a little. "Actually I think he was searching your cabin. I was out saying goodbye to the sheriff." She saw a flicker in his eyes, but he didn't comment, so she continued. "Walt started to walk out your door right in front of me. He looked...surprised. But he had the gun, and I guess he decided to grab the chance to have a little chat with me."

Luke had stopped pacing. He stood right in front of her, his gaze intense. "Tell me what he said. Every word."

Rachel repeated what she remembered. Luke listened, frowning.

"You said the sheriff was here. Did he see Walt, too?"

"Yes, but before I could explain who he was, George heard some code over his radio that meant he was needed, so he took off. I don't suppose he paid that much attention."

"No, probably not," Luke agreed. "But most cops have a good memory for faces. He might be able to recognize Krupinski again. Who knows? That could come in handy."

The strain of standing here, carrying on a relatively normal conversation with Luke after all that had passed between them, was beginning to tell on Rachel. She longed to escape for just a few hours, to sink into a hot bath and close her eyes. She couldn't wash away all evidence of the two men who'd touched her in very different ways this last hour, but she could try.

"Is there anything else?" she said.

"Just one thing." He shoved his hands into his pockets. "I'm going to move into the lodge tonight."

Whatever she'd expected, this wasn't it. "You're... what?" she repeated.

Luke looked at her white face, her pleading eyes, and damned himself. But about this he couldn't back down. Whatever was happening had gathered momentum. He knew he wasn't the only one to feel a sense of urgency. And to someone in a hurry, Rachel had to be a target.

He tried to explain, "I want to be closer to you. You're not safe alone in that old monstrosity. There must be empty rooms where I can sleep. Ones that I could hear you from."

She opened her mouth as if to protest, and Luke flinched inside. Did she already hate him so much that she couldn't stand to have him that close? But after a pause she twined her fingers together in front of her and said steadily, "All right. I'll make up a bed."

"Thank you."

"No," she denied in an absurdly polite way. "I owe you the thanks, not the other way around. Now may I go?"

That last, childish request made Luke feel as if he'd been punched in the stomach again. He looked at her and saw dark circles under shadowed eyes, a face made plain by its pallor, a fight to save some last remnants of self. And all he could do was nod.

Rachel turned and walked wearily across the grass toward the parking lot. But she'd gone only a few feet when she stopped and turned around. "Oh, I almost forgot, Luke."

He waited in the doorway.

A small, malicious smile curved her lips. "You'd better come up with a story of your own. Don't you think?"

A story?... Damn. His fingers flew to his cheek, which was decorated with a scrape. Amused warmth blossomed in his chest. Rachel might be down, he knew, but she wasn't beaten.

"We were holding hands climbing those stairs," he said, straight-faced. "We both slipped. It's really romantic, when you think about it."

She gave her head a little shake and just looked at him for a moment. Then in an odd voice she said, "You know something, Luke? Sometimes I positively hate you. And sometimes . . . I like you.'' With that she turned and walked away.

Smiling, he watched her go. He waited until she was halfway to the lodge before he said in a voice too soft to reach her ears, ''You know something, Rachel? I always like you.''

Rachel sat up in bed that evening, her legs crossed under the warm quilt, her back supported by a heap of pillows. The small lamp beside the bed cast a golden glow on the open diary she held in her lap.

With a sigh she turned another page. Any lingering sentiment she'd felt for this last, most personal vestige of her dead husband was rapidly fading into boredom. Was her life as limited, as single-minded, as Jack's had apparently been?

Rachel wriggled a little deeper into the pillows, conscious of a few aches the bath hadn't taken care of.

She stretched out her legs under the covers, then with a start realized she had begun to merely skim over the entries. She couldn't afford to do that. Just one word, one brief notation, was all she'd need to prove his innocence. Or his guilt. Even that, she was coming to believe, would be a relief. Either way she would be free once more.

Rachel didn't start to read again right away. Somehow she was unsettlingly aware of Luke's presence in the lodge. He was little more than a wall away. In fact, he'd considered the layout and insisted on the cubby that was closest to hers. He'd also noticed at the end of the hall the seldom-used door that connected the upstairs of the lodge proper with the tiny hall outside her bedroom. He'd demanded that it be unlocked. Rachel had been about to protest his high-handedness when she'd remembered the night Walt had called. She would have given a great deal then to have had Luke so close. And Walt *had* promised to be back.

But knowing Luke was so near also put her on edge. Every few minutes she found her mind drifting from the pages of the diary. She imagined Luke undressing, sliding into the prim, ruffly bed with its cold sheets. She wondered if he slept in pajamas. Then she would groan and make herself read the next entry.

She'd started with what had been written a year before the heist and had come almost immediately to that winter's absence. It was so peculiar. There was simply a date in late November and then one in early April, with no explanation, no break. The handwriting didn't vary.

Rachel had worked her way through the ruled pages of one thin volume, and was now a third of the way through the following one. She came again to November and the next of those startling, maddening breaks. She'd read through these dates when Luke first arrived, but now she did it once more, slowly. Nothing. Only humdrum details as Jack considered applications for summer employees, increased food orders for the kitchen, thought about the earthshaking addition of one item to the restaurant menu.

Then, only a few pages further on, dated a couple of weeks later, she found it. She read the notation, moved to the next and then stopped. Incredulous, she looked back. All he'd written for that day was "Put my future under the bridge. Ought to be safe."

Openmouthed, she stared at those few ambiguous words. Ambiguous and incriminating. He'd hidden something. Something so valuable he considered it his future. Something he had never mentioned to Rachel, whom he had married less than six months later.

Over and over she read the words. It occurred to her that she ought to be angry, astonished, yet she wasn't. She had scarcely been aware of the doubts that had begun to erode her certainty of Jack's innocence. Now, with scarcely a flicker, those doubts turned into acceptance of his guilt. She even had a sense of its inevitability.

Rachel stared unseeingly at the flower-printed paper that covered the sloping ceiling as she tried to come to terms with what she now knew. How could she have been so wrong about a man? Even when she had known that the marriage was failing, that she'd made a terrible mistake, she had never guessed at Jack's inner depths. She'd come to consider him harsh, uncommunicative, insensitive, even unlikable. But it boggled her mind to think he'd lived a secret life on such a scale. If he had truly loved her, why hadn't he ever told her any of it? And if he hadn't loved her, why had he asked her to marry him?

Rachel blinked and returned her gaze to the words on the paper. Would she ever be able to trust her own judgment again?

Feeling numb, she read several more pages. There was nothing more. Jack was back to worrying about finding enough summer employees. At last Rachel slipped in a marker and closed the book.

Now what? It was eleven o'clock. Luke was probably in bed already. It wouldn't make any difference if she waited until morning to show him. But she knew she wouldn't be able to sleep for a while. Maybe he'd still be awake. She could slip through the door and see if his light was still on.

Rachel pulled on a bathrobe over her nightgown, then left the room.

A crack of light showed in the hall. Not knowing whether to be relieved or apprehensive, Rachel stepped forward on her bare feet and lightly tapped on the door.

"Rachel?" His voice was sharp, wary.

"Yes, it's me," she said. "Can I come in? I have something to show you."

"Sure."

When she opened the door he was laying his gun back on the night table. A small tremor ran through her. When most people heard a knock on their doors, they wondered mildly who the caller might be. When someone knocked on Luke's, he reached for a weapon.

The gun's ugly presence was incongruous in the room. Luke was stretched out on the bed, two pillows piled behind him, his ankles crossed. He wore his pants but no shoes or socks, and his shirt was unbuttoned, baring a smooth, muscled chest. A book lay open, facedown beside him on the bed. The relaxed, sensual picture he made was at odds with the weapon he'd so carefully set aside and his alert, calculating look.

"Is anything wrong?" he asked.

She shook her head, hesitating just inside the door. She realized that she had the thin notebook clutched to her chest in a death grip, and made herself step forward and hold it out.

Luke sat up and swung his feet to the floor. "Jack's diary," he said quietly. "You found something."

Rachel nodded. His eyes didn't leave her face as he reached out to take the book from her unresisting fingers. To her surprise, he didn't immediately turn to it. Instead, he asked in a low, gentle voice, "Are you all right, Rachel?"

"Yes, of course." She felt stiff, impatient. "I have the place marked. See what you think."

Frowning, he held her gaze for another instant, then at last looked down, flipping the book open. He read silently, and when he glanced up again, Rachel saw a gleam of satisfaction in his eyes.

His voice was rich with the same emotion. "He gave himself away. I knew he would."

"Yes, he did," Rachel said colorlessly. "Well, I wanted to show it to you. I think I'll go to bed now."

She turned, but Luke moved swiftly. Before she reached the doorway, he was standing there, blocking her way. "Let's talk about it, Rachel."

Determined not to look at his face, she focused on the fine hairs that curled on his chest. She suddenly felt unutterably weary. "You know as much as I do," she said.

"That wasn't what I meant." He wrapped his hand around her chin and forced it up until she had no choice but to meet his eyes. With a small shock she saw the compassion in them. "How does this make you feel?"

"I . . ." She compressed her lips and her lashes fluttered. With horror she realized she was on the verge of tears. "I..." She swallowed hard, tried again. What emerged was little more than a choked whisper. "I guess I'm not surprised."

His gaze was disturbingly intent. "But you still feel angry and betrayed, don't you?"

"Yes." She knotted her fingers painfully together. "Yes, I do! Good God, how can I help it?"

"Are you angry at him? Or me?"

Rachel looked blankly at Luke. "At him, of course! Even if you'd never come, if I'd never known, Jack would still have been what he was. How can I blame you for that?"

For a frozen, intense moment Luke's thoughts were unreadable. Then a flare of powerful emotion in his eyes gave him away, and through fingers that still gripped her chin Rachel felt the tension leave him. His mouth curled into a humorless smile. "I've worried about that."

"I—I can see." Rachel was shaken. She'd known that he was attracted to her, perhaps even liked her. But this revealed hidden depths that she hadn't dreamed of. "I'm not that unreasonable," she clumsily reassured him. "You're only doing your job. And . . . you were right about him."

He dropped his hand to his side, releasing her. "I thought you might hate me for making you see that."

"For a while I thought I would," she admitted, turning a little away from him and wrapping her arms around herself. "But I've come to realize that you had no choice. It was...irrational for me to think the government ought to shrug and forget millions of dollars just to save my feelings. Besides... I needed to know what Jack was really like. In a way, well, it frees me to get on with my life."

He zeroed in on what she'd said. "Why did you need to be freed? What was holding you?"

"Oh..." Rachel shrugged. Unable to stay still, she walked restlessly over to the small window and looked out at the darkness. "Memories, responsibilities..."

"Guilt."

She started. How much had he guessed? Turning her back on the window, she met his gaze across the room. "What makes you say that?" she asked sharply.

"You told me how often you feel guilty. Guilt is a fine emotion for immobilizing a person. I've been wondering why you're still here." His gesture encompassed the whole resort, the isolation, the dead end her life had run into. "Why aren't you starting your first year of law school right now?"

"I wasn't ready. Anyway, I'd have to sell Sahale first." It was something she hadn't even considered until the past few weeks. Immobilized was the right word for how she'd felt. She would have been grateful for the violent severing of the bonds that had held her here, had it not been for the damage it had done to her confidence. She added, "Finding a buyer might not be easy."

"No," Luke agreed, shutting the bedroom door and taking a step toward her. "But you didn't really tell me what I wanted to know."

Rachel had nowhere to retreat to. Her back was to the sill, and the closed door made her feel caged. Lifting her chin, she said, "Aren't I entitled to a few secrets? Don't you have any?"

That was a killer of a question, Luke thought. He smiled wryly. "In other words, back off, buddy."

"Something like that," she said.

He stopped in the middle of the small room, not trusting himself to be any closer to her. What he wanted was to take her into his arms and tell her everything would be all right, but he knew how dangerous that would be. He contented himself with a simple "Okay, Rachel. But you know... You can tell me anything. Anything at all. I'll understand."

She stared at him, her eyes wide with pain, then turned her back to look out the window once more. The lamplight laid a golden sheen on the glass, however, and in it he could see her reflection.

He wondered if she had any idea how seductive she looked in that old-fashioned flannel gown. He had tried to imagine what she slept in, and come to no conclusions. Knowing what she wore during the day, he hadn't been able to picture her in anything filmy or flouncy. Naked—ah, he'd been able to see that, all right. He clenched his jaw now as he tried to dispel his fantasy and hoped that she was looking at the darkness and not at him.

The practical nightgown suited her. The problem was that for him its very practicality made thinking about what was under it irresistible. But then, he decided ruefully, he was so hungry for her that even the sight of her bare feet turned him on.

It was time for him to think about something else, before he grabbed her and flung her onto the bed. He walked over and picked up the notebook. The triumph he'd felt when he'd first seen those spare, revealing words had vanished. Now he had to try to work up some enthusiasm.

"Do you know what he means?" Luke asked abruptly.

Rachel was momentarily disoriented. What was he talking about? But then she saw the book in his hands. With an effort she pulled herself together. It would be easier if they weren't alone in a small bedroom, her in a nightgown, him half undressed, she thought fretfully. She should have waited until morning. She had come for comfort, for understanding, and because temptation had drawn her. If she had any sense she would retreat now.

"No, I really don't," she said. "Although I suppose... well, it almost has to be the bridge out in front, don't you think?"

"I don't know," he said. "You tell me. Is that the bridge that comes to mind when you think of Jack?"

"*No* bridge comes particularly to mind when I think of him," she said tartly. "He didn't spend hours standing out in the middle of it gloating, if that's what you mean."

"Not exactly." Luke snapped the book shut and handed it back to her. "We'll start digging tomorrow. I don't like it, though."

"What do you mean, you don't like it?" Rachel had an absurd feeling of outrage, like someone who'd expended a good deal of effort on a gift, only to be told it didn't please.

"What the hell does he mean by *under* it?" Luke demanded. He began to pace, as he always did when his mind was in overdrive. "Those piers rise right out of the water. The banks are so damned steep. There's the narrow strip buried under driftwood, but—"

"The waves crash right over that in winter," Rachel interjected.

Luke shook his head impatiently. "And salt water would ruin almost anything. Even assuming the tide didn't shift the sand underneath so that whatever he buried could never be found. But I'll have to look even if it means crawling on my belly in the sand."

Reluctantly Rachel considered in practical terms what was written in the diary. She'd been so concerned with what it meant to her that she hadn't really thought about what Jack had actually been saying. But Luke was right; the bridge out in front wasn't a logical place to hide anything. Unless . . .

"Could it be something so small it's tucked up under the boards?" she ventured. "On one of the joists?"

Luke paused, glancing over his shoulder at her with eyes that held the emotionless, calculating look of a hunter. "That's a thought. Or maybe he's talking about the highway bridge. The banks aren't as steep, and they're brushy. It has more possibilities, except it's not on his land. Are there any others, Rachel?"

She watched him move restlessly back and forth within the confines of the room, stopping before he could bang his head on the sloping ceiling, prowling almost to the door, then around the bed and by Rachel, so close that she could have touched him. In his bare feet, he walked with a catlike tread that was disturbingly sensuous. She also found it unnerving, a reminder of the violence he was capable of.

She said edgily, "Of course there are others. Remember that one hundred fifty inches of rain a year I keep mentioning? With all that water having to find the ocean, there's a stream or river every mile or so. There must be hundreds of bridges around here."

Luke swore under his breath. "But some of them must be more likely than others."

"Well, yes, of course. The two right here. And there are a couple of small wooden ones on the hiking trail that starts just the other side of the highway. Jack actually built them, I think."

He'd stopped on the other side of the room to look at her. When she hesitated, he waited, his hands shoved so deep in his pants pockets that the fabric was pulled tightly over the long muscles in his thighs. Rachel was painfully conscious of his bare chest and lean stomach.

Averting her gaze, she said, "Jack had a couple of favorite hikes up in the rain forest. Although that's in the national park, of course. If he'd gotten caught digging there..." She stopped. "If *you* get caught digging..."

"You mean 'we.'" He showed his teeth in a smile she didn't like. "I need your help. Let's get this over with, Rachel."

Her mind dredged up an appalling picture of herself standing in ice-cold water, her arm aching as she held up a flashlight to provide illumination for Luke to dig by. Rustlings in the darkness kept her nerves quivering as she imagined that every shifting shadow was Walt, waiting to step out with a gun.

She balked. "You don't need me."

"I can't do it alone." He looked impatient. "Rachel, this is the trickiest part. We're not the only ones after this gold. We have some information now that Krupinski doesn't. If he guesses that we're searching under every bridge in the county, he might find the right one first. Or he might just wait for us to find the right one. And then there's that joker in the deck that worries me. I don't want *anybody* to know what we're doing. Besides, working in darkness isn't my favorite occupation. I'm going to need you to hold a light for me, if nothing else."

Her worst suspicions had been confirmed. She ought to simply refuse. But she couldn't let him go alone. All she would do would be to lie awake in bed, wondering what he had found. Or who had found him. She had to know what was happening. To opt out before the end wasn't for her.

But . . . "Now?" she asked doubtfully, looking down at her nightgown.

"Well . . ." She sensed that he was collecting himself. "No," he said finally. "Tomorrow. We can poke under your bridge in daylight. And the highway one, too. We'll be less conspicuous that way than we'd be at night with a lamp. But the others'll have to be searched under cover of darkness. Especially—" a quirked brow acknowledged her earlier dismay "—the ones in the park. I'd just as soon not have to explain myself to the Park Service."

If only that were the least of the dangers! Rachel simply nodded. Her mind had decided abruptly that it didn't want to cope anymore. She'd had enough for one night. "I'm tired. I'd like to go to bed now."

He looked at her, his eyes narrowed. She couldn't tell what he was thinking. "All right," he said after a fractional pause.

Rachel had to walk within inches of him on the way to the door. She was almost past when his hands closed on her arm.

"Rachel . . ."

"Yes?" She stood, outwardly stiff but trembling inside.

His voice was soft. "We've all made mistakes about someone."

She refused to let herself yield. "There are mistakes. And then there are mistakes."

Luke said with quiet intensity, "Don't let this haunt you."

"How can I help it?"

"Trust yourself enough to let go. Love again. You're not twenty-two anymore. You can see yourself better."

"Maybe myself," she said bitterly. "But not necessarily other people. Let me go, Luke. I'll help you search. But don't expect me not to feel angry."

"I don't expect that," he said. "Just remember what you told me once. Most people *are* worthy of trust." His fingers released her.

Without another word she left him.

Chapter 8

W e have an audience," Rachel observed quietly.

She and Luke stood under the bridge in front of the lodge. A fine mist dampened the air, making her hair curl wildly underneath the thin hood she wore. Luke had already thoroughly examined the bridge itself and probed the upper reaches of the crumbling bank. Now, despite the weather, he had rolled his jeans up above his knees and waded into the creek's low but very cold water. Rachel shivered on the bank, watching as he probed the hard sand with a pole. Her senses were attuned to the man who was strolling onto the bridge above.

Luke turned his head casually to glance at her. "Who? And where?"

"Henry Kirk," she returned in a low voice, nodding upward. "Thataway."

Luke poked around the cement block base of one of the pier supports. A good minute later he looked up and waved.

"Hi," he called. "Am I making you nervous? I promise the bridge isn't going to fall down."

The slender dark man who was leaning over the railing smiled uneasily, as though the direct approach had taken him by surprise. "No, no, I'm just curious. What *are* you doing?"

Good question, Rachel thought. Luke was right, though; it would have been much harder to answer if anyone had happened to stumble on them doing the same thing in the dark.

Luke gestured vaguely. "Just checking the supports. Winter storms are hard on the bridge. Come this time of year, we like to make sure everything is solid and the wood hasn't rotted." He grinned. "I should have waited until a warmer day, though."

Henry Kirk was edging away. "That's very interesting. Well...uh, excuse me."

Luke waved amiably, then went back to probing. Rachel watched the strange guest beat a retreat toward the cabins. She couldn't see that they had any other observers. She assumed that a few guests were on the beach, but none were visible in the creek's narrow outlet. The creek was popular only on warm days, for wading and floating on inner tubes and skipping stones. The upper structure of the bridge could be seen from the bay window of the coffee shop, but the place where she and Luke stood was hidden except from the windows of the now-empty rooms on the upper floor of the old shingled lodge.

Again Rachel shivered, from a combination of chill and nerves, both of which contributed to the second thoughts she was having about the wisdom of her accompanying Luke. But even though morning had brought reluctance in its wake, she hadn't been able to make herself bow out. Somehow she'd felt as though he needed a sentry, or maybe just moral support, even if she couldn't actively contribute. And it was true that he didn't look as though he was enjoying himself very much.

Eventually he finished, by which time he was positively gray with cold despite the heavy sweater he wore.

"The things I get myself into," he muttered, gratefully accepting the towel she proffered. After using it, he hurriedly pulled on his socks and boots. "Hell, where next?" he said, running the towel over his damp hair.

Rachel poked with her toe at one of the driftwood logs that the ocean had stripped of bark and polished to a silvery gray, then deposited here in the curve of the Sahale. She said doubtfully, "I can't imagine...."

"No, I can't, either." Luke's brooding gaze followed hers. It would have been nearly impossible for a man to shift even one of the logs, much less the pile. And yet, come the first violent winter storm, the ocean would play with the logs as if they were toys, rearranging the pile, discarding a few logs and adding others. Rachel found it inconceivable that Jack had buried anything of real value where nature's careless, cruel hand could so easily tear it from its hiding place.

"It *must* be somewhere else," he said, shaking his head.

Rachel walked silently beside him as they retraced their steps toward the beach. She looked at Luke out of the corner of her eye. He didn't seem discouraged, merely preoccupied. There was something purposeful in his long stride and the set of his shoulders.

She and Luke emerged on the grassy bluff. The resort lay deserted around them, damp in the heavy mist. The bridge they had just been under stood hunched in the rain, stolid and defiant. A few empty cars sat outside cabins, and smoke from the chimneys curled up to merge with the gray sky.

Rachel had gone several steps before she realized Luke wasn't with her. Turning, she looked back to see him frowning at the span, with its sturdy railings and plank walkway, which was just wide enough to handle a car.

If she hadn't been positioned as she was, she would never have seen the flicker of movement between two trees on the other side of the creek, behind the cabins. It was something green, but not quite the right shade, and why should anything green be moving, anyway? she thought. Then she saw that the green was the muted color of a slicker and that a rifle was pointed at Luke.

"Luke!" she screamed, launching herself. He'd begun to turn when she tackled him, sending them both crashing hard to the wet ground. Even as they were falling she heard the explosive crack of the rifle. Luke wrapped his arms around her, and the moment they were down he rolled above her, protecting her with his body. She felt him fumbling as he reached up under his sweater and withdrew a revolver from a shoulder holster she hadn't realized he was wearing.

Still lying on her, he braced his elbow and fired back. Rachel slapped her hands over her ears and buried her face in the wet grass. She had a feeling of déjà vu that was not at all pleasant.

"He's getting away!" Luke said suddenly. Without more ado he was off her and running across the bridge in a crouch. Holding her breath, Rachel lifted her head to watch. Luke's footsteps echoed hollowly on the planks, but in the distance the underbrush crackled as the fleeing gunman pushed his way through. Luke returned a few minutes later, shaking his head. With a grimace he pulled up his sweater to put back the revolver.

By that time Rachel had sat up, her arms wrapped around her knees. Luke's eyes were wary as he stopped in front of her and held out his hand. She allowed him to pull her to her feet, and stifled a groan as some new aches and pains made themselves evident.

With what she thought was admirable moderation, Rachel remarked, "This is growing old."

"You're telling me. Did you get any better look this time?"

Rachel shook her head.

Luke sighed. Then, as he took in her appearance, humor gleamed in his gaze. "You look like a drowned rat."

"Thank you. That's very romantic." Rachel shivered, then surprised herself by chuckling. "So do you."

Luke wiped ineffectually at the smear of mud that decorated one cheek. He grinned. "I suggest we part ways here. I think we can both use a hot shower and change of clothes. If you can filch some fresh clams from the restaurant, I'll make us some chowder for lunch. How's that grab you?"

"As an improvement on standing here." Rachel started to move away but suddenly stopped, her heart sinking. "Except that I'm going to have to call the police. Aren't I?"

Luke looked around. "I'm not so sure anybody noticed. Unless they did up in the lodge. The rain probably muffled the sound, and none of the near cabins are occupied, are they?"

"No, I guess not." Cold and tired, she concluded that she could live happily without the fuss. Especially since she knew how useless it would be. "I'll keep my fingers crossed."

She discovered that a couple of employees thought they'd heard the sound of gunfire. Rachel was able to pass it off by saying that she thought hunters were responsible this time.

"Though I'm not sure exactly where they were." She was relieved when her story was accepted.

She spent the afternoon on resort business. She and the chef discussed ideas for entrées to add to the menu. This was a good time of year to experiment a little, trying the new dishes as specials.

She was also experimenting this winter with closing down the lodge entirely for two days a week. Only a few cabins were occupied during the week, and those were equipped with kitchens. Winter guests tended to be self-sufficient anyway. Weekdays, the coffee shop simply wasn't doing the business to justify its being kept open. Nor did it make sense for Rachel to pay a receptionist to sit around all day, taking the occasional reservation for the next summer. So the entire staff now had Mondays and Tuesdays off, and Rachel herself minded the shop, answering the phone and being available for guests or the rare tourist that pulled in on impulse.

Attired this time in a slicker, Luke had gone to explore under the concrete highway bridge. Half of Rachel's mind was on him all afternoon. Not that she had wanted to accompany him. The rain had picked up to a steady downpour, and she doubted that the bridge offered much protection. All the same, one person would be less conspicuous than two. She was a little put out, though, not even to have had a chance to present her excuses. Immediately after lunch, Luke had informed her brusquely that he didn't require her presence that afternoon. Rachel thanked him tartly for his consideration, to which barb he didn't even respond.

The hours crawled by. She kept thinking about how calmly she'd handled being shot at again. Maybe it was something that became less traumatic with repetition. The odd thing was that this morning she hadn't been frightened for herself. Over and over she recalled the moment when she'd realized the rifle was aimed at Luke. She had never felt anything like the terror that had swamped her. Thinking about it even now was enough to make her tremble inside. She was astonished at how humbling and even frightening it was to realize how essential somebody else's well-being was to her.

And right now he was out alone somewhere in the rain, vulnerable to another attack from a faceless enemy. *Not faceless,* she told herself quickly. It had to be Walt. She'd seen the sick fury on his face. He was trying to murder Luke, not because it would help him gain the money, but because he'd been thwarted and now wanted revenge. Rachel tried not to let herself argue against her theory. Walt was scary enough, but at least he had a face, a voice, a presence.

Finally she excused herself from the housekeeper, with whom she'd been discussing the linen they needed to replace before spring. She had probably just made a fool of herself, anyway, asking the poor woman to repeat everything she said. When Rachel returned to her empty apartment, she opened Jack's notebook once again. The most useful thing she could do would be to find another clue.

As the dinner hour approached, Rachel began to listen for the sound of Luke's footsteps. Surely he would at least stop by to tell her what he'd found. Jack's less-than-riveting prose failed to hold her attention, and she found her eyes drifting from the page.

At last she gave up and put down the notebook. She walked out to the lobby. The receptionist was eager for a chat, so without urgency they went over the day's business. Lois mentioned that the sheriff had telephoned that morning, and Rachel made a mental note to return his call. Finally she asked casually, "Have you seen Luke?"

The older woman frowned as she thought. "No, I don't think so. Not since he passed at lunchtime. Is there a problem? I was just going to pack up and head home, but if you need me, I could—"

"No, no!" Rachel smiled. "There was just something I wanted to ask him, no big deal. Go home."

"Okay." Lois began to tidy papers. She gave Rachel a sly smile. "I like Luke."

"Do you," Rachel returned dryly. She wondered what the conservative, motherly woman would think if she knew what Luke did for a living. But the only comment she made was a noncommittal "He's been a big help."

Lois opened her mouth as though to say something more, but then closed it, her expression changing as her gaze shifted to a point beyond Rachel's shoulder. Rachel turned around and suppressed a gasp. Henry Kirk stood only a few feet away.

"Yes?" Rachel said more sharply than she'd intended.

"I'm sorry. Did I startle you?"

There it was again, that hint of mockery, Rachel thought. Determined not to let him see the effect he had on her, she made her voice both pleasant and a little formal.

"We were just talking. You weren't interrupting anything. Can I help you?"

"Oh, I wanted to mention that I heard some gunshots this morning. I was out walking. And I wondered..." He shrugged.

A chill crept over Rachel. How had she managed to entirely forget about him this morning? Where had he been when the shots were fired? Had he donned a slicker and taken his rifle for a stroll in the woods? Once again, the timing had been right. He had known where she and Luke were and that they would eventually have to appear on top of the bluff. He could also have noted that it was unlikely there'd be any witnesses.

She forced a smile. "We've been having some trouble with hunters who are trespassing on our property, even though it's posted No Hunting. You might remember, the day yo arrived we'd had an incident. I'm afraid this was just another one. Did you by any chance see anything that might be of interest to the police?''

She almost held her breath as she waited for his answer. Even if he was an innocent bystander, she was in big trouble if he had seen Luke in action and said so in front of Lois. How would she explain the story she'd told this morning? On the other hand, she thought, trying to sort through the various ramifications, if he *was* the gunman, surely he wouldn't mention having seen Luke. His goal would be to try to establish his innocence, not put himself in the spotlight as a witness.

Rachel wasn't sure whether to relax or become tenser when he said, ''No, I'm afraid I didn't see anything. I was down on the beach. In fact, I saw you and that man go up the stairs. So I worried when I heard the shots.''

''Thank you for your concern,'' she said. ''But really there wasn't anything to worry about.'' Deliberately Rachel smiled again. ''I hope you're enjoying your vacation despite all the rain.''

''Oh, yes, I don't mind it.'' He returned her smile and made no move to leave.

''Have you been hunting yet?'' She was conscious of Lois silently closing up shop behind the counter.

''Yes, but I haven't even seen an elk. I'm not that serious about it, anyway. It's just an excuse to get out into the woods.''

''Well, good luck,'' Rachel said vaguely. She began to turn away. She was anxious to put some distance between her and this strange guest.

Through the window she could see that it was already getting dark outside. Where in God's name was Luke?

''Uh...I wondered...'' the guest began.

She glanced back, her nerves tightening.

"Is there any chance I could offer you dinner tonight? If you felt like leaving, we could drive on up to Forks or over to Lake Quinault Lodge."

Rachel hid the fear his suggestion provoked. She couldn't think of anything that would make her get into a car alone with him.

"What a nice offer," she said insincerely. "But I'm afraid not. I really can't be away from the lodge, and I do already have plans for tonight, anyway. But thank you."

"Maybe another time?"

"I can't make any promises," Rachel said. "I'm very busy, even at this time of the year. If you'll excuse me right now...?"

She was very conscious of him still standing there, watching her as she walked down the hall. She didn't remember ever having felt so uncomfortable turning down a date. She knew that it was partly because she wasn't sure about his motives. He might simply be attracted to her. But what better way to get her alone if he had something more sinister in mind? Damn! Should she put on a raincoat and go hunting for Luke? But if somebody saw her disappear under the bridge, wouldn't they wonder? It was growing late. If she waited a bit she could slip out unseen under cover of darkness.

She was just putting on her raincoat when a quick knock sounded on her door. With a rush she answered it. Luke stepped past her into the living room. Indignantly she saw that he'd already showered and changed. His jeans were damp, but the heavy flannel shirt he wore under his raincoat was dry and clean, and his hair was slicked down as though he'd just washed it.

Rachel planted her hands on her hips and glared as he slung his raincoat over the hook on the tree. "How long have you been back?" she demanded.

"Back?" He looked at her in surprise. "Oh, maybe an hour. Why?" Then he took in her expression. "Don't tell me you were worried about me."

"Of course I was! I was just about to come out looking for you!"

"I'm flattered," he said gravely. "I didn't think you cared."

Narrow-eyed, Rachel searched his face for signs of amusement. "I wasn't sure what to do with your body," she said. "Maybe you should tell me who to call—just for future reference."

Luke grinned. "You certainly have a way of making a man feel good. I'll tell you what. If I die, you can be creative. Do whatever you want with my body. Stuff me, hang me over the fireplace. Toss me into the attic with all the other useless things."

Rachel rolled her eyes. "You're a big help. Just tell me what you found, okay?"

For the first time she noticed the weariness on his face. "Absolutely nothing," he said shortly. "Which is hardly a surprise. There's no way I can dig up every inch under there. I poked a little, looked for disturbed ground—although after three years it probably wouldn't be disturbed anymore. Without some idea where to start, it's damn near hopeless."

Rachel was silent for a moment. "What if you never find it?"

His smile was crooked. "Then we haul Krupinski in for assault. You sell the resort and get on with your life. I take a cut in pay."

"You're kidding!"

Luke's grin wiped out the tiredness on his face. "I'm

kidding. The rest of it I mean. But . . . we'll find it, Rachel. Have confidence. Now, tell me about your afternoon.''

So she did.

Henry Kirk. Henry Kirk. The name ran like a litany through Luke's mind, keeping rhythm with his digging. The beam of the flashlight wavered in the darkness, barely illuminating the muddy hole. Behind the bright spot of light, Luke could just make out Rachel's silhouette. She was silent, even the sound of her breathing cloaked by the constant patter of the rain on leaves and on the boards of the small footbridge.

Water oozed into the hole each time Luke's shovel left it. He had to pause to wipe his face with his wet sleeve, because the mixed rain and sweat were affecting his vision.

Henry Kirk. The shovel ground into the soil. Luke grunted, throwing all his weight onto it. Who the hell was Henry Kirk, and what did he have to do with anything? Luke was accustomed to functioning with blind spots, but this time it bothered him more than usual. Somebody was doing his damnedest to kill him. His spine crawled every time he had to walk across an open space. Under that highway bridge this afternoon, he'd felt like a fly being watched by a spider. For all he knew, he was already stuck to the web.

The shovel grated against something hard, and Luke dropped to his knees. With his bare hand he felt the obstruction, rough and rounded—a rock. A damned big one, he could tell from the shape of it. So much for this hole. Pushing himself tiredly to his feet, he began to shovel the dirt back where it had come from.

Why was somebody trying to kill him? What did anyone have to gain by getting rid of him?

Krupinski didn't like him, Luke knew. The man might be just far enough out in right field to want to knock Luke off just for the hell of it. But somehow that didn't feel right.

Krupinski wanted the money badly, and he had to know he couldn't get away with murdering a federal agent.

The only motivation that made sense was that someone wanted to isolate Rachel, making her more vulnerable. Luke was a threat just because he was *there*. But who, damn it, *who*?

He stamped on the ground, flattening the evidence of his digging into muddy indecipherability.

"So much for this bridge," he said, almost startling himself with the sound of his voice. "How are you doing?"

"Fine," Rachel answered tersely, aiming the beam of light toward the narrow trail, instead of at his feet.

Luke gave his head a shake and wished he'd left the hood up. Water was dripping down his neck. Rachel probably didn't feel any better. "Come on, be honest," he said.

"Honest? You want honesty?"

"Yeah, why not." He made his way up the muddy bank onto the trail. Rachel's stoic silence was beginning to make him feel guilty for having dragged her along. A chance to really let him have it might warm her up.

"Okay," she said with spirit. "I'll tell you. I'm cold, I'm wet, I'm tired. My arm aches from holding up this miserable flashlight. I've lost all feeling in my toes. When I'm not scared, I'm bored. How's that for honesty?"

"Pretty good," he said cheerfully. "I'm not having too much fun myself."

"I'd have thought you were weird if you were." She led the way on the trail, but the darkness was so dense that if it hadn't been for the weak beam of light playing along the ground in front of her, he'd hardly have known she was there.

They walked in silence for a minute. "How far's the next bridge?" Luke asked.

"Maybe half a mile."

"Wonderful," he muttered.

"This is a pretty hike during the daytime. That is, when it's not raining."

Luke didn't argue. He shifted the shovel from one hand to the other so the colder one could get a turn in his pocket.

Rachel stopped in front of him so suddenly that he bumped into her. Then they were plunged into darkness as she switched off the flashlight. "Listen," she whispered.

Then Luke heard it, too, not far behind them: the crackle of a branch breaking, the rustle of leaves. Reacting semi-automatically, he grabbed Rachel's arm and pulled her with him off the trail, ignoring the slap of wet vegetation. They stumbled into the tall, rounded barrier of a fallen log and crouched behind it.

The crashing grew louder, until Luke could distinguish the sound of breathing as well. He tensed, straining his eyes to see in the darkness, fighting the urge to grab his gun. He groped for Rachel's hand and found the flashlight there, clutched tightly. He had to pry it out of her fingers.

Aiming it at the trail, he waited. The sound of a loud snort startled him even though he had begun to suspect the truth. A pursuer wouldn't have let himself be heard coming for a quarter of a mile. Luke switched on the light. In the glare of its beam he caught an elk sporting a full head of antlers. Luke had the impression that several smaller animals were behind. The elk froze for a fraction of a second, then bolted. Luke turned off the flashlight and chuckled at the crashing sound of their passage.

Rachel surprised him by saying softly, "He was beautiful."

"Yeah. I wonder why they were blundering around in the middle of the night." With a groan he straightened to his feet. "For that matter, why the hell are *we* blundering around in the middle of the night?"

"Good question." Rachel sneezed.

Luke boosted her over the log, mildly surprised to find that he enjoyed touching her even in these conditions. He could feel her suppleness as she scrambled over the huge fallen tree, and in his mind flickered a picture of her moving just as beautifully when they'd made love.

In his distraction, Luke dropped the flashlight and had to grope for it in the wet loam. Grimacing, he wiped his hand on his soaked jeans, then slid over the log. The gun in its holster dug into his rib cage. Usually he forgot he was wearing the damn thing.

Rachel's voice came quietly out of the darkness as he found his footing. "You know, if Henry Kirk had seen that elk, he'd have shot him. Most of the men I know would have. Did you see those antlers?"

Luke pictured again the proud animal caught in the glare of light. The thought of the elk falling, crumpling to its knees in a death agony, appalled him.

Just then a wet branch stung a trail across his face, bringing him back to the present. To Rachel he just grunted a response.

"Do you hunt?" she asked.

Luke held out a hand to help her up onto the trail. "No," he said brusquely. After a moment he added, "I don't enjoy killing."

Rachel sounded tentative. "Have you... ever killed a person?"

Luke didn't like the direction the conversation was taking, but he knew he had to be honest. He stopped and turned to face Rachel, pointing the beam of light downward. Above it her face was shadowy, pooled in darkness, but he thought maybe he'd be able to read strong emotions.

"Twice," he said in a hard voice. "I had no choice either time. I'd do the same again. Once the man had just shot my partner. The other time... Well, it doesn't really matter. What does is that I see those scenes over and over in my head. It's like I filmed them. They're so clear, and they move in slow motion. I can see it all happen again, but I can't change anything. I see my partner's face, their faces...." He paused, then finished abruptly, "I hate killing. I don't even kill a bug if I can help it."

She stood silent for a moment, then reached out and briefly caressed his cheek with a hand that was wet and cold, yet miraculously gentle. In a small gruff voice she said, "This is one of those times that I like you."

That was all, but it was enough for Luke. Rachel had just heard the worst, knew that he'd killed, and could still touch him with loving sweetness. The relief was overwhelming.

They were standing close in the rainy darkness. Her face was tilted up so she could see his, or at least peer up toward where she knew it was. He closed his free hand on her chin. She didn't try to move as he looked down at her. "Thank you," he said huskily, and kissed her.

Her lips, trembling under his, tasted of rain and were soft and warm and accepting. Heat ran through Luke's body, making him forget for a pleasurable, tempting moment where they were, forget the rain and the slippery trail, the darkness and the danger and their goal. Most of all he forgot that he shouldn't be kissing her at all. He wanted to plunge his tongue into her mouth and taste her more deeply. He wanted to pull her against him so he could feel more of her warmth.

But it was the very tenderness of her response, the reason for it, that recalled him. A river of icy rain found its way inside his collar and ran down his back. He pulled away, let his hand drop, thinking wryly that a cold shower had been just what he needed. *Damn it, she's offering me sympathy and human understanding, not love,* he thought.

"Let's get this over with," he said hoarsely, swinging around and heading up the trail.

Rachel picked up the nearly forgotten shovel, which she'd almost tripped over, and stumbled after him. Luke had already opened a distance between them, but she'd become so accustomed to the darkness that she hardly minded. Seeing the elk had given her a curious lift, and Luke's kiss had done even more, although the haste with which he'd pushed her away was deflating.

She thought about what he'd told her, and what it revealed about him. He was a man with a frightening potential for violence and danger, yet he'd seen beauty and life in the magnificent animal, not the petty victory of inflicting death. She hadn't lied when she said that made her like him. But Luke was a constant puzzle to her, a contradiction in terms. A man who'd killed and yet who valued life. A man of shadows and impermanency and deceit who had integrity, who was solid and decisive and kind, who could laugh at himself.

Rachel shook her head. She was wasting her time thinking about him. She couldn't share her life with a man of his profession, no matter how much she loved him.

As she realized what she'd just thought, Rachel stopped right where she was, jolted into shocked awareness. For a moment she was scarcely conscious of the vast darkness or the rain blurring her vision.

Love him? Did she really?

Yes, of course she did. Why else was she out here in the middle of the night, cold, wet, tired and frightened? She'd made all sorts of excuses, but they were nonsense. The only reason she was here was that she couldn't let Luke come alone. She loved him.

The tumult and bewilderment she'd felt these last weeks suddenly made sense to her. On one level she'd known all along how she felt. She couldn't have made love to him with such joy and abandon otherwise.

But she felt no joy now at her realization. She had once before thought herself in love. She had been terribly, tragically wrong about Jack Brewer. Was she as wrong about Luke? She wondered desperately if she was fatally drawn to the same qualities over and over.

The feeble beam of the flashlight Luke carried up ahead had begun to seem like a mirage. Rachel forced herself into motion again. She almost immediately stubbed her toes on an exposed root in the trail, then slipped in the mud trying to regain her balance. Suddenly she felt smothered, as though she were struggling through a vat of ink.

"Luke," she croaked.

The light ahead wobbled and stopped. "Did I lose you?" Luke called. "Sorry." The illusion of impenetrable blackness gave way when he turned the beam to illuminate the path.

"I'm sorry," Luke repeated when Rachel was within touching distance. "I should have checked over my shoulder."

"No, it's my fault," she said quickly. "I was...daydreaming."

"Really." His tone was dry as he looked around. "I wish I could do that. I feel like I'm having a nightmare."

So did she. It occurred to her that this was when she should wake up, never knowing how it would end, grasping for the tendrils of memories left, but relieved to find reality around her. But this nightmare had to be lived to an end that would be at best bittersweet, at worst shattering. It had changed reality, so that nothing would ever be quite the same again.

On the other hand, Rachel thought with surprise, maybe her life had *needed* shaking up.

"We must be almost there," she murmured, trying to orient herself. A thread of sound that underlay the steady dropping of the rain told her she was right. "Would you like me to take a turn digging?"

"Not unless you want to."

"Sure. I've always longed to dig up buried treasure."

Luke grinned. "Now you're getting into the spirit of this."

Well, why not? Rachel thought, feeling inexplicably giddy. How often did a person get the chance to dig under bridges in the middle of the night, not to mention get shot at? She might as well *try* to enjoy it.

So she told herself, until the weak beam of light in Luke's hand suddenly flickered. The next moment it died, plunging them into utter darkness punctuated only by the insistent drip of rain and the sound of their own breathing.

Chapter 9

Before Rachel had a chance to panic, Luke's cheerful voice floated to her out of the darkness. "Ah, foresight, foresight!"

Through stiff lips she said, "What do you mean?"

"I have an extra battery." There was a pause as he fumbled inside his raincoat. "I think."

"You *think*?" Her voice rose, ending on a squeak.

"Just joking," he assured her with annoying good humor. "Ah, here it is. Now the trick is to get it in—without dropping it or getting it too wet."

Rachel blindly reached out. Her hand encountered the stiff, wet fabric of his raincoat. "Can I help?" she asked. She was proud of how calm and collected she sounded. With a little encouragement she could easily have had hysterics.

The blackness was absolute. It made her feel horribly exposed, as though only she were blind, and eyes were watching from every direction.

"Sure," Luke agreed. "Come closer and hunch over my hands. You'll make a great umbrella." His fingers guided her. "And hold this." *This* seemed to be the battery. Rachel clutched it as tightly as though it were the crown jewels.

Luke began to whistle a tune as he worked. Rachel realized gratefully that he must be trying to distract her. The sound made her aware that Luke's lips must be nearly touching the top of her head. Suddenly she smiled, recognizing the song. "Zip-a-dee-doo-dah, zip-a-dee-ay, My oh my, what a wonderful day . . ."

"How about 'It's raining, it's pouring . . .'?" she suggested.

She felt his laugh against her hood. Then, "Voilà!" he announced. When only darkness ensued, he added, "I think."

Rachel rolled her eyes. "You inspire such confidence." Actually, he did, and astonishingly so, she thought. Even if he didn't get the wretched flashlight working, she was suddenly quite certain she'd survive the night with her sanity intact. Luke would probably keep her laughing despite her misery.

"Give it a shake," she offered helpfully.

"Thanks," Luke muttered. Nonetheless, Rachel heard a faint rattle as he took her advice. The light obligingly came on, flooding their feet with brightness.

Rachel blinked as her eyes tried to adjust. "Voilà," she murmured.

Luke chuckled. "Do you kick candy machines, too?"

"Only when they defy me."

That was when Rachel realized that about all that separated her from Luke was the flashlight. She'd huddled so close to him that she could make out the individual bristles on his chin. He was looking down into her face, too, and had abruptly become very still. Although Rachel couldn't see the expression in his eyes, an indefinable but very tangible tension stretched taut between them. She could actually feel the heat from his body. She swallowed hard, unable to take that step back.

At last Luke drew in a ragged breath. "We'd better get on with it," he said roughly.

"Yes." Rachel cleared her throat. "Yes, of course."

The next afternoon, Luke sat in Rachel's living room, elbows propped on his knees as he skimmed the papers spread out on the coffee table, then tossed them onto an untidy heap on the floor and grabbed more from the box to give them as cursory a look. There was nothing here but garbage, he realized. Invoices, correspondence, receipts, all years out of date. Luke would have liked to start a bonfire with the stuff, but he couldn't afford to. Somewhere in one of these boxes might be the one letter that would answer all his questions.

Luke's mood was not good. He was very conscious of the silence from the next room, where Rachel was working on a new brochure for the resort.

It irritated him that his concentration was so poor. Even more, he was annoyed with himself for the length of time this job was dragging out. Usually he was carried along by the excitement, by the feeling that he might find that buried "treasure" any minute. And there was an intellectual challenge to this kind of job that would be capped by the triumph of deciphering the clues and outwitting the perpetrator. But then, he'd never before had an emotional stake. His anxiety to get this over with had long since supplanted any feeling of excitement, and the reams of paper before him didn't represent challenge; they were a chore.

A sense of urgency was mounting in him. He wanted Krupinski behind bars, Rachel safe. He wanted to be able to stroll to the beach without expecting a bullet in his back. He wanted to be able to drop a letter of resignation onto his boss's desk. And most of all, he wanted to be able to court Rachel, to argue and laugh with her and kiss her with a clear conscience.

But his eyelids felt gritty and his mind fuzzy. He felt as if he was wasting his time. He couldn't believe he was going to find anything here. With a sigh he leaned back on the couch and rose. Maybe he'd better start planning tonight's expedition, as damn-fool as it was. He was wryly amused at his own eagerness to have an excuse to interrupt Rachel.

She looked up when he appeared in the doorway. Her eyes were wary, and his jaw tightened as he noticed the dark smudges beneath them.

Luke pulled up a chair beside her. Brochures were spread across the dining table, and she'd made notes on a lined tablet. At a glance he could see that she was right about needing a new brochure; the ones in front of her looked old-fashioned, with photographs that were less than sharp and far from compelling. They wouldn't have inspired *him* to want to vacation here.

"How's it going?" he asked with a nod at the notes she had made.

She just shrugged. Since she looked as tired as he felt, Luke doubted he was interrupting a creative frenzy.

"I bought a map," he said abruptly. "Can you pinpoint the next most likely bridges?"

A ripple of emotion crossed her face, and he wouldn't have been surprised to hear a groan. But she said reluctantly, "I guess so."

Luke pushed the brochures aside and spread a detailed topographical map in front of her. She surveyed it without enthusiasm.

"Has it occurred to you," she said, clearing her throat, "how . . . well, how *unlikely* it is that we're going to stumble on anything this way?"

Luke slumped lower in his chair. "Yeah, it's occurred to me," he said sardonically. "To tell you the truth, I feel like a complete idiot, wandering around randomly digging holes in the ground."

"It's not that bad," she protested without conviction. "We do know whatever he hid is under a bridge."

"Yeah. One of hundreds. Hell, thousands! And maybe we're misinterpreting him. Maybe he was speaking symbolically! God, I'm embarrassed to phone into my office and admit how I'm spending my time."

"But what else could you do?"

Luke's shoulders moved in a dispirited shrug. He didn't answer. They sat in silence for a moment while Rachel stared down at the map without giving the impression that she was really seeing it.

Out of the blue she asked, "Would you know if Walt had been arrested?"

"I'd be called," Luke said. She'd pinpointed one of his sources of frustration. Why in God's name hadn't Krupinski been picked up? This was a rural area. How hard could it be to find a stranger? With an effort he pulled himself together, sitting up and leaning his elbows on the table. "Well, what do you think?" he asked, flicking a finger at the map.

"I don't have the faintest idea," she said flatly. "I've come to realize that I didn't know Jack at all. So how am I supposed to know what he would have done?"

"You must have known him!" Luke couldn't help the sharpness that crept into his voice. "On some level, anyway. If you had any kind of marriage—"

"We didn't," she said simply.

There was silence for a moment.

"What do you mean?"

"Just what I said. We had a lousy marriage. If he hadn't died, I'd have left him."

Luke stared at her, his brows drawn together. He had to replay her words in his mind before he took them in. A dizzying wave of relief washed over him. She wasn't in love with her husband. There was one less obstacle for him to fight. But on the heels of his relief came anger. He said explosively, "Why didn't you say so before? Damn it, you've acted like you were protecting your dearly beloved!"

"Well, how did you expect me to act?" she flared, looking disconcerted by his anger. "I didn't know you! And I *was* married to him, after all! I felt like I owed him something."

Luke moved impatiently. "Why would you think that? No, let me guess. You felt guilty because he died and you didn't love him."

She lowered her gaze to the table. "No," she said in a small voice. "Not exactly."

"Then why? I don't understand."

Rachel stirred under the intensity of his stare. "Does it really matter?"

"Yes," he said tersely. "It matters to me."

His tone made her flinch, but she continued to stare down at the map. He didn't let his expression soften. Why had she misled him?

As though the silent force of his demand had triumphed, she at last gave a helpless shrug. "Partly it's like I said. Jack was dead, and there wasn't anybody but me to defend his . . . well, his honor. I didn't really *like* him by the time he died, but I thought he was basically an honest man. He was respected around here. And—" she shrugged diffidently "—I was the closest person to him. He left me everything he owned." She heard her own words and grimaced. "Well, I

A Shiver of Rain

thought he'd left me everything he owned. And I probably wasn't a very good wife. So I felt—'' she shrugged again ''—in debt.''

Luke leaned back in his chair and crossed his arms. ''That makes sense. Up to a point.''

''There's something more,'' Rachel admitted. Still she hesitated, and Luke saw something like fear in her eyes. What was she afraid of? His reaction? That would imply that she cared what he thought. An icy core in his chest began to melt. As he waited, a muscle twitched at the corner of his mouth. He was suppressing too much, he knew. But it was beginning to look as though she had been hiding even more.

''When they came to tell me about the accident, that Jack was dead...'' She swallowed. He watched her fingers writhing together, squeezing until her knuckles were white. The words came out in a burst. ''I was relieved. I didn't feel sad or shocked or anything normal. For that first second I felt a huge explosion of relief. It made me dizzy. The policeman who'd come thought I was in shock. I can remember him helping me to a seat and making me tea and being so nice, and all the while I was trying not to laugh, because I felt free.'' She looked fiercely at Luke. ''Now do you understand?''

''Yes.'' A wave of all-consuming tenderness swept over him. ''Perfectly. Death never seems very real at first. You were suddenly, painlessly free of a trap. I can't think of anything more natural than feeling the way you did.''

Tears shimmered in her eyes and her voice trembled a little as she said, ''Really?''

''Really.'' He reached out and took her hands in a warm, enveloping clasp. ''If I know you, you spent plenty of time grieving for Jack, once the fact that he was gone seemed real to you.''

A shadow crossed her face as she looked back, but she said, "Yes, but... Oh, to be *glad* someone died, because it made things easier for me...!"

"It was a natural reaction," he repeated firmly. "Good Lord, Rachel, who hasn't had thoughts they're ashamed of later? I certainly have! None of us are saints. Anyway, I really believe that what counts are actions, not thoughts."

She gave a watery chuckle. "Sort of like a man who admits that he lusted in his heart for other women but it was okay because he was faithful to his wife?"

Amusement relaxed his tension. How like her to find something to laugh at, even in the midst of distress.

"Exactly. And there's something else I want you to think about. Now that you know Jack was not only a crook but a double-crossing one, aren't you glad that he didn't die with you still thinking him perfect? It goes to show that your judgment isn't so bad, after all."

She looked startled, then thoughtful. Luke let her contemplate for a minute, moving his thumbs in an absent-minded caress on her palms. Finally he asked, "Now that you have that out of your system, do you feel better?"

"Yes," she said with faint surprise. "I guess I do."

"Good." His voice hardened. "Then you can tell me why you left me believing you were still madly in love with him."

He felt the startled tremor that ran through her. She tried to jerk her hands back, but he didn't let them go.

Temporarily accepting defeat, she let her hands lie limply in his clasp, but defiance sounded in her voice. "I never said anything that would make you think I was still madly in love with him!"

"Maybe not directly," he admitted. "But indirectly—hell, yes, you did. Every time I criticized him, you leaped for my throat."

"I felt—"

"I know. Like you owed him. But that's not good enough. Come on. There's more to it than that."

"That's not what I was going to say," Rachel told him with dignity. "What I thought was that if I admitted to you what Jack was really like, it would strengthen your case."

"Knowing him, why didn't you stop to think that maybe my story *was* true?" he asked with no softening of his tone.

Rachel compressed her lips and didn't say anything.

"Damn it, Rachel." Luke let her hear his anger again. "We made love. Couldn't you be honest?"

"If that's what you want, I'll *be* honest!" she said, suddenly angry, too. "I didn't tell you how I felt about Jack because I thought it would make you despise me. I couldn't face that. So now you know. Does that make you feel good?"

They stared at each other. "Yeah," Luke said slowly. "Yeah, it does. And that probably doesn't say much for me, does it?"

Rachel lowered her gaze first. "I—I don't know."

Luke waited, studying her averted face. Did she understand what he had just told her, how much he'd admitted? Or was she still angry because he had essentially shoved her up against a wall and shaken the truth out of her?

He was stunned by the force of his own feelings. He had known he wanted her, had even come to terms with the knowledge that he was falling in love with her. He'd learned to know frustration intimately. Acting as though he'd never made love to her had shown him the limits of his own control. But in the past half hour he'd felt relief so profound it made his head swim, anger that had hurt, tenderness and understanding, and at the end a sweet, twisted triumph, because she did care. It was disturbing to discover how much he was at the mercy of his emotions.

Still he waited. Finally Rachel made a decision of sorts, because she said in a voice that was almost matter-of-fact, "I think we should try this trail right here, up the Hoh River valley." Her finger indicated the point on the map. "It's quite a ways from here, but . . . Jack liked it."

Luke cleared his throat, accepting the diversion. He decided it wasn't time yet to force a moment of truth. But waiting wasn't going to be easy.

"All right," he said, his voice sounding harsh in his own ears. "Rachel, you don't have to come with me tonight."

Alarm showed on her face. "Don't be ridiculous!" she said pugnaciously. "Of course I'm coming."

Luke studied her for a moment, then inclined his head as he struggled against the desire to sweep her into his arms. "If you insist."

At least it didn't rain that night, although that didn't help a great deal. When the trail ventured into the open, Rachel could see the nearly full moon between scudding dark clouds. It was colder than it had been the night before, and the ground under the trees was still wet. They were in the rain forest here, which meant that the cedars and spruce and Douglas firs reached monumental heights, and under their stately canopy the growth was lush. Ferns nestled in every nook, and moss hung in swags and streamers from the branches.

Greenery was everywhere. And all of it was wet, eternally dripping. On some stretches of the trail it might as well have been raining.

Fortunately the track ran along flat ground. Rachel was able to follow the beam of light ahead without thinking about every step. What she did think about was the scene that afternoon.

Luke had been relieved; she couldn't be mistaken about that. Or about the anger that was so uncharacteristic of him. He had to have known what he was saying at the end, when he'd admitted that he wanted her to care what he thought.

Rachel didn't know how to feel after that. Determinedly ignoring the glow that had warmed her all afternoon, she tried to tell herself that she didn't *want* him to be in love with her. It was going to be hard enough for her to see him go in the end, without knowing that he hurt as badly as she did. But what other outcome could there be?

Even if she could trust her own feelings for him, be sure why she was attracted to him, she and Luke just didn't fit together. She despised guns and violence and subterfuge; they were how he made a living. Even if he quit his job, she would always know what he was capable of. His competence, that dangerous air, made him a reassuring companion now, but she couldn't imagine living with a man who reached for a gun as a normal response to a knock on the door.

Of course, she'd come to know him under unusual circumstances, she reluctantly had to remind herself. He had told her that he hated guns and killing. She couldn't forget his essential kindness, the idealism that motivated him, the pleasure he took in small things, like building a solid fence or watching the sandpipers skitter over the wet sand.

She wished suddenly that she knew more about him. What did his apartment look like? How did he spend his days off? Did he want to have children someday?

Well, why not ask? she thought.

"Hey, Luke," she said. His face was a dim blur when he glanced over his shoulder and slowed his pace. "Can we talk?"

Rachel sensed his scrutiny but felt safe from it in the darkness. He shrugged. "Why not? What do you want to talk about?"

She began obliquely. "You said you live in Falls Church. That's just outside D.C., isn't it?"

"Right over the Potomac. I have an apartment, but I'm not actually there very often."

It was nice talking as they moved through the darkness, she mused.

They talked about their childhoods, his in a loving family that encouraged independence, hers essentially barren, colored with fantasies about the father she'd never known.

Eventually she found the courage to ask something she'd been wondering since that afternoon. "Why were you so upset about my not being honest?" The question sounded abrupt to her. She hurried to fill in the silence. "I mean, you must lie a lot on your job. More than usual. But you sounded so—" the word came to her unbidden "—outraged."

He checked his stride, and she bumped into him in the dark. Then he walked away, the shovel bobbing on his shoulder, the flashlight casting its beam ahead on the narrow trail.

She decided he wasn't going to answer.

He suddenly said harshly, "Maybe that's why I don't like dishonesty. I live with too much of it. And . . . I have an uncrossable line. Some lies are necessary when I'm undercover. Some aren't. I haven't lied to you. I don't lie to anyone more than I can help. It works better, anyway, to let a person assume something." There was a brief silence. He continued, his voice rougher than usual, edged with something indefinable. *Anger, maybe?* she wondered. "Believing in honesty has gotten in the way of my career. I'm used on a certain kind of job, but at the department they know

damn well they can't trust me to cover up the dirty doings
of some public official. I'm good at what I do, but I'll never
make it to the next notch. There are too many games being
played and I'm not a player.''

Rachel absorbed all this. Somehow it didn't surprise her;
early in their acquaintance she'd concluded that he might
not be telling her everything but that what he did say was the
truth. His gaze was too direct, his manner sometimes too
impatient, for her to think otherwise.

He said no more, but she understood what was unspoken: he wouldn't tolerate lies in personal relationships,
either.

When Rachel at last made it to bed that night, she was still
thinking about what he'd told her. They'd ended up not
even digging. The two bridges on the trail, which had been
one of Jack's favorites, were tiny, built of peeled logs that
barely cleared the stream. Upon examination she and Luke
saw there was simply no place for him to have hidden anything. Rachel couldn't help being relieved. She had felt like
a criminal herself, skulking through the national park in the
dark with a shovel. This wasn't exactly what she'd had in
mind when she'd recommended Luke visit the rain forest,
she thought wryly.

Although they had avoided the exertion of digging, she
and Luke had hiked more than five miles and gotten thoroughly wet despite their slickers, and she had acquired a
blister on one heel. A hot bath and a cup of tea had helped
only a little.

Rachel lay in bed longing for sleep but unable to close her
mind to the look on Luke's face as he'd said good-night to
her in the hall outside the door. He'd been gaunt with tiredness, his wet hair plastered to his head. Nonetheless there
had been a light in his eyes that had reawakened that honey-

rich feeling in her belly. His voice had been gruff but tender, and she had known that he'd kept his hands at his side, that he'd turned and walked away down the hall, only because of the very tight rein he had on himself. Rachel wasn't at all sure that she wouldn't simply have melted into his arms if he had reached for her. The scene between them this afternoon had opened a Pandora's box that she, at least, wasn't ready to examine too closely.

At last exhaustion claimed her, and she slept heavily. When she realized in a very far-off way that a voice was calling her and hands were shaking her, she fought both, too fuzzy to think rationally.

"Rachel! Damn it, wake up!"

Her brain felt padded in cotton balls, and she instinctively curled up and tried to pull the covers over her head. Luke didn't let her hide. He wrenched back the covers, letting in a nasty cold draft.

Rachel squeezed her eyes shut and snatched at the blankets, but she was beginning to awaken. Luke's face was taut with anxiety, and he wore only a pair of pajama bottoms that rode low on his hips, exposing quite a lot of beautiful male body. Cursing under his breath, he was leaning over her, reaching to haul her up. Rachel was shaken by the desire to slide her arms around his neck and pull him down onto the bed with her.

Only... What was he doing here at all? She sniffed cautiously and bolted upright. They would have banged heads if he hadn't jerked back.

"Smoke!" she cried.

"No kidding." He grabbed her robe and thrust it at her. "I've called the fire department already. I thought I was going to have to carry you out."

"I'm a deep sleeper," she explained unnecessarily. She ignored the robe and reached for a pair of jeans that lay across the trunk at the foot of the bed, scrambled into them and stuffed the tails of her flannel nightshirt into the waistband. "What's on fire?"

"The lodge." Speaking crisply, Luke was already in the doorway. "I can't be sure, but I think it started in one of the bedrooms by the stairs. Do you have some hoses?"

She looked around for her slippers. "Yes, I'll go out and start hooking them up. You'd better grab something else to wear."

"Rachel..." Faint gray tendrils of smoke drifted past him. "Wait for me. Somebody might be out there."

Aghast, she watched him vanish into the hall. He was saying that somebody might have set the fire. If so, one purpose could be to drive them out into the night, vulnerable targets. Yet they had no choice. The smoke was a more tangible danger, the volunteer firemen could be slow and she refused to let the magnificent old lodge burn to the ground without a fight.

Taking advantage of his absence, Rachel hurriedly put on shoes and socks and a sweater over her nightshirt. It seemed only a blink of an eye before Luke was back at her side, wearing jeans, a dark T-shirt and running shoes. He was fastening the shoulder holster over his shirt as he came. The last buckle completed, he shrugged into a heavy flannel shirt to hide the gun, leaving it unbuttoned.

"All right, let's move," he said.

They went out through Rachel's private entrance. The moon showed between flitting dark clouds above the ocean and a faint yellow glow from the sodium lamps out front filtered around the edge of the building. The bedroom windows upstairs on this side of the lodge were dark. Thank God those rooms were all empty! A month earlier they would have been occupied.

The moment she and Luke emerged, he gave her a sharp nudge in the side, indicating they should move into the deeper shadows that ringed the lodge. Slipping past her so that he led the way, he seemed to become part of the darkness. Rachel followed, her nerves prickling as with all her senses she searched the night around them for motion. Now she could smell the smoke, hear a distant crackle.

They rounded the lodge into the nightmarish glare of dancing orange flames that were weirdly distorted by the still-intact windows of two rooms. For an instant Luke held her with a tight grip on her upper arm as his gaze swept the parking lot and the darker silhouette of the small grocery store.

At last he released her. "Okay, where are the hoses?"

Rachel led the way at a run to the storage shed. For a moment she had trouble remembering the combination for the lock and had to take several deep breaths before she managed. Her hands shook as she helped Luke unreel the neatly coiled hoses, then drag them across the gravel to the outside faucets.

Rachel knew that despite the recent rain, the wooden structure itself had to be as dry as tinder. She had always dreaded fire, knowing the building could go in minutes.

Luke fastened the hoses to the faucets. She felt a rush of relief when water gushed out. Following his example, Rachel trained her stream of water onto the roof and walls around the flames. Almost immediately the eerie orange light appeared in another window.

"We've got to get some water right on it," Luke called. "I'm going in. You stay here."

With that he disappeared into the lodge, trailing a hose behind him. She tried to stay calm, directing the stream from her nozzle in a rhythmic sweep, but terror gripped her.

What if the roof fell in or the fire leaped behind him? She should have stopped him, she thought desperately.

Her pulse thudded furiously when she heard the sound of a siren in the far distance. At last, the huge truck screeched to a stop behind her. Rachel couldn't tear her gaze from the flicker of the fire, the pitiful stream of water that only just reached the shingled roof.

"Anybody in there?" a voice asked urgently in her ear.

"Yes, Luke. My—my assistant." Gratefully, Rachel saw huge blasts of water cascading over the roof and two fire fighters running for the front door, pulling the hose behind them.

She dropped her own hose and began to follow, but the firemen had barely reached the porch when Luke emerged, bent over in a fit of coughing. Rachel ran to him and he straightened, closing his arms tightly around her as he hauled her up against him.

The hose that was snaking from the truck bumped against their ankles, recalling them to reality. His arm still around her, Luke pulled her away from the building. From twenty yards or so away, they turned to stare at the lodge. Was it her imagination? Rachel thought the flames were already lower, dying under the barrage of water.

"I think it's going to be okay," Luke said quietly in her ear. "The bedroom doors were all shut, which helped confine the fire. Looked to me like three or four of the rooms'll be badly damaged, but if you're lucky it won't be structural."

Rachel ignored his reassurances, turning on him fiercely. "You scared the hell out of me!"

He looked down at her in surprise. "What are you talking about?"

"Going in there like that! What if the roof had caved in?"

"Damn it, Rachel! What did you want me to do, let the place burn down?"

"Yes!" she cried, her eyes stinging from the smoke and the tears that burned inside her lids. "Yes! I'd rather lose the lodge than have your death on my conscience!"

"You mean you'd feel guilty about me?" He was mocking her, but his voice had an angry undertone.

Rachel blinked rapidly, then wheeled away from him to stare with blurred vision at the lodge. Not caring that she was being contradictory and illogical, she choked out, "No, I wouldn't! People who do dumb things deserve what they get."

There was a momentary silence; then, astonishingly, he laughed. "Hey, now you're getting the right idea!" When she turned to glare at him, his grin faded and he said gently, "I really wasn't in any danger. I promise. I just soaked the hall so the fire couldn't jump. I didn't realize you'd be frightened."

"I..." Her throat closed and she couldn't continue. Barely above a whisper she managed to say, "I—I'm sorry. I guess, while you were in there, I realized that you do dangerous things all the time. It's natural for you, isn't it?"

They stared at each other. Luke's mouth tightened grimly. "I don't make a habit of fighting fires."

"That's not what I meant."

At last he shrugged, his face closing. Without moving a muscle, he gave the impression of having stepped back. Even his voice was more distant. "There are risks in my job. You know that. But probably no more than those guys take." He nodded toward the firemen who were clambering up a ladder to direct the water into the gutted windows.

Rachel suddenly realized how unutterably weary she was. Her gaze followed his. "What a mess," she murmured.

"That's what you pay those outrageous insurance premiums for," he reminded her.

"I guess so." All the same, she was unable to feel anything but forlorn. Rachel tried to reassure herself that everything would look better tomorrow. Things could have been much worse. What if guests had been sleeping in those rooms? Or a sniper had been waiting out here in the darkness when she and Luke emerged?

That thought inspired her to take an uneasy look around. Once she'd been gripped by the need to fight the flames, she had managed entirely to forget the danger that might come from another source.

She saw for the first time that a dozen or so guests clustered to one side, staring at the scene. She really ought to go speak to them, she thought, almost grateful to have a purpose. She'd taken a step when she saw Henry Kirk. He stood, as he always seemed to, in peculiar isolation a few feet from the group. The others were dressed in the hodge-podge people pulled on when they hurried from their beds: nightgowns under parkas, slippers with jeans. Only Henry was completely, nattily dressed, all the way down to socks and a woolen scarf wound around his neck. He'd either been already dressed when he heard the commotion or sufficiently incurious to take his time. He was looking not at the drama being enacted in the light of the twin beams of the fire truck but at Rachel.

"Rachel." The man approaching wrenched her attention from the peculiar guest. Will Pierce was chief of the volunteer fire department, as well as a logging foreman. He often stopped at Sahale for a cup of coffee or breakfast.

"Will, hi." She forced a smile. "Thanks for getting here so fast."

He ignored that. "We've got the fire out now, although we're dousing it to make sure of any last sparks. But Rachel, there's going to have to be an investigation.'' He shook his crew-cut head, looking worried. ''I can smell gasoline up there. I don't think there's any doubt we're talking arson here. But why? Good Lord, why?''

Chapter 10

It was another hour before the firemen, satisfied that the fire was permanently out, had packed up and left. Rachel soothed the guests with reassuring words and shooed them back to their cabins. All the while, she was uneasily conscious of Henry Kirk watching her. She didn't let her facade crack, however, and even managed to include him in one of her pleasant smiles as she apologized for the disturbance.

Rachel tried to convince herself that if he had set the fire, he would have surely had the sense to pretend he'd been roused from bed like the other guests.

At last she and Luke were left alone to slump wearily into chairs in her living room. The acrid smell of the smoke had permeated even here, but Rachel was hardly aware of it. Her mind kept returning to the fact that while she and Luke slept, someone had jimmied a lock, then crept into the lodge, splashed gasoline around, flung a match and fled without being observed, apparently uncaring that two people slept in the old building.

She was startled when Luke's voice took up where her thoughts had left off. "This had to be Krupinski."

"Why?' she asked.

He ran a hand tiredly over his unshaven jaw. "Because he didn't really try to kill us. Not to say it couldn't have had that effect if I were a heavier sleeper. But still, if he'd wanted us to die, he could have ensured that. The fire could have been set so that we were trapped in our rooms. We have our lights on every night. If he's watching, he knows which bedrooms we were sleeping in. No, unlike the shots, I think this was meant as a warning."

"I guess that makes sense," Rachel said uncertainly. "Could the shots have been intended to scare us, too? After all, we weren't hit. We assumed we were supposed to be, but..."

Luke grimaced. "It's possible. But, damn, those bullets came close."

Silence followed. Rachel didn't have anything to add. Her mind seemed to be working in a sort of ponderous slow motion. Most of all, she was becoming aware of the late hour and their isolation, of the tension between them. She would have given anything to stumble into the haven of his arms, to lay her head on his chest and weep. And thoughts like that were very dangerous.

She hunched her shoulders and crossed her arms, saying abruptly, "I guess you can't sleep in your room tonight."

"It smells pretty bad," he agreed. His hands were shoved in his pockets, and he seemed to be waiting.

"Well...maybe the cabin?"

His voice was implacable. "Not without you. You're not staying here alone."

She couldn't seem to tear her gaze from his eyes, which had an odd glitter. "Surely nothing more will happen tonight," she said.

"Probably not. But I'm still not leaving you alone. Anyway, has it occurred to you that your bedroom probably stinks to the high heavens, too?"

"Oh," she said blankly. "I—I suppose you're right. I can start airing out tomorrow."

"But not tonight." His voice was gentler now. "Bring a sleeping bag if you don't trust yourself under the covers with me, but let's go get some sleep, okay?"

"You mean . . . in the cabin?"

Amusement showed briefly in his eyes as he inclined his head.

He wasn't being very much help, just standing there looking at her that way, Rachel thought resentfully. He appeared to have made up his mind about something, but what?

"I guess I don't have any choice," she admitted. "Let me get my stuff."

They parted at the top of the stairs, Luke going on to his room. Rachel wrinkled her nose at the pungent odor as she collected her toothbrush and a fresh nightgown—as fresh, that is, as anything she owned. She had a suspicion that merely airing out the rooms wasn't going to do the job. Her eyes were watering after she'd been in the small bedroom for only a minute.

At last she opened her closet and stared at the sleeping bag on the shelf. She'd been determinedly thinking about everything *but* Luke and their sleeping arrangement. Nervous excitement had been coiling in her, however, weakening her resolve.

Rachel shut the closet door and hurried out before she could change her mind. Luke was already waiting at the bottom of the stairs. His gaze moved over her, and she was quite certain he noticed the absence of a sleeping bag, but his expression didn't change. For that she was grateful.

They walked across the gravel parking lot without talking. The faint crunch of their footsteps was the only noise but for the sigh of the wind in the treetops and the muffled roar of the surf.

Even those sounds were shut out once they'd entered the cabin. Unused for some days, it was cold and damp. The bed was still made, and some of Luke's clothes hung in the small closet. There had been no reason to explain to her employees about Luke's move to the lodge. Both for the sake of her reputation and to confuse any watchers, Luke had pretended to be still living in the cabin.

She jumped nervously when Luke spoke. "Ladies first." He gestured toward the bathroom. The glint in his eyes told her he was as conscious of the situation as she was, but otherwise his demeanor was stolid.

Maybe, Rachel thought with mixed hope and disappointment, he would be a perfect gentleman and stay on his own side of the bed.

"Uh, thank you," she mumbled. Still clutching her toothbrush and gown, she made a wide circle around him and found sanctuary in the tiny bathroom. She took her time there. It felt strange to put her damp toothbrush into a cup and know that Luke's would probably join it. Even stranger was the idea of stepping out into the cabin—where the bed was the most prominent piece of furniture—in her nightgown and bare feet. But at last she decided she couldn't put it off any longer.

Luke had taken advantage of her absence to strip to his jeans. He looked lean and very masculine, with long, supple muscles that shifted as he straightened to face her. Rachel stood rooted in the bathroom doorway, her gaze riveted to his chest. His skin was smooth and brown. His jeans fitted loosely, riding low on his lean hips so that very little was left to her imagination—or her memory.

Rachel forced herself to look Luke in the face. A hot light smoldered in his narrowed eyes, and his mouth was tightly compressed.

In a gritty voice that was unbearably sensuous, he said, "If you don't mind."

"Mind?" she repeated stupidly. "Oh. Oh, I'm sorry." She was horribly conscious of the warmth that rushed to her cheeks as she moved out of his way. When the bathroom door closed behind him, she realized she was trembling.

On the other side of the door, Luke stared at himself in the small mirror, hardly recognizing his own face. His teeth were clenched. He was damn near shaking from the force of his desire for her. She was wearing another one of those flannel nightgowns, prim and proper at first glance, but far from it to a man who looked hard enough. The sturdy fabric had softened from repeated washings so that it clung to her small breasts and slender hips and thighs. And the way she had looked at him . . .

Damn, he wanted her! He'd decided tonight that he had to have her, whatever the cost. The last straw had been the look on her face when she had rushed into his arms as he stumbled out of the smoky building. She loved him. Even if she refused to say so in words, she had admitted it with her eyes and the arms that gripped him ferociously. What scared the hell out of him was the anger that had followed. Worse yet, the coolness, the withdrawal. And she was right about him; he couldn't argue. He didn't regard himself as reckless, but danger had been such an integral part of his job so that he no longer thought twice about it. Danger was part of life. But he could see the fear, even repulsion in her when she was confronted with the side of him that wasn't easy-going and amiable and humorous, the side that was a hunter.

If he gave her too much time, she would reason herself out of loving him. If he were totally unselfish, he would let her do that. But he needed her too much to let her walk away now.

He ducked his head under the faucet and let the stream of hot water wash away the soot and grime and sweat. After toweling his head dry, he made himself take the time to brush his teeth, but all the while he was listening to the silence from the other room. When he opened the door, he was irrationally relieved to see her still there, although he wasn't sure where he had thought she'd go in her nightgown and bare feet.

She had climbed into bed, but sat upright against the headboard with the pillow behind her and the covers clutched tightly above her breasts. Some of his own tension receded as a smile twitched at the corners of his mouth. She looked like a frightened virgin. He had the feeling that if he moved too suddenly she'd be out of that bed like a shot.

Moving unhurriedly, he turned off the overhead light, leaving on a bedside lamp. After checking to make sure both doors were locked, he eased out of his jeans and tossed them onto a chair. He didn't need a second glance at Rachel's big dark eyes to tell him to use a little discretion and leave his shorts on.

He saw her quiver when the bed gave beneath his weight. Luke would have liked to coax her out of her nerves, to tease her and make their lovemaking gentle and lighthearted. But he wanted her so badly that if it hadn't been for the tenderness that was softening the blunt edges of his hunger, he thought he'd already have grabbed her. How was he supposed to find the restraint to be gentle and patient when he was burning with desire?

But he loved her, so he would. It was that simple, he realized.

He rolled onto his side, holding himself up on one elbow. The sheets were cold. He and Rachel could warm them up nicely, he thought.

"Rachel . . . are you frightened of me?"

The velvet-dark pools of her eyes were veiled when her lashes swept down. When she looked up again, her expression was rueful. "No, of course not. If I'm scared, it's of the way you make me feel."

He had to clear his throat, but his voice was gruff. "That works both ways, you know."

"No. No, I didn't know," she said.

Luke couldn't believe they were in bed together conversing as they might have chatted over the dinner table, a careful distance separating them. Now that she'd relaxed her clutch on the covers, he was achingly conscious of the way her breasts rose and fell under that soft flannel.

"It scares me to be out of control," he said, surprising himself with his desire to be completely honest. "With you I feel that way. That's why I've tried to keep from touching you. In my job it's dangerous to lose control. I should have had Krupinski that day, but I let him go because I thought you were hurt."

She took that in. "That's why you looked angry."

"Yeah. I guess I was, at myself."

"Oh." He watched her study him. In her eyes was renewed confidence, as well as a sensual awareness that made his muscles tighten. "Then why are we here?" She meant the question to sound innocent, he knew.

"I think you know that," he replied.

"I'd like to hear you say it," she said.

From between clenched teeth he growled, "I need you, Rachel."

Her smile brimmed with feminine triumph and desire as acute as his own. "I guess that's good enough," she murmured, and slid down in the bed as he reached out to crush her in his embrace.

All his restraint was shattered, and he let it go without regret. He ravaged her lips and with his tongue aggressively claimed possession of her mouth. He rolled her beneath him, vaguely annoyed by the blankets clumped between them. But her breasts pressed against his bare chest and the nipples were taut beneath the fabric of her gown. He tangled one hand in her silky curls while with the other he cupped her breast, roughly caressing it as his thumb teased the nipple.

Moaning against his mouth, Rachel arched her back. Her arms encircled his neck, and now her hands moved restlessly, stroking and kneading and tugging him closer. Her body was passionately, electrically alive under his, both pliable to his touch and tense with urgency. He couldn't remember ever having felt such explosive desire. He could have separated her thighs and buried himself in her that instant.

But he wanted her as ready, as hungry for him as he was for her. And there was that nightgown.... He could have cheerfully yanked the gown down to her waist and ripped it off. Instead, he lifted his mouth a fraction from hers, then nipped at her full lower lip.

"I'm going to learn what every inch of you feels like," he muttered, his voice still rough and barely recognizable to his own ears. He felt as much as saw the smile that trembled on her lips. Her neck was unbelievably slender, the skin satiny, the racing beat of her pulse adding jaggedly to his excitement. Rachel flung back her head and made a small whimpering sound when his mouth found the hollow at the base of her throat.

It took more concentration than he'd thought himself capable of to unfasten the tiny round buttons of her nightgown. She sat up, helping him as he eased the gown off her shoulders and bared her to the waist. His hungry gaze took in the small firm breasts, the dusky centers of puckering nipple. Even her shoulders were slender and graceful. He had tortured himself with the memory of her unclothed body, but she was more beautiful than he remembered.

"You're perfect," he said with fierce pleasure, looking down at her.

She gave a shaky smile. "So are you."

He made a harsh sound in the back of his throat, then bent his head to take sweet possession of her breast. Clutching desperately at his shoulders, she moved beneath him in a way that drove him wild. Even as he grazed her nipple with his teeth, Luke was kicking the covers aside so he could tangle his legs with hers.

Rachel was growing frantic with need. His mouth and tongue and teeth on her breasts were sending shafts of almost painful pleasure through her, and his hand seemed to be moving with excruciating slowness as it slid down her flat stomach, over her waist and the curve of her hip. He was deliberately toying with her, his fingers brushing the soft center of her desire, caressing the inside of her thighs before teasing her again in a way that made her squirm to capture his hand where she needed it. Against her breasts he murmured words of endearment, his voice low and hoarse with urgency. Somehow his shorts had gone the way of her gown, so that his naked body was hard and lean and demanding against her. She had never felt like this before. Spirals of desire were coiling tighter and tighter until she thought she had to have him inside her or die.

"Please!" she begged in a raw whisper.

As though in response, he moved his attentions lower still. His tongue teased a torturous, fiery pattern on her belly, and when he lifted his head, the look on his face made her catch her breath in her throat. Burnished with a sheen of perspiration, the skin seemed to stretch tightly over his cheekbones. His eyes were molten with need, and unruly locks of damp hair hung over his forehead. His gaze clung to hers, communicating in a way that made Rachel's blood sing.

Then he brought his mouth back to hers and drunkenly sampled its most private depths. At the same moment her body arched convulsively as he drove inside her, piercing her with a sweet fire. For a second he paused, deep within her, and then, as if compelled, began to move in a wild rhythm. Rachel gripped the damp, muscled expanse of his back as she molded her body to him and raised her hips to meet his thrusts.

When she fell over the brink, she gasped out Luke's name as though he were her only anchor. A tremor seemed to shatter her into fragments, filling her veins with liquid fire. The convulsions that wracked her brought Luke to the end as well. A deep, guttural cry burst from him as he buried himself in her one last time. The explosive pleasure on his face filled Rachel with profound joy.

Too late she realized what a mistake she had made. The first time she had been able to dismiss what they had experienced as the natural aftereffect of fear. This time it would be much more difficult for her to find a rationale, a neat little compartment into which she could put her feelings. Because she and Luke had done far more than enjoy each other's bodies; they had made love in the truest sense of the word. And Rachel didn't know what to do about it.

When she awakened, morning light was filtering around the edges of the curtains and Luke was gone. Rachel lay there for a moment, feeling chilled. Except for the hazy memories of curling into his hard, warm embrace, she might have slept alone. Suddenly eager to be somewhere else, she jumped out of bed.

As she hastily pulled on the jeans and sweater she'd worn the night before, she wrinkled her nose. The smell of smoke that clung to them evoked a shudder full of memories. Outside, she discovered that the clouds had been whipped away by the wind, leaving the sky a crystalline wintry blue.

Hurrying across the parking lot, Rachel shivered in the cold breeze, reminded that it was late November. Luke's presence became immediately apparent when she circled the lodge; the windows and doors of her apartment were wide open, allowing the cold wind to blow through the rooms.

Huddled in a parka, Luke sat on the couch in the living room, a box of papers beside him. For a moment she stood in the doorway, unnoticed, watching as he impatiently scanned a sheaf of invoices, threw them aside and snatched up another piece. The breeze had flung the discarded papers all over the floor. A frown tightened his face, and from across the room she could feel the tension that drove him.

"Good morning," she said.

He looked up, and immediately his face softened. "Morning, love."

The light way he said it gave her a pang. Rachel couldn't help remembering that despite the passion they'd shared, he hadn't said he loved her. She had trouble believing that all he wanted was a roll in the hay, his cry of need had been too powerful, the look on his face too intense. On the other hand, things were always different in the morning.

He seemed to read her mind. His voice low and husky, he said, "I didn't like leaving you to wake up alone. But I couldn't sleep after it got light, and I wanted to get to work."

"I understand," she said hurriedly. "I didn't expect a champagne breakfast."

"Though one would have been nice." He gave her a crooked smile and rose to his feet. "A kiss would be even better."

He stopped in front of her, grasping her by the upper arms. His lips sent a shock of electricity through her. The kiss was gentle, even sweet, without the sexual intimacy of the night before. Yet in its way it was more reassuring than passion might have been.

When he released her, she swallowed and stepped back. "Uh, have you had breakfast?"

His smile was swift, as his attention was already returning to the pile of papers. "Just coffee. I'm not hungry. You go ahead."

Taking him at his word, she went first upstairs to shower and change clothes, then into the kitchen to make a quick bowl of cereal and a cup of tea.

She would have been hurt by Luke's preoccupation if she herself hadn't shared the underlying apprehension and urgency that fueled it. Afterward she, too, went right to work, beginning with phone calls. Blackened holes exposed several of the upstairs rooms to the weather, and rain would only exacerbate the fire damage, further soaking the charred timbers. She was eager to have the cleanup and reconstruction work begin. She could finish reading Jack's diaries later.

Around midmorning, fire and insurance inspectors arrived to begin sifting through the blackened mess. Rachel showed the two men up, then left them. She was depressed by the sight of the burned-out room and couldn't seem to escape the gasoline and charcoal smells, which lingered in her nostrils.

As she walked back through the living room, Luke didn't seem even to notice. He was raking his fingers through already rumpled hair and mumbling under his breath. The whirlwind of papers around him had mounted, and she knew he had found nothing.

Just as she reached the kitchen, the phone rang and she answered crisply.

The sheriff's voice was brusque in her ear. "George here. I hear you had a fire last night."

"Yes, I'm afraid so." Rachel propped her shoulder against the wall.

"You're not hurt?" he asked sharply.

"No, nobody was," she assured him. "I'm told it looks like arson, though."

"Something funny is going on out there." He sounded angry. She gave him the credit of assuming his tone was a reflection of his concern for her. "Damn it, Rachel, you're too trusting! Those supposed shots—and now a fire, too! Are you sure you know everything you should about that new assistant of yours?"

Her mouth twisted wryly. What a question!

"George, Luke is the one who discovered the fire and woke me up. He probably saved my life. And he was on the receiving end of the shooting. He's not the one I need to worry about."

"Then who is?"

She didn't want to sound stupid and make George suspicious. So she said tentatively, "I've been wondering about that crank I called you about. If he's still in the area—"

"You haven't heard from him again, have you?"

Rachel hesitated. She would have broken her word to Luke in a second rather than be left at Walt's mercy, but what good would that do now? "No, I haven't," she said at last. "Still, it's coincidental that he should threaten me, and then a couple of such strange incidents would happen here, don't you think?''

The sheriff agreed, sounding thoughtful, then promised to do some further checking around. He let her change the subject, and she took the chance to ask for his recommendations on local contractors.

Rachel was frowning as she hung up. George had said nothing about the directive to find Walt Krupinski that Luke had told her about. If Luke was telling the truth, there must be a search under way for the man. Obviously George hadn't connected her nameless crank and the stranger his deputies were watching for. Well, why should he have? And she couldn't enlighten him without giving Luke away. It was all so complicated, she thought with frustration.

By early afternoon she got as far as walking through the damaged area a couple of times with contractors who promised to get back to her with bids. The charred smell stayed with her afterward. She tried not to think too much about how the once-charming rooms looked. She told herself she could make them attractive again but knew in her heart that it would never be the same. She couldn't afford the time to search out distinctive, individual pieces and lovingly restore them. With the insurance money she would sweep through antique stores and commission new rugs and quilts from local crafts people. But there would be a newness in these rooms that couldn't be wiped away, a newness that would recall the ugly memory of fire and the hate that had sparked it.

Rachel knew that she would be leaving all of this soon. Whatever happened with Luke, it was time for her to move on. She didn't know whether the resort would have been sold by then, or where she would go, but one way or another she would be enrolled in law school next fall.

As the day went on, she couldn't help noticing and being disturbed by the general air of fear about the resort. At lunchtime the coffee shop was nearly empty. Guests were staying away. Employees, knowing the fire had been deliberate, whispered in corners, looking nervous. Rachel felt curiously detached. She tried to reassure them, but how could she make promises when she knew quite well that the danger wasn't over?

A sense of urgency gripped her. If the fire had been intended as a warning, an omen, it had certainly been clear. She was afraid to think about what might happen next, because if anyone was to be hurt, it would most likely be Luke. Someone seemed determined to get rid of him.

Rachel kept a surreptitious eye on Luke all day. She was grateful that he made no effort to go out. She wasn't sure she could have survived the fear if she had glanced into the living room and found him gone.

Finally she settled down there with the last volume of Jack's diary. Though she didn't expect to find anything, she felt the same compulsion she knew was driving Luke: time was running out.

Luke glanced up. His eyes were red-rimmed, and for a moment he looked blank, almost as though he didn't recognize her. Then he wearily leaned back against the couch, his gaze wandering over the strewn floor.

"I've made a hell of a mess in here, haven't I?" he remarked.

Rachel gave her head a quick shake. "It doesn't matter. Have you found anything?"

"Not a damned thing." He flung his arms above his head and stretched. "Another hour or two and I'll have read every word your husband ever wrote."

Quietly she said, "And then what?"

He didn't answer for a minute, then shook his head. "Then it's time to admit defeat and call in the cavalry. I wanted to keep this quiet for your sake, Rachel. That won't be possible if we have to really tear this place apart."

Her smile was small and a little painful. "I don't care anymore. Do what you have to."

Luke studied her face for a minute in silence, then nodded briefly. In what she suspected was a deliberate attempt to change the mood, he grinned. "Look at it this way. You'd have spent the next ten years sorting all this junk. Now you'll have some empty closet space."

She curled her lips in response. "True. Maybe I'll start collecting my own junk."

"Like what? What's your weakness?"

"Books," she said without hesitation. "If I could afford to buy everything I wanted to read, I'd be buried in books already. What about you?"

"I like books, too. But my little fantasy is to have a perfectly equipped workshop. I told you I like to build with wood. It's tougher without the right tools. I'd like to create every stick of furniture for my house. All custom-made, sanded to a sheen. There are so many woods I'd like to experiment with." Hearing his own enthusiasm, he shrugged ruefully. "You asked."

"Yes." She found it easy to picture him working in complete contentment over a table saw, patiently rotating a slab of wood, rubbing a caressing finger along the grain. Building something that would last for generations. Or perhaps hold the next generation. She'd seen plans in magazines for cradles and even cribs. Hands that were deft with wood, tender on a woman's body, would also be gently loving with a baby.

He interrupted her train of thought with a groan. "Well. Back to work." With a visible effort he gathered himself and hunched over the coffee table again. Rachel saw him rub his eyes before he was able to focus on the print.

Her sigh soundless, Rachel followed his example and flipped open the notebook. It was strange how irrelevant it seemed that Jack had written it. She'd begun to feel as if her life with him had been an eternity ago. Now he felt to her like the stranger she knew he'd been.

"High wind today," she read. "Electricity out for *two* hours. Complained to PUD. They need to make us a higher priority. Produce delivery late, too. Carlson's is going to have to clean up their act, or I'll find another supply."

Carlson's was still delivering fresh produce to Sahale, and Rachel was perfectly happy with their service and the quality of the produce, much of which was grown locally in season. Jack had been hard to please, and it had taken her a while to learn that she wasn't the only one who found him that way.

The next hour passed for Rachel and Luke in surprising harmony. The atmosphere in the lamplighted room was almost cozy as early winter dusk wrapped the lodge in darkness. She could no longer smell smoke. Luke had shut the windows and doors some hours before and even built a small fire in the fireplace. She gazed at the flickering flames and thought how ironic it was that the sight could be comforting. As she looked up, she wondered why she'd never replaced the painting over the mantel, with its opaque grays and dark mood. It had brooded over her on too many lonely evenings.

She was skimming the diary now, only a few months from Jack's death. There was no reason to think he would obligingly describe where he had hidden the pilfered wealth. After all, he'd been writing only for himself.

Then she came to an entry that hit her like a wall. Incredulous, she reread it. Jack had made contacts about selling

Sahale, the resort he had supposedly loved. At the end he had added cryptically, "Tell R. I've applied for a new loan and that's why they're looking the place over?"

The words burst from her: "Why, that . . . that . . . !"

"S.O.B.?" Luke supplied helpfully. He stood with deceptive laziness and strolled over. Nodding at the notebook, he inquired, "Is his offense strictly personal? Or is it something I'd be interested in?"

"He was going to sell this place!"

"That's a surprise?"

"No, I suppose not," she admitted reluctantly. "But to think he was planning that, even having prospective buyers look the place over, and all the time he was lying to me! You know—" the realization was almost a relief to her "—he had no intention of taking me with him when he left! He was going to walk out of here rich, and free as a bird." Her laugh was angry. "At least I know now why he wasn't interested in marriage counseling!"

"You told me you were ready to leave him, too," Luke reminded her.

"After exhausting every effort to make the marriage work!"

He sat on the arm of the chair, looking down at her. His eyes were intent on her. Rachel knew he was trying very hard to hide his tension, but despite the relaxed pose, his body was taut.

"How do you feel about this?" he asked.

"You mean, am I brokenhearted? No! But I *am* mad as hell! I feel like such a fool, remembering how earnest and gullible I was!"

"We're all gullible sometimes," he said quietly.

"Yeah. Some of us are just more so than others."

The wheels were turning in his head, and Rachel could see the moment he came to a decision. Abruptly he said, "I told you I killed a man after he shot my partner." He waited for her nod. "Well, we walked into that situation because *I* was gullible. I took some assurances at face value. Afterward I thought about hanging up the job, but I didn't. I figured that mostly I'd done things right. Nobody is perfect."

"And your partner didn't die," she said with sudden certainty.

Something flickered in his eyes. He said wryly, "You've figured me out. No, John didn't die. If he had, I wouldn't be able to sleep nights. And I would have quit the job." He grimaced. "Which might not have been a bad thing."

"Tut, tut." Rachel wagged a finger at him. "Remember, guilt is a destructive emotion. You wouldn't want it to rule your life, now would you?"

After a moment of astonishment, he threw back his head and laughed. A grin still lingered about his mouth when he reached out, grasped her chin and tilted her face up. Warmth and something more were in his eyes. His voice had a husky undertone. "You're good for me, Rachel. I like you."

And I love you, she thought as his lips came down on hers.

He came to her bed that night as though he had a right and was sure of his welcome. She had washed the sheets and blankets from both upstairs beds to get rid of the pervasive smell of smoke. Not wanting to make assumptions, she had casually mentioned to him that he could have the other room.

She thought he looked amused for a moment, but his only response was to stretch out his long legs under the table and comment idly, "Then I'd better go back to the cabin and pick up my toothbrush."

"No!" Startled at her own vehemence, she tried to moderate her tone. "I'll get you a new one from the gift shop."

He understood without her explaining. "We can't hide in the lodge forever."

"No, but—" she bit her lip "—I've had a bad feeling today."

"Me, too," he admitted.

Hesitantly she asked, "You don't want to go search under any bridges tonight, do you?"

"No. That was an exercise in futility, if I've ever indulged in one. There's got to be another answer. Maybe a good night's sleep will help."

Maybe that was all she needed, too. Too little sleep might explain that feeling of apprehension that had hung over her all day. The tired mind often distorted reality, she reflected.

Without more discussion, Rachel took the first turn in the small upstairs bathroom. As she showered and brushed her teeth, she couldn't help being reminded of the night before and wondering whether Luke would be waiting outside the door. But the hall was empty.

Her room was dark, and she was curled up under warm covers when the crack of light from the hall widened until Luke stood in the doorway. He wore only jeans. The one unpleasant note was the holster, which dangled loosely from his hand. Without a word he clicked off the hall light. A moment later she heard the sound of him setting down the gun on the stand, and then the bed gave beneath his weight.

When his arms encircled her and his mouth found hers, Rachel responded eagerly. She wouldn't let herself think at all, only feel. The memories of her nights with him would be precious, even if they were all she had.

Their lovemaking was different tonight, slow and lazy and tender. Desire washed over her hot and thick, leaving her not so much urgent as languid under its spell. Their tongues and breath mingled, their hands caressed and kneaded and learned each other's bodies. They made love as though they had all the time in the world, defying the possibility that this was all there ever would be.

Eventually, of course, their need became too much. The deliberate, provocative rhythm grew uneven, frantic, and a climactic crescendo left them shuddering with pleasure.

Afterward, in the dark stillness, Luke cradled Rachel in his arms. She nestled into his embrace, savoring the closeness, wishing it could last forever. She was grateful for the darkness, warm and heavy around them. She couldn't see Luke's face, so there was no need to interpret his expressions or imagine she was seeing things that might not even be there. Nor could he see her. He would never know about the smile that trembled on her lips or the tears that dampened her lashes.

Rachel awakened with the first, reluctant light. Luke still slept deeply, his hair standing out in spikes, his lips moving occasionally as he murmured to himself. Rachel wondered what he was saying. Was she in his dreams, or did he forget her in sleep?

Without disturbing him, she freed herself from the warm weight of his arm. As quietly as possible she gathered her clothes and slipped out to the bathroom to dress hurriedly, shivering in the early-morning chill. Downstairs she took the time for a hot cup of tea and two pieces of toast with blackberry jam.

When Luke still hadn't appeared, she bundled herself into a parka. Her routine had been horridly interrupted lately. It had been several days since she had even walked around the loop to see how everything looked. She'd given the two maids instructions about winterizing the empty cabins, but neither girl had much experience. Normally Rachel would have been checking up on them.

This morning seemed to her a good time. The night had passed without incident; she doubted that in her winter gear she would even be recognizable from a distance. As Luke had said, they couldn't hide out indefinitely. And her fears had disappeared with the night.

She left a note on the table. Outside, frost sparkled on the grass, and the salty tang in the air seemed sharper than usual. Gray clouds hung ominously to the northeast, no doubt depositing snow in the mountains. Except for the background noise of the surf, the resort was completely quiet. Smoke curled from a couple of chimneys, but nobody was stirring outside yet.

It was at the far end of the loop that Rachel noticed a cabin door standing slightly ajar. This particular cabin was set apart from the others, isolated by a stand of firs. It was also one of those that was supposed to be empty.

Her first instinct was to retreat. She stood well back, staring at that door. The windows, etched with frost, were empty. Then she saw that the doorstep was covered with a razor-thin crackle of ice. Nobody had stepped there yet today.

Reassured, she started forward. The maids had probably been working here yesterday and not latched the door properly when they left. She would glance in, make sure everything was all right and speak to them later.

The thin, rough ice cracked under her weight. The sound sent a little ripple of nervousness through her. Maybe she should go back and get Luke.

But then, through the opening, she saw the body. Head turned to one side, he lay sprawled facedown on the bed, unquestionably, violently dead. Even from here she could see the bloody hole in his temple. What was more, she *knew* the man, who stared sightlessly at the door, his expression frozen into a snarl. It was Walt Krupinski.

Chapter 11

Luke saw the note right away. Anxiety seized him the moment he'd finished scanning the brief contents. What had she been thinking of to have gone out by herself?

Uttering a muttered oath he sat down to pull on his boots. He would have liked a cup of coffee, but didn't take the time. Grabbing his parka from the rack by the door, he hurried outside.

Damn, it was cold, he thought. He shoved his hands into the pockets of the parka and hunched his shoulders to bring the collar up to his ears.

He was across the parking lot when he saw Rachel coming down the lane at a half run, and he knew immediately that something was wrong. She was breathing in quick gasps, stealing glances over her shoulder.

Instinctively Luke groped for his gun, then remembered he didn't have it. *Very smart,* he chided himself. Even as he closed the distance between himself and Rachel with long strides, he looked round, hunting for that tiny sign of something amiss. Nothing.

Rachel's eyes were wide and horrified, her face unnaturally pale under the knit hat except for bright spots on her cheeks from the cold. She clutched Luke's sleeve.

"He's dead. Walt Krupinski. I found him."

"Where?"

"The last cabin. The door was open. He—he was shot."

"You're sure he's dead?" Luke took a step that way, but her grip on his parka sleeve held him.

"Very sure." She shuddered. "He was cold."

Luke swore. If somebody had to kill Krupinski, why the hell did they do it where Rachel would find the body?

He took her cold hands and squeezed, willing warmth into them. "Rachel," he said, his voice gentle but compelling. "I want you to go back to the lodge and call the police. Don't tell them you know who it is. Just say you've found a man shot to death in one of the cabins. Then make yourself a cup of tea. I'm going to take a look, but I'll be right with you. Okay?"

She nodded. "Yes, all right, but Luke, don't we have to tell—?"

"Yeah, it's time for true confessions. But only to your friend the sheriff. With a homicide, he'll show up. You leave it to me."

With a small push he started her on her way. The dazed look on her face stayed before his mind's eye as he walked in the opposite direction. A man had died, and he ought to be thinking about that. Instead, he couldn't help wondering what effect this would have on how Rachel viewed him. His job and all that went with it had been repugnant to her before, but still distant. A few minutes ago she'd seen immediate reality. His reality. Violent and sordid. Sometimes sad. Not tragic in a grand sense—how could it be, when the man who had died was such a lowlife? But still, he'd died by someone else's hand. Even Walt Krupinski deserved better.

What would Rachel see? The men Luke had killed before their time?

With his shoulder he carefully pushed the cabin door farther open, doing his best not to destroy any potential fingerprints. Inside the cabin, he managed to block thoughts of Rachel from his mind. As he stood looking down at the shell that had been Krupinski, his assessment was professional, clinical. With one finger he tried to move the cold stiff hand. Under some conditions he could have made a pretty decent guess as to how long the man had been dead, but the weather made it tougher. It had been damned cold the night before. Still was, for that matter.

He couldn't see anything out of place in the room. There was no sign of a scuffle. Luke lifted Krupinski's thin jacket to see a shoulder holster and the butt of a gun. It didn't even look as if he had been reaching for it.

Had he been surprised by somebody who shot him before he even realized he had company? But then how could Krupinski's presence be explained at all? Luke looked around again, his gaze narrowed. Was there something special about this cabin? He himself had made a reasonably thorough search of all the empty cabins, including this one.

If he'd been on the run, Krupinski might have been planning to sack out here, figuring it was empty and nobody would notice. But where were his things: extra clothes, toothbrush, car?

Any suitcases could have been taken by the killer. But Luke could think of another explanation for Krupinski's being here. This cabin was isolated. It would be a good place to meet someone for a quiet talk—someone who had shot him unexpectedly. The same someone who'd been taking potshots at Luke. But who? Damn it, who?

After glancing into the small bathroom and the closet and finding exactly what he expected—nothing—Luke left the cabin. He strolled around the loop, studying the vehicles pulled in next to cabins. Near the end, he found what he was looking for. A few parking slots were screened from the lodge by the small grocery store. One spot was occupied by a blue sedan. The windshield was iced over, the hood patterned with frost, so Luke knew it had been here for some hours at least.

It was an oldish Chevy, but in nice shape. Anonymous, the kind of car nobody noticed, nobody remembered. Luke searched his memory and pictured Walt's car disappearing in a cloud of dust around the bend after Luke's futile dash across the parking lot. In his mind he could see the shape of the rear lights. Circling the car, he looked at the back. *Bingo.* It had to be Krupinski's car.

Using the edge of his sweater, he opened the unlocked door and slid into the driver's seat. Luke was careful not to touch the steering wheel; if a decent set of fingerprints could be found anywhere, it would be there. The back seat was empty. He cautiously opened the glove compartment and found only papers for car rental to one Philip James. The trunk would have to wait, since the homicide cops wouldn't appreciate finding the lock picked. Besides, Luke didn't expect to find a thing.

The one anomaly was the open door of the cabin, Luke reflected. If the killer had closed it when he'd left, the body might have gone undiscovered for days. Well, maybe the killer had just gotten careless. Or maybe he didn't care when the body was found. If he had a good enough alibi or was unlikely as a suspect, it wouldn't matter. The other possibility was that he'd left in a hurry.

Luke shrugged, slammed the car door with his shoulder and headed for the lodge. He checked his stride at the sound of a car engine, then lengthened it as a park service pickup passed on the highway without slowing.

Rachel was going to need him. He knew the sight of Krupinski's obscenely dead body would be hard for her to forget. Only time would blur the image and make it less likely to be in the forefront of her thoughts.

The trouble was, *he* didn't want to be seen through that distorted image. He wanted her to see him, all of him. He had a sick feeling it wouldn't be that way. She had enough reservations about him; seeing death at its most grotesque might easily confirm them.

He was opening the front door of the lodge, intending to cut through, when the first police car pulled into the parking lot. No siren, no flashing blue lights, Luke noticed. Either they'd had the sense to be discreet or Rachel had asked especially. Luke didn't pause.

He did hesitate before the door to her apartment. Recognizing his own cowardice, he grimaced and opened it.

Rachel turned anxiously at the sound. She hadn't even taken off her parka, he saw, and was huddled in it with her arms crossed as though it were freezing in here instead of at least sixty-five degrees. He would build a fire and hunt up some brandy.

"Did...did you see—" she swallowed "—it...him?"

"I saw." He took her hands. "You're cold as ice." Bad choice of words, he thought ruefully. Krupinski had been cold, too.

"Cold?" She looked blank, her eyes almost vacant. She hadn't even noticed that she was cold. She started to pull her hands away and huddle up again. Luke watched, helpless. He could warm her body, but not her soul. And the endless questions still to come would chill her further.

Suddenly she lifted her head to look at him. Her brown eyes shimmered with the first wave of tears. "Oh, Luke! It was so... horrible! How could someone do that to another human being?"

"I don't know," he said wearily. That was a question he had never been able to answer, even for his own satisfaction. "It was quick, Rachel. He might never have even known what was happening."

"And he would've done the same to someone else, wouldn't he?"

The observation surprised him. Her critical faculties hadn't entirely shut down. "Yeah. Krupinski wasn't a man you should waste too much sympathy on. Don't forget your own experience with him," he said.

Her eyes seemed to be shaded now by a memory; his own feelings hardened as he remembered Rachel's cheek, swollen and purple. No, Krupinski was no loss to society.

"Luke?" Her voice quivered.

He looked down at her. "Yeah?"

"Hug me, will you?"

He fiercely wrapped his arms around her, drawing her against him. Despite the parkas both wore, he could feel her shivers, her brittleness. He held her tightly, his cheek against her soft curls, until it seemed as though her shivers were lessening, her tension easing.

Inside, he was exultant. She had turned to him, asked for his warmth and his comfort!

A loud knock resounded through the room, and Rachel jerked, then stiffened in his arms.

"The police," Luke said quietly, forcing himself to relax his grip as she stepped back and visibly gathered herself. "I'll let them in."

Rachel's head ached. She took another sip of tea, but it was too strong and tasted unpleasant. Still, it warmed her throat as it trickled down. She edged closer to the fire, feeling the heat as a sting on her cheeks, but not bone deep, where she needed it.

Reminding herself that Walt Krupinski had been a genuine louse didn't seem to help. It wasn't his death in particular that was upsetting her; it was Death with a capital *D*. Death by violence, death when it was most unexpected. She remembered lying on the ground, her cheek pressed to the dirt, with bullets skipping by.... She shuddered and wrapped her arms around herself.

Luke risked that kind of death every day on his job. How could he bear the fear? Well, maybe he didn't feel fear. Maybe he was a fatalist, but she wasn't! The night before came back to her, the explosive passion and heart-stopping tenderness, all wrapped in the cocoon of night. Luke was so alive, and she felt ill at the thought of him crumpling before a bullet. No! She couldn't live with him with that fear.

Of course, he hadn't asked her to, and she had no reason to think he would. No reason but the look in his eyes, the way he made love to her as though for him the world began and ended there.

Rachel stood restlessly and walked to the window. The thin glaze of ice on the glass was melting, dripping. Outside on the frosty grass Luke stood talking to the sheriff. They were both big men, particularly in their heavy parkas. She found it hard to read their emotions. Their heads were close together, their hands shoved into coat pockets. But their body language was telling; instead of looking at each other as they talked, both faced the parking lot, where an ambulance and police cars were the center of a hive of activity that she preferred not to think about.

She was only grateful that it was Monday and she didn't have to deal with staff. She was willing to bet that there would be more than one resignation on her desk Wednesday morning. And who could blame them?

She was fortunate that Sahale had only a handful of guests right now, mostly late-season elk hunters. As a group they had taken the news of murder very calmly. What the publicity would do to next season's reservations was another matter.

The routine that followed a homicide was in motion. A detective had questioned her in detail. The coroner had come and gone. Minute evidence was now being gathered for the lab. Half hysterically Rachel thought of technicians analyzing her dust.

Through the wet glass she saw the sheriff make an abrupt, choppy motion with his hands while he vehemently shook his head. Luke's expression was hard, unapologetic. He was demanding cooperation, Rachel guessed, and the sheriff was reluctant to give it. Heaven knew George had reason to be angry. She wasn't looking forward to facing him again. He'd understand, of course. What choice had she had? Still, her lies would jar their relationship, she knew.

At last, reluctantly, she turned her thoughts to the central problem. Who had killed Walt Krupinski? She made herself face the fact that Luke was capable of it. Could he have done it, if he'd feared Walt was beating him in the race to find the gold? She'd read often enough in the newspaper about the government doing some dreadful covert things. What if they had decided Walt was an inconvenience? On trial, he would have talked about the gold and where it was going, which might have gotten some people in trouble. Was it even remotely possible that Luke had been *ordered* to dispose of him?

She was obscurely comforted by her instantaneous, forceful rejection of the idea. Not Luke! He would never have done it. He wasn't, couldn't be, a cold-blooded killer! She'd learned enough about him to know how idealistic he was. He would never have violated his own moral code.

The conversation out on the grass seemed to have come to an end. Luke nodded abruptly and the two men began walking toward the parking lot. Rachel hated to imagine what was happening there. She turned back to the fire and the cup of cooling tea, which had left an aftertaste in her mouth.

Who could possibly have reason to want Walt Krupinski dead? She wondered if the police would be talking to Henry Kirk. Maybe it would turn out that somebody had seen something. A car pulling into the resort in the middle of the night, or one left on the verge of the highway, might have been noticed. But in her heart she knew it wouldn't be that easy. The employees would have been most likely to notice something odd, but even the last kitchen help had been gone by ten last night. And what were the odds of one of the few guests having seen anything? None were even in a unit near the end, where it had happened. Anyway, if the killer was the same man who'd shot twice at her and Luke, he had a gift for slipping in and out unseen, as though he had no more substance than a ghost.

Rachel sank into a chair and stared at the low flames licking hungrily at the logs. With a crackle, a shower of multicolored sparks shot up, then blinked out like fireworks in a night sky. Her mind kept running over the same path. Who could possibly know about the gold, know who Walt Krupinski was, see Luke as a threat? Who?

The sheriff left shortly after talking to Luke. He stuck his head in to say goodbye to Rachel, but his manner was strictly impersonal. When she tried to apologize, he shrugged.

"Some things you can't help." Brusquely he added, "Detective Myers will be in charge here. You talked to him earlier, didn't you?"

"Yes. George, I hated having to lie to you."

Again he ignored her attempt to apologize. "I'll be keeping an eye on the investigation. You ought to be safe enough here with Warren."

Left alone, Rachel consoled herself with the thought that she could talk to him another time. His mind was probably more occupied with Luke's revelations and the murder than with the trivial lies she had told him, anyway.

Hours passed before the parking lot began to empty. Luke glanced in several times, his brief smiles reassuring. Twice the chief investigator returned to ask her more questions. Rachel began to pray he would go away. She wanted to forget, and instead he was forcing her to remember.

She gathered that the detective had been let in on the secret of Luke's identity and Walt's reason for being at Sahale. Although Luke stood silently in the doorway when the investigator asked her questions, she had the impression that Luke would have been deferred to if he'd made any effort to take charge. Instead, he watched and listened.

At last the stocky, dark-haired detective let her know he was leaving. "Needless to say, we've sealed off the cabin. Don't go in, and don't let anyone else in. It may be as much as several weeks—"

"There's no hurry," Rachel interrupted. "We were closing it for the winter, anyway."

"Fine," he said crisply. "Warren, I'll let you know anything we find out."

"Thanks," Luke said. The two men shook hands with apparent cordiality and the detective left. In the silence that followed Luke looked at Rachel, his brows raised. "How are you feeling?"

"Oh, I don't know." She shook off his question almost irritably and paced to the window to stare out. The lowering clouds seemed to suit her mood. How *did* she feel? She wasn't sure. But suddenly the room felt stuffy. She needed fresh air. "I have to get out of here." Her voice held a panicky edge.

"I could use a break myself," Luke said calmly. "How about a walk on the beach?"

Rachel agreed and grabbed her coat, eager to move, to stretch her legs, to feel alive. They went out the side door and across the lawn. The sky had clouded over, and the air was heavy with a promise of rain or even snow. The solitary, harsh call of a seagull drifted toward them, and Rachel noticed how high the Sahale was running. Swirling with undercurrents, the water lapped against the jagged driftwood heap that was wedged in the curve below the lodge.

They were at the stairs leading down to the beach before Rachel felt a belated stirring of caution. She paused uncertainly. "Do you think this is safe?"

Luke glanced at her. "Yeah. The place has been swarming with cops all day. I can't picture the murderer hanging around waiting for us to go for a walk on the beach."

Put like that, it did sound a little silly. Rachel nodded and started down the steps. The day was too cold to go barefoot, so as she started across the beach she ignored the sand that inevitably sifted into her shoes. By unspoken agreement she and Luke headed toward the harder, wet sand left by the retreating tide.

A sudden gust of cold air stung her cheeks and whipped her short curls around her face. Instead of tucking herself into her collar, Rachel lifted her face and spread her arms. She strode into the wind, reveling in the feeling. She felt lifted out of her depression, as free as the gulls that dipped and wheeled above the choppy ocean. By habit Rachel scanned the beach as they walked. Among the pebbles and damp seaweed and broken shells she often found a perfect sand dollar or even a Japanese float, particularly in the winter.

Slowly she began to lose her tension. What Luke had said the day they talked down here was true. There was something so big, so eternal, about the ocean that her own problems began to seem petty and finite.

In a way, Rachel realized, she was frightened and resentful of the forces that had taken over her life. Sometimes she felt as though she were in the midst of a nightmare. How could all this be true? Being shot at, finding a dead body, making passionate love to an undercover federal agent who could easily disappear from her life as abruptly as he had appeared in it…. Here, walking on the beach as she'd done hundreds of times, she could almost believe none of it was real. But the funny thing was, she also felt free, freer than she had ever been in her life. It was as though all of this had wrenched her from her moorings. She could choose her own direction now. Which was far simpler than it sounded when her heart called her one way and her reason another.

She stole a sidelong look at Luke. As though sensing her scrutiny he turned his head to meet her gaze. His eyes were gray and bleak, his face tired.

On impulse Rachel took her hand out of her pocket and slipped it into the crook of his arm. Some of the tiredness left his face and he smiled, squeezing her hand between his arm and body. They continued to walk without talking, but the small contact was companionable. She matched his stride, sometimes her hip lightly bumped his. It was a nice feeling.

The beach stretched ahead and behind them like an endless pale ribbon, empty except for them. Driftwood logs were thrown randomly against the base of the bluff, which was twenty feet high and made of crumbling orangish clay cut by an occasional narrow canyon. Now that the resort had been left far behind, there were no signs of human habitation.

Rachel had glanced back and noticed how diminished in size even the huge rock stacks were when Luke said suddenly, "Rachel, I'm discouraged as hell."

He sounded lifeless, not himself. He'd talked about giving up, she thought in alarm, but did he mean it?

"You mean about finding the gold?"

His mouth twisted and he hunched his shoulders. "Worse. I'm beginning to wonder if it's even here. I'll tell you, maybe we've all made a monumental mistake. Maybe your husband wasn't Bill Sand at all. I haven't found even a sliver of real evidence since I got here to prove that he was."

"But . . . what he said about the bridge?"

"Could be interpreted a million ways. We read into it what we wanted to see."

Rachel was getting confused, even a little angry. "He was planning to sell the resort, remember? And he was gone every winter, just like you said."

"God." His steps slowed and he rubbed his fingers against his forehead. "I was so damned sure he was Bill Sand, I never made any effort to look for proof that he wasn't. We could have checked the airline records, any number of things. Maybe he had a nice little pied-à-terre someplace warm, just like you suggested. Maybe he even had a woman there, and that's why he was going to sell and move without telling you."

Wrenching her hand away, Rachel stopped in her tracks. She watched him walk several steps before he realized she was no longer with him.

"But you told me you *knew*!" she cried. "You didn't have a picture, but you had evidence! Remember?"

He was facing her, the wind blowing his hair back from his face. In his eyes was the bleakness she'd seen earlier, and more.

"I thought I knew," he said. "I still think I'm right. But I could be wrong. That's what I'm saying, Rachel. I could be wrong."

Panic rose in her chest, almost choking her. She stumbled a couple of steps backward as though she'd been given a hard push. "This is a fine time to tell me!" she yelled. "Do you know what you've done to my life? How could you make a mistake like this?"

"I didn't say it was a mistake!" Suddenly he was shouting too. "But, damn it, nobody is perfect!"

"Perfect!" Her voice rose another octave and she stared incredulously at him. "Perfect!"

That was when, mysteriously, a giggle bubbled in her throat, followed by another. A minute later she was doubled over with laughter. She collapsed onto the sand, laughing until tears appeared in her eyes. Through the blur she saw Luke, staring at her with such astonishment that she began to laugh at his expression instead.

"I'm sorry," she managed to get out at last, between chuckles.

"Can you let me in on the joke?" he asked, his tone acerbic.

"There...there really isn't one." She wiped her damp cheeks with the back of her hand. "It was just the way you said it. Maybe I'm a little hysterical. But do you know, we were actually having a fight! Really kind of a childish one."

He shoved his hands into his pockets. "I noticed."

Rachel became aware that the sand was wet and soaking through the seat of her jeans. "Ugh," she mumbled, scrambling to her feet. She wiped ineffectually at her bottom.

For the first time all day there was a spark of sexual interest in Luke's eyes as he watched. "Would you like some help?"

She wrinkled her nose. "What kind?"

He swatted her lightly, his hand lingering for an instant. "This kind."

"Oh, Luke." There was a smile in Rachel's voice. Standing on tiptoe, she slipped her arms around his neck. "I *am* sorry." Not waiting for his response, she brushed her lips over his.

He put his hands on her hips and held her slightly away from him. His expression was grave. "Rachel, you have every right to be mad."

"About what?" Her tone was astonishingly frivolous, almost gay. "Because you aren't perfect?"

"Is that funny?" The words had a snap to them.

She swallowed another giggle. "Of course it isn't! Not the way you mean. It's just...oh, Luke, if there's anybody in the world less perfect than me, I don't know who it is! I'm the one who married a crook! And you're apologizing to me!"

"Rachel, damn it!" He dropped his hands to his sides and made a jerky motion as though he intended to turn away but couldn't make himself. "Think what I've done to you! What if I was wrong? Can you just forget all this, like it never happened?"

"No." She smiled. "Luke, we both know you aren't wrong. Jack did it. The gold is here somewhere. He was a louse, and you've done me a favor. So quit feeling guilty."

There was a peculiar look on his face. "You're so sure?"

"Very sure," she said firmly.

A small wry smile curved his lips. "Thank you," he said huskily.

"You're quite welcome." They smiled at each other for a long moment. Then Rachel tucked her hand into the crook of his arm again. "Shall we head back?"

His sigh was almost imperceptible. "Why not?"

They began to walk, retracing their footprints in the damp, hard sand. The wind gusted now into their faces, and Rachel noticed how quickly the clouds had closed in.

She was cold and getting tired. That made it a strange time for her to be hit quite forcibly with a fresh realization of how attractive Luke was. She had felt his presence all day, but hadn't really *looked* at him. Now the wind blew his short hair back from his face, exposing it in stark relief. Even as she was studying him he gave her a sidelong, rueful smile. A warm glow started in her stomach.

Rachel remembered with astonishment that she had once worried that he was like Jack.

The ridiculous but touching argument they'd just had showed how wrong she had been. Jack had never really cared about anyone but himself. In Luke's position, he would have been angry at his failure to find the money. Luke was upset not because he had failed but because he might have hurt her.

That she'd worried at all showed what a low her confidence had sunk to. Even then she'd known Luke better than that. He was a study not in contradictions, as Jack had been, but in complexity, and he was nothing like Jack.

Feeling curiously comforted by her conclusion, she said aloud, "Tell me what you found out this morning." She was vaguely surprised that she wanted to know, and pleased at how remote her discovery of the body seemed. What she wanted most of all was to hear Luke's voice, talk to him, know what he was thinking. "Do they have any idea when Walt died? Did anyone hear a car or anything?"

Luke shook his head. "Nobody heard or saw anything. Which somehow doesn't surprise me. A silencer might have been used. But even if it wasn't, with the door closed, those thick log walls, nobody occupying any of the nearest cabins..." He shrugged. "As for the time, the coroner thinks late evening, somewhere between nine and eleven. Perfect planning for someone intending to commit a murder. Late enough so that there wasn't much activity around here, or chance of being seen. But unlike in the middle of the night, nobody would think twice about a car coming or going. My guess is he parked out on the highway and slipped through the woods."

"Yes." She was silent for a moment. "Do you think Walt intended to meet him?"

"Yep. I think they knew each other. Which is tough to figure. I can't help thinking about the third partner. But, damn it, Willis took a grenade in his gut! He's dead. He can't be wandering around." Luke gave his head an impatient shake. "I don't know. Maybe Krupinski shot off his mouth while he was finishing out his enlistment, and whoever he told about the gold decided to cut himself in. I'm beginning to think he's welcome to it, if he can find it."

"But what if he can't?"

Luke didn't answer. Rachel shivered, only partly from the cold. A fine, sleety rain had begun to fall, stinging her face and soaking into her parka. She hunched her shoulders and buried her chin in her rolled collar, blinking to clear her eyelashes.

"Your friend the sheriff." Luke sounded as though he was musing aloud. "How competent is he?"

"I don't know," Rachel said honestly. "He has a good reputation as far as I know. But he was only elected three years ago, and I don't really know what his background was. Jack and he got to know each other in Vietnam." She crinkled her brow as she tried to remember. "I think George was an MP there, so I guess that's how he got started as a policeman."

"Is he from around here?"

Moving cold lips, she answered as well as she could recollect. "I think he moved here not long before I did. At least, that's the impression I had. Jack worked hard at helping him win the election." She added wryly, "Which isn't much of a recommendation, is it? But believe it or not, Jack was involved in a lot of respectable community activity. Anyway, the incumbent sheriff was totally incompetent, and George had an impressive-sounding background. I think people are happy with him."

Luke grunted. Rachel wasn't sure whether the sound indicated skepticism or an unwillingness to expose his mouth to the weather long enough to speak intelligibly.

"Does his background matter, anyway?" she asked. "I mean, there are so many other people involved in the investigation. Surely if they're competent..."

Luke shook his head. "He'll make the important decisions." What she could see of his face looked unhappy. "I hate being at the mercy of local cops."

"Couldn't you call in some big shots?" she asked. "FBI or... or something?"

"Nope," Luke said, sounding faintly amused. "Not even 'or something.' If the murder had happened in the national park, the federal government would have jurisdiction. As it is..." He shrugged to make his point. After a moment he continued in a brooding voice. "But Myers seemed willing enough to work with me. And your state crime lab has a good reputation. Hell, I don't know what I'm worried about.''

''You and George don't like each other, do you?'' she said quietly, gazing up at a soaring gull.

Luke shot her a glance. For a while he didn't answer. When he did it was with a terse admission. ''We'll never be buddies.''

They trudged along in silence after that. Ahead, the resort came into view, for which Rachel was grateful, since she was freezing. Her mind had begun to wander. *Mad dogs and Englishmen,* she thought, but decided she did know when to come in out of the sun. Just not out of the sleet. But a walk had been a good idea, even if the weather had deteriorated on them. She felt worlds better than she had.

They turned to angle across the beach toward the stairs. Rachel slowed as she struggled with the uneven footing in the softer sand. From here she could see the outlet of the creek, turgid and gunmetal gray until it spread into a wide fan to cross the beach. The bridge stood solid and gray, the lodge above hunching in on itself, the shingles aged to a pale silvery gray, the roof a steep peak, the windows looking empty and sightless.

She seldom had occasion to be on the beach in this kind of weather. A chill crept up her spine as she gazed at her home with new eyes and realized how ominous it could look. The warm glow of light within and the charm of the old building were still there, but her feelings had been colored by the murder. Suddenly she could see the eerie painting that hung above her fireplace. It superimposed itself on the scene until the two were one, mysterious, with that creepy impression of something ominous lurking behind the obvious.

Rachel gave her head a quick, hard shake. That damn painting had nearly given her nightmares. She refused to let it distort the way she saw reality. There were no dark shadows, only an icy rain. She made herself remember the sunny days—even that morning, before the storm moved in, with the frost sparkling on the ground and the tiny-paned windows of the lodge etched with beautiful, intricate patterns.

But then, as her thoughts made another leap, she suddenly saw Jack, as vividly as though it had been yesterday, standing in the living room in front of the painting. He was smiling as he looked at it. It was a peculiar little smile, filled with pleasure and satisfaction. He had often stood there like that. It had bothered her then that he should so love a piece of art that was admittedly powerful but also disturbing.

Now her steps slowed further as she stared at the bridge and the lodge in the driving rain. Luke had drawn ahead, apparently unaware that she was no longer with him.

"Luke," she said, then with more urgency, "Luke!"

He stopped and turned. Only the top half of his face was visible. When he saw her expression, his own changed. His eyes became instantly alert; his head lifted like an animal scenting danger.

"What's wrong?" he asked sharply.

"I know where it is," she said. "I know where Jack hid the gold."

Chapter 12

Rachel and Luke crouched on the floor before the frame, which lay on its face on the rug. The tension in the room was electric. Luke had already ripped the paper covering off, and it was immediately obvious that they were looking at the back of a very old canvas. With exquisite care Luke eased it from the frame. Sinking back on his heels, he tilted up the stretched canvas. As the golden glow of colors appeared, Rachel drew in a slow, wondering breath. Beside her she heard Luke's sharp intake of air, his muttered exclamation. Triumph and something less definable filled her chest.

In the foreground, seated on an overturned Grecian column under a tree, was a mother nursing a baby. An old man with a white beard looked on. The tones were jewel-like, the woman's curves ripe in the manner of the time even as her face was serene and saintly, her eyes modestly cast down. Tiny cracks covered the surface. The colors were darkened with age, a little yellowed, yet still remarkable, with the shades of light and dark bringing uncanny life to the scene.

She couldn't begin to identify the artist, although vague memories from an art history class in college made her certain the painting was sixteenth century, of the Italian High Renaissance.

"How could he bear to hide it?" Rachel murmured. But in her memory she saw again Jack's smile and realized he hadn't cared about the painting; he had cared only about its value. His tastes, when she thought about it, had run more to the modern.

"Titian." Above her, Luke announced the single word with deep satisfaction. Twisting her head to look up, Rachel saw the jubilation on his face. Eyes glittering, he was staring at the painting, talking as though to himself. "I'll bet it's a Titian."

But then his gaze shifted to her face. He laughed softly at her astonishment. "No, I wasn't an art curator in another life. But I've been involved in a few cases of art theft," he explained. "Once we recovered a stolen Titian. This has the same feel to me."

Rachel plopped to the floor, crossing her legs. "Is it stolen, do you think?"

Luke's answer was dry. "Undoubtedly. But valuable nonetheless. The market in stolen art is thriving."

"I've read about it," she said absently, without taking her gaze from the canvas. What had been an abstract world of crime to her had suddenly become real and very distasteful. This painting should hang where everyone could see it, not in a silent, sterile room for one greedy man's gaze.

"It was a good investment for Jack," Luke said. The triumph in his voice was gone, leaving a clinical tone. "I'll bet it has appreciated since he bought it. Have you seen the prices at auctions lately?" He shook his head in amazement, adding, "This is small, and not well-known, but I think we've definitely found our millions. The only catch is, if the painting is stolen and has to be returned, Uncle Sam is going to be the one left empty-handed. That's going to make a lot of people unhappy. I'm glad it's not my problem."

The telephone rang. Rachel scrambled to her feet. "I'll get it."

The caller turned out to be the sheriff, who told her that he needed to talk to her and Luke again about the investigation.

Rachel agreed reluctantly. She couldn't think of anything on earth she wanted less than to spend another few hours talking about Walt Krupinski. Besides, what could she tell George that she hadn't already gone over with Detective Myers?

"Are you coming now, George?" she asked.

"Tomorrow morning will be soon enough."

A sudden, dismaying thought popped into her mind. Would Luke still be here then? Panic lodged in her throat, making it impossible for her to speak. Why hadn't she realized what finding the painting meant? Luke had what he'd come for. The end she had tried not to think about was here.

The sheriff was saying something. *Oh, God,* she thought with fresh dismay, George didn't know about the painting. She would have to tell him they'd found proof that Jack had been a crook. George would take it hard. He and Jack had been good friends for nearly twenty years, with trust and obligation on both sides. Finding out how much of their relationship had been a lie would have to be a blow for him.

"Rachel? Is something the matter?"

"No, no! It's just that I have something to tell you." Taking a deep breath, she plunged on. "George, I know this is going to upset you, but..." There was no way to say it but bluntly. "We found the money Jack stole."

"Where?" he demanded harshly.

"It's a painting," she said quietly. "It was hidden under the one hung over the fireplace."

There was a long, impenetrable silence. At last he spoke again, sounding stunned and a little distant. "So Jack did have it after all."

"Yes. I'm sorry, George," Rachel said with deep pity, but sensing how useless her sympathy must be. "I know how you must feel."

He didn't respond to her attempt at comfort, which neither surprised nor offended her. Instead, his voice gritty with shock, he said abruptly, "I'll talk to you later, Rachel," and severed the connection. It was a moment before she replaced the receiver.

In the living room, she found that Luke had lifted out the modern oil of the bridge and propped the two paintings side by side against the couch. He was standing in front of them, but when she appeared in the doorway he turned his head to look at her quizzically.

She responded to the unspoken inquiry. "That was the sheriff."

"Did you tell him?"

She gave a brief nod.

Luke's expression grew thoughtful, but there was compassion in his eyes as well. He didn't comment, however. He seemed to know instinctively when it was best not to say anything. She thought wryly that it gave him an advantage over mere mortals who rambled and bumbled their way along at ill-chosen times. His silence now was merely part and parcel of his ability to stand back, to become detached from a scene when it suited him.

Of course, Rachel thought with a flash of resentment and pain, *he has no emotional involvement in any of this. It's just a job to him.*

The resentment vanished in an aching wave of loneliness that separated her from him even though he was still physically present. How could she say goodbye with any dignity? she wondered with despair.

As she stood there, Luke's attention wandered back to the two paintings. He crouched easily in front of them, resting his forearms on his knees.

Grateful that he wasn't looking at her, Rachel tried to take slow, even breaths, calming her panic, making herself face her fear. It was as though a terrible chasm of emptiness had opened before her and she would fall into it if she took a step.

She had lived these past, too short weeks for the moment, refusing to let herself envision the future. Now her mind raced back over their time together. She saw herself and Luke laughing together, arguing, vehemently explaining their views. She saw the tenderness in his eyes when she had exposed her deepest hurts, heard the rawness in his voice when he told her about the men he had killed, the waste he sometimes thought he was making of his life.

She had never been able to talk to anyone as she could to Luke. She found it incomprehensible that he might walk away and that she might never see him again.

She tried to make herself think of all the sensible plans she'd made. After selling Sahale, she would have all the money she needed. She would begin a new life with law school, just as she had always dreamed. And she would have time to recover her emotional equilibrium, to regain confidence in herself.

If only it all didn't sound so bleak, so lonely!

"I'll bet Jack commissioned this specially," Luke said suddenly. "Unless he cut it down to size?" He ran his fingers along the rough edge of the thin masonite board on which the bridge was painted.

Rachel made herself look down at the bleak depiction of the bridge, with its veils of gray. Somehow it no longer had the power to make her feel anything. Her sense of failure had for so long been a rope also twisted with strands of guilt and grief. Now failure and guilt were gone, leaving only regret for the lost years and a lingering uncertainty about her ability to judge people.

She managed to consider Luke's point. It helped, she discovered, to think about something prosaic.

Jack's choice of the masonite board instead of another stretched canvas made sense. It was less than a quarter of an inch thick, and since it didn't have to be fastened in any way to the valuable painting beneath, there was no risk of damage. The back had been covered by brown butcher paper, on which had been affixed a card bearing the title of the bridge painting and the artist's name:

P. Cannell, *Gray over Dark*.

The frame itself was very old, of heavy carved wood with gilding that had crackled with age. Rachel had no idea if it was the original, although the heavy opulence seemed in keeping with the sixteenth century.

"I can check the receipts," she offered, grasping for something to focus on. She had to get a grip on herself before Luke turned and looked at her. I have ones for all the paintings."

He said wryly over his shoulder, "Do you have one for a Titian?"

She forced a smile in case he was looking, then went over to sit at her desk. In one cubby was a small wooden box that held a sheaf of receipts and appraisals filed by artist's name. *Gray over Dark* was the only painting by that artist that Jack had owned. She took in the date and the price, both of which were scrawled in an unfamiliar hand.

"The timing is perfect," she said.

"I'm not surprised." After a brief silence, Luke straightened decisively. "Listen, I'd better call in. We're going to want to get insurance on this right away. And it'll need to be crated adequately for shipment. I can't exactly carry it onto the plane."

The professional at work, Rachel thought, and pain squeezed her chest. He was going to leave just like that. And there was nothing she could say.

Luke seemed to become aware of her unusual silence, because instead of heading for the telephone, he walked toward her, a small frown creasing his brow. He stopped in front of her, so close she could feel the warmth of his body. When she stubbornly refused to meet his eyes, he closed one hand on her chin to lift her face. She stiffened, resisting the pressure of his fingers, longing all the while to throw her arms around his neck and bury her face in his chest.

She and Luke both heard the sound of a car at the same time. Summoning her reserves of emotional strength, Rachel twisted neatly away. She was proud of her steady voice. "It's Monday, remember. I'd better see who that is."

"We need to talk." His voice was gentle, but unyielding.

"Later," she said, slipping quickly from the room.

Inside, she was breaking apart. If he had to leave, she wanted him to go *now*, just to climb into his car and drive away. She told herself she couldn't bear to hear excuses and vague promises, at which she would have to smile and act as though she believed him.

But in her heart she knew that wasn't how it would be. What she really feared was that he would ask her to go with him. Panic squeezed her again. She wasn't ready for this kind of decision! She loved him, but hadn't she been certain she loved Jack, too? Yes, she was older and wiser, but should she take that kind of risk again, when she had made such a dreadful mistake the last time?

With Luke's help she had begun to regain faith in herself. Someday she might even believe that it was possible to have made such a fundamental error in judgment and yet still have confidence in herself. But not yet. And this was hardest of all, because she had never been as emotionally vulnerable to anyone as she was to Luke. She was painfully confused, because on one level she was sure of him. He was nothing like Jack! But there were other kinds of mistakes. Two well-meaning people could still be mismatched. And that would hurt her beyond recovery.

What would it really be like to share his life? she wondered, tentatively trying to imagine something she hadn't let herself consider until now. Even if she could reconcile herself to what he did, to the secrets and the violence, what would it be like on a day-to-day level? To have to smile and say, "Have a good month at work, dear?" to a man who was disappearing undercover? Or welcome him cheerily back when he arrived tired and gaunt, with shadows in his eyes? Or mourn when one time he didn't come back, forever picturing his last moments, what the bullet or knife or car had done to his body? But wouldn't it be worse to spend her life wondering what had happened to him, never knowing even whether he lived or died?

She was drawn from her self-defeating thoughts by her surprise at discovering the sheriff's unmarked car parked in front and the sheriff himself already stepping onto the porch.

"George!" she said, holding open the heavy door. "Come on in! I didn't expect you."

He tried to smile, his bulky shoulders moving in a shrug. "Just wanted to see it with my own two eyes."

Rachel hesitated, biting her lip, then nodded. Surely Luke wouldn't mind.

The lodge was very quiet, the door to the gift shop closed and the restaurant dim and deserted, without the usual warmth and bustle and tantalizing smells. In the apartment, Luke stood in front of the desk, exactly where Rachel had left him. Their eyes met before his shifted beyond her shoulder. He didn't appear pleased, but when he looked at her again, his expression was resigned.

"Sheriff." He nodded coolly.

The sheriff matched the nod with an equally curt one. He crossed the room and stopped in front of the two paintings that were propped against the back of the couch. Rachel went to Luke's side, watching with pity as the sheriff looked for a long time at the painting. The only sign of emotion was in his hands, which curled into impotent fists. Rachel understood his anger very well.

The sheriff turned at last, his movements slow and as if defeated. But when he faced them, one of his hands held a gun. Shocked, Rachel stared down the short barrel, feeling the world compress to a pitiless dark hole.

It took all Luke's self-possession to stand still, his hands at his sides. He longed to go for his gun or to smash that broad, meaty face in with his fists. Searing anger curled in his gut, but it left his mind working coldly, calculatingly. That was how it had always been with him. The only difference this time was the fear. He'd had guns pointed at him before. He was discovering that it wasn't the same at all when that gun was pointed at the woman he loved.

He'd been a damned fool. His instincts had screamed for him not to trust this man. Why the hell hadn't he stayed silent that morning, let them cart Krupinski's body away without entrusting them with his own identity or the story behind Walt's presence at Sahale?

From the beginning he hadn't liked it that the sheriff was Jack's best friend. If Jack had confided in anyone, this was the man. But because of the uniform, Luke hadn't seriously considered the sheriff a suspect. He was disgusted at his naivety. The result was that he and Rachel were looking down the barrel of a gun held by the law enforcement officer who would be in charge of the investigation into their murder.

The sheriff smiled unpleasantly. He seemed to be enjoying himself. "It was good of you to find my...retirement funds, shall we say?"

Out of the corner of his eye, Luke saw bewilderment mixed with horror on Rachel's face. "George..." She was pleading for this not to be happening, Luke knew. "I don't understand."

Again he smiled, cruelty underlying his mock regret. "Let me introduce myself. Chuck Willis. Jack's old partner, although he would have liked to forget that. But I earned this." He nodded toward the painting without taking his gaze from them. "The name I've been using is borrowed. Pity I can't give it back now that I don't need it anymore."

It all came crystal clear in Luke's mind. The grenade that had supposedly killed Willis had been American. Not an accident at all. A messy death had covered a change in identity. Damn the Agency. Hadn't they checked dental records, fingerprints, whatever was left? Or had they docilely accepted a dog tag?

"You mean you...killed someone?" Rachel sounded both appalled and incredulous.

"He took a grenade in the belly," the sheriff said indifferently. "Don't worry—he died quickly. And, conveniently for me, there wasn't enough left of him to bury." Self-satisfaction oozed into his voice. "I'd chosen him very carefully, you know. I spent a couple of months finding the perfect identity, but it was worth it. He had a useful background, his enlistment was done. I waited until he was flying out that night. It wasn't hard.''

Rachel looked sick. The callousness was enough to make anyone feel that way, Luke thought. More immediately relevant was the fact that the man's willingness to murder once in cold blood made it highly unlikely he would show any mercy now. The only positive aspect to the situation that Luke could think of was the sheriff's desire to chat. He should have gunned them right down, but he was enjoying the chance to brag.

But he wasn't a complete fool. The gun waved toward Luke. His voice hard, the sheriff said, "Open your shirt, very carefully."

Not seeing any alternative, Luke did as directed.

"The gun, please. And don't be foolish."

Luke slowly took out his gun.

"On the floor. Kick it toward me—gently."

Outwardly relaxed, Luke bent forward, following the instructions. God, he hated being so helpless. He at least wanted to see it coming when he died. But nothing happened. He straightened, and the sheriff aimed again at Rachel as he stooped to recover Luke's gun, then shoved it into his belt.

Why didn't he just shoot them? Luke wondered. But whatever his reasoning, the more time he gave them, the more likely it was that they'd have a chance. Luke shifted slightly, feeling the pressure in the small of his back where a second, smaller weapon nestled. He didn't always wear it, but with the gathering sense of danger these last days he'd made a practice of taking double measures.

Rachel shot him a panicky glance, which he met with as much reassurance as he could muster.

He would have given a great deal to do something, say something, but he didn't dare. The bastard must like

Rachel, or else he wouldn't have enjoyed bragging. She could take advantage of that and lengthen their odds. But would she realize it?

He saw a flicker of something in her eyes, and she wrenched her gaze away. Luke felt like cheering when she addressed the sheriff in a calm and even sympathetic voice that quivered only a little.

"Why did you and Jack wait so long to spend your money? After taking so many chances, I'd have thought you'd want to enjoy it. Or did Jack double-cross you, too, like he did Walt?"

A nasty expletive amply described the sheriff's opinion of Jack Brewer. "I tracked him down and he told me things had gone wrong on the European end, that he'd had to run empty-handed. I didn't believe him, especially after the roadblocks he'd put up against my finding him in the first place. But what could I do? He offered to help me run for sheriff, make me respectable, and I accepted. I wasn't going to let him out of my sight. He wouldn't have gotten away with it. But then he had to go and die."

"If you didn't believe Jack, didn't you ever look for it?" Rachel asked. Luke knew what a lousy liar she was, but she was nicely managing a tone of polite, understanding interest. He could see how rigidly she held herself, but he could also see her pride. She wouldn't crumple and beg. She was using her head, giving them time. The only problem was, so far the gun was steady as a rock, with her the target. If Luke made even the smallest movement, Rachel would be dead.

"Yeah, I looked right after the funeral," the sheriff said, smiling slightly. "I'm afraid I left you a little bit of a mess. Actually, I've left you a couple. Krupinski didn't bleed too badly, though, did he?"

"No, not too badly," Rachel said with admirable calm. "Was it you who shot at us? And set the fire?"

"Not the fire. Krupinski was a fool. What if he'd burned up the painting? But the shots... I didn't like your friend here." He looked coldly at Luke. "I still don't like him, but I wouldn't have tried to kill him if I'd known he was a fed. Until I had my hands on this—" he jerked his head toward the painting "—shooting a federal agent was too dangerous. This place would have been crawling with his buddies if I'd eliminated him."

"It still will be," Luke remarked. "I've already made a call. A couple of FBI men are on their way."

The sheriff smiled. "It's too bad all they'll find will be two dead bodies. Which *I* will have discovered. Speaking of which..." He glanced around the room, at the wide sweep of windows. On one side was the ocean, on the other the highway and wooded ridge beyond it. The view clearly made the sheriff nervous. Luke tensed, balancing on the balls of his feet, but it was too dangerous to try anything now.

"Outside," the sheriff said suddenly, but not as though it were an order. He seemed to be reflecting aloud. "I think your friend here is going to have shot you," he told Rachel. "The gun will have gone off in the scuffle, taking care of him, too. Maybe one of you will have gone over the bluff. Yeah. Nice touch."

"Why don't you just take the painting and go?" Rachel said quietly, not moving. "We can't stop you. There's no reason to kill us. It'll just make more trouble for you."

He laughed shortly. "I'd never get away. Now, no more talk." His voice had hardened. "Outside." He gestured with the gun, and the jerky motion made Luke more wary. The sheriff was becoming tense.

But they had to move. It was now or never. Luke walked forward very slowly, keeping his body language deliberately nonthreatening. He waited until he was abreast of the

couch and the sheriff had taken a couple of steps back to
maintain some distance.

Then, in a split second, he shoved Rachel behind him and
snatched up the painting. It was a perfect shield, maybe
three by five feet.

Snarling, the sheriff raised the gun, but Luke waved the
painting in front of his body, bobbing and weaving behind
it so he didn't leave any one part of himself exposed for too
long. "Going to shoot me through it?" he mocked, prepar-
ing to play a deadly game of cat and mouse. Every nerve he
had seemed to be standing on end. The canvas wouldn't stop
a bullet if the sheriff's fury triumphed over his greed.

He considered telling Rachel to grab his gun, but she'd be
too slow in using it. He'd never forgive himself if she died
trying to be a heroine at his behest. But while he held the
painting he didn't have a hand free to grab the damn thing
himself. He didn't dare break eye contact with the madman
in front of him; his only hope was to read any glimmer of an
intention before it crystallized into action.

Trying to make herself as tiny as possible behind Luke,
Rachel was both terrified and angry. The sheriff had mur-
dered two people and was planning to murder her and Luke,
and he expected them to walk passively to their death.
Oddly, in the way petty things have of seeming to matter
more than important ones, what rankled the most was his
casual confession to having been the one who'd ransacked
her rooms. She'd had a vivid flash of memory—the pages
torn out of books she'd saved from her childhood, the
shattered dishes and jam ground into a favorite dress.
Wanton, hateful destruction by a man she'd believed was a
friend.

She couldn't just hide here, waiting to be saved again by
Luke. The sheriff was screaming obscenities, telling Luke
explicitly which parts of his anatomy he planned to shoot,

and Luke was taunting him in return. Rachel couldn't imagine what he had in mind by deliberately enraging the sheriff. Maybe it was an attempt to divert his attention long enough for her to get away. She wouldn't disappoint him.

Luke had carefully maneuvered them in a semicircle, so that the French door that led to the outside was no more than ten feet away. It looked to her like a hundred yards. But she couldn't let herself think, or she would freeze. With a fervent, silent prayer, Rachel bolted. She was lunging for the doorknob when she heard a crack and felt a wind whip her hair. The door swung open and she fell through, sobbing for breath. The wet sleet slapped her in the face, made the two wooden steps treacherous. She slipped and fell forward, so that she landed hard on her hands and knees on the small brick patio. She scrambled forward, not daring to look behind her, but before she could regain her feet, a hand snatched her by the collar and twisted until she gagged. She struggled frantically until she felt the pressure of the cold gun against her temple.

What little she could see of it was so frightening that she pressed her eyes shut, a whimper escaping from a well of fear so deep she couldn't control it.

"Let her go." Luke's voice, almost unrecognizable, was an icy whiplash.

Rachel opened her eyes. Through a glassy film of terror she saw him at the foot of the stairs, only a few feet away. He still held the painting, but in the other hand was a gun. His gaze didn't waver from the sheriff's, as though he expected by sheer willpower to compel his obedience.

"Let's trade," Luke suggested in a cold, hard voice. "If you kill her, you can't have the painting."

"I'll kill you both!" Rachel could hear her captor's hysteria, feel it in the gun that trembled against her head.

"God, please, please!" she whispered. Tears slipped down her cheeks, mingling with the icy rain that had already soaked her hair and thin flannel shirt.

Her only grip on reality was the sight of Luke's face. He looked dangerous, his anger so icy it might shatter. And she loved him. She loved even this side of him so much that it hurt.

If only someone would hear them or wander around the end of the lodge, she thought, frantic. But the hope was almost nonexistent. This narrow stretch of lawn between the steep drop to the creek and her part of the lodge couldn't be seen from the parking lot. The sheriff knew that no employees were here today. Only four of the cabins were occupied, and who would be out for a stroll in this weather?

Suddenly she realized what Luke was doing. While he was talking, he'd been edging his way over to the edge of the bluff. Now, with a swift movement, he lifted the painting over the low split-rail fence so that it dangled above the precipice. Rachel jerked in instinctive protest. Luke now stood exposed, without even the illusion of protection.

"Let's trade," he called to the sheriff again. "Killing us isn't going to do any good if you can't walk away with the money."

The sheriff began to curse again, words that might have been shocking another time sliding into a monotonous, incomprehensible jumble. He half dragged Rachel as he took long strides toward the fence so he could look over. She stumbled and almost fell, but he pulled her up by the collar.

They could all see the thirty-foot drop now, the tumble of jagged driftwood below and the high waters of the creek merging sullenly with a salt water tide. The painting would never survive the fall.

Rachel could feel the sheriff's fury and indecision, his hunger for the wealth that was slipping away. The gun barrel was grinding into her temple, hurting. Luke hadn't looked at Rachel yet, but now, for a fleeting second he did. In his eyes was an electrifying blend of love and fear. Her numbness crumbled before his fear. How could she ever have wondered what she meant to him, what he would sacrifice for her?

She had begun to shake from the cold, and her teeth were chattering. She clamped down her jaw, terrified to make any tiny movement that might anger the sheriff. The brutal shove on her back took her completely by surprise. With stunning force she landed on her outstretched hands, which slid out from under her on the wet, icy grass. She ended jarringly on her face, but she was beyond feeling pain. She rolled over to see Luke begin to pull the painting back.

A spark of fire leaped from the sheriff's gun, and Rachel screamed. But Luke didn't seem to be hit. He fired in return. As though in slow motion, the sheriff recoiled, reeled backward, staggered against the low fence. The graying, time-rotted rails splintered apart and he seemed to hang in space with a look on his face that Rachel would never forget. Then he vanished over the edge.

The silence that followed was eerie. Luke dropped the painting to the grass as though it had ceased to be of importance. He walked forward slowly and stopped where the fence ended in a gaping hole. For a long time he just looked, the gun hanging loosely from his hand. When he turned to Rachel, his face was weary, his wet hair plastered to his head. His eyes were dark with anger and resignation and sadness. With astonishment and then a burst of love, she realized that despite everything Luke hadn't wanted to kill the sheriff.

She stumbled to her feet as he came toward her. The look
on his face changed, and he shoved the pistol into his waistband and snatched her into an embrace so tight it hurt. He
was shaking a little, or maybe it was only her. All she knew
was that he was warm and alive and that she loved him.

The next instant he bent his head and kissed her with a
desperate, devouring passion that she answered from the
intensity of her own relief. When at last the kiss ended she
caught only a glimpse of the strain on his face and the
haunted look in his eyes before he leaned his cheek against
the top of her head.

In a low, hoarse voice he said, "I didn't know it was possible to be so scared."

Rachel tried to speak and failed. The best she could do
was to hug him harder. It seemed to be enough. How could
it not be? Right now, just being able to hold each other
again was a miracle.

The next few hours were a rerun of the morning. The resort crawled with policemen, and Rachel and Luke repeated their story again and again. FBI men appeared and
then departed with the painting, which had been carefully
crated and seemed undamaged by the wet. Once Rachel took
an incautious glance out the window. A body bag was being
carried across the floodlit lawn. Biting her lip, she hastily
turned away, blocking from her mind a picture of the man
in it.

But then her gaze met Luke's, and her own feelings were
forgotten in a rush of love and pity. He stood looking out
the window, watching the procession pass. One of the policemen said something to him, but he didn't hear it. His
face was impassive, but his eyes were bleak. When Rachel
touched him lightly on the arm, he blinked and looked at
her. He seemed to search her face for some answer she didn't
know if she could give, but what he saw seemed to satisfy

him, because she felt the taut muscles in his arm relax, saw the ghosts in his eyes retreat.

At last everyone else was gone. Looking beaten, Luke slumped on the couch, head down. Rachel went quietly into the kitchen and dumped her umpteenth cup of tea into the sink. Without much interest, she studied the contents of a cupboard. Surely something to eat would revive them, but she wasn't really hungry.

A sound behind her made Rachel turn, startled. Luke stood in the kitchen doorway, shoulder propped against the jamb. They looked at each other for a minute, then he grimaced. "I can't believe we're finally alone. This has been the longest day of my life."

"Yes." She thought back to the morning and its horrific beginning. With a shudder she tried to focus again on the rows of cans and boxes in the cupboard. She had a vision of steam curling up from homemade soup, the smell of freshly baked bread. But she was too tired.

The words that popped out of her mouth caught her by surprise. "Poor Henry Kirk. All he wanted was to date me."

"He'll never know we suspected him." Luke's voice became rough but uncertain. "Rachel, will you come here?"

His vulnerability tore open her carefully constructed veneer of control. Two steps and she was in his arms again, soaking up his strength, feeling despite everything the spark of physical reaction.

One big hand captured her face and lifted it so that he could see her expression. "I love you," he said in that same voice, which hardly sounded like his own.

"Oh, Luke." Her mouth began to tremble. She was going to cry. "I love you," she whispered. The words were a beginning, but they sounded like an end, too.

Quietly he said, "I know," but she saw the swift alarm in his eyes, the wariness. He was afraid. "I can't do without you,'' he said with an intensity that made her forget everything but his needs. And hers. ''Marry me, Rachel.''

She couldn't tear her gaze away from his. Primitive exultation swept her, because he cared so much. A million things passed through her mind: the sweetness of their lovemaking, the dangers of his job. Her qualms. But above all there was the look in his eyes, and the brush with death. She'd learned something about taking risks. Out there in the sleet, Luke had risked everything for her. And she had discovered that if love didn't have any guarantees, neither did life. And without one, the other wasn't worth much.

She blinked away tears. ''Yes.'' Her answer was barely audible, a murmur of sound. She swallowed, tried again, stronger. ''Yes, I'll marry you.''

Luke looked blank for an instant, as though he'd been braced for her refusal. Then profound relief altered the lines of his face. He closed his eyes as he got a grip on himself. When he looked at her again, his gaze was fierce, his voice ragged. ''I thought I was going to lose you.''

Rachel reached up to caress his cheek. ''We almost lost each other,'' she said.

He made an odd sound and bent to kiss her, his mouth hard and desperate. Her lips parted, meeting his fierce need with soft acceptance. He held her so tightly that her breasts flattened against his chest and she felt every taut line of his body as though it were part of her. Beginning in her chest, where a last, icy core seemed to melt, a tide of slow, thick warmth ran through her until her knees began to quiver. Everything that had gone before was forgotten. Only this moment mattered. She was dizzy with happiness and a sort of astonished disbelief that she could be so lucky. She felt only the searing passion of his mouth, the rough, hungry touch of his hands on her back and hips, molding her closer to him.

But then, by slow degrees, the bruising force eased; the kiss became gentler. His fingers tangled in her hair while the other hand held her at the waist. With his tongue he tasted her mouth as though he'd never known such sweetness. The kiss made promises of passion and need, but of tenderness, too.

When Luke lifted his head he was smiling, and his eyes glowed so softly that Rachel thought she could fall into them and never surface. His mouth, which could look so hard, was full and sensuous, with a gentle quirk that made her heart lurch.

"I've been a fool," he murmured, shaking his head. He moved his gaze over her face as though memorizing the curve of her cheekbone, the velvet passion in her eyes, the quivering softness of her mouth. "Holding myself back, afraid to lose control. What I was really afraid of was that you wouldn't love me."

"But I always have," she protested shakily. "You must have known."

"I thought you might hate me when this was all over. I know there's a part of me that frightens you. And..." His mouth twisted and a shadow darkened his eyes. "When you're dependent on someone to protect you, it's easy to think you're in love with them. Afterward, when you don't need them anymore..."

Beneath his elaborate explanation Rachel heard the uncertainty. She thought she understood the reason why he wasn't sure of her, and it hurt. She pressed her hands against his chest and pushed, although he didn't let her go.

"Damn it, Luke!" she cried. "It's because I was dumb enough to marry Jack, isn't it? Now you think I pick men for the wrong reasons! Well, let me tell you—"

Giving her a little shake, he interrupted her firmly. "What I think is that your taste has improved remarkably. And after all," he added, straight-faced, "who can judge that better than me?"

Her temper sizzled and went out like a fire doused with water. A reluctant smile curved her mouth as she thought how characteristically Luke that remark was: bracing, self-mocking, humorous and definitely right. The wretched man was always right!

"Just don't forget I love you," she informed him a little pugnaciously.

"Heaven forbid," he murmured, amusement deep in his eyes.

"Because your job is going to make you a lousy husband," she informed him. "But I'm marrying you anyway and I'm going to put up with it, because..." She drew the word out, paused to tantalize.

The gleam of amusement became laughter. "Because?"

"Because..." She relaxed her arms and began to move her splayed hands in caressing circles on his chest, seeking his shirt opening so she could feel the warmth of his skin. "Because I like you," she said innocently. "Why else?"

The curve of his mouth became more sensuous than amused. "There wouldn't be a little lust involved?"

"Well..." She leaned forward to press a loving kiss at the base of his throat. With mock reluctance she admitted, "Maybe a little."

"Good." Luke reached down to cup her buttocks in his hand and press her against him. "Because I have to admit to a little lust myself."

Her hips touching him so intimately, she tried for a tone of casual surprise. "Really? I'd never have guessed."

He leaned forward as though to kiss her but stopped a hairbreadth from her mouth. "Oh, by the way," he said, his voice low and husky. "Before you resign yourself to being, stuck with a lousy husband, I should tell you I'm hanging my job up. I think I'll go into private practice."

It was a moment before the words penetrated. Then, "What?" she demanded, jerking back.

He began to repeat himself, but she interrupted him. "Are you doing this for me?"

"No. It's been coming for a long time. I'm burned out. I'll admit I wasn't sure when I came here. And making a decision on my job got mixed up in my feelings for you. I didn't think I could have you unless I changed my life."

Rachel made herself say it. "But you can."

"That...makes me feel good. But I'm going to quit anyway." When she didn't say anything, he smiled coaxingly. "Listen, lady, how would you like to hang your shingle up with mine in, say, about three years?"

He was offering her the world, her dreams and his. Her answering smile was shaky and filled with newly unfurled joy. "Sounds good."

They looked at each other for a long moment, smiling, saying things with their eyes that words seemed inadequate for. At last, in a gritty, shaken voice, Luke said again, "I love you, Rachel."

"And I love you," she said fervently.

Then there were no more words as Luke swept her up in his arms and headed with long strides out of the kitchen, toward the stairs. Rachel laid her head on Luke's shoulder and thought dreamily that tonight they wouldn't have to hide in the darkness. She wanted to see Luke's face, have him see her. Because there wouldn't be any tears this time. She'd faced all of her fears, real and imagined. Tonight there would be only love and passion.

* * * * *

Silhouette Desire ®

CHILDREN OF DESTINY

A trilogy by Ann Major

Three power-packed tales of irresistible passion and undeniable fate created by Ann Major to wrap your heart in a legacy of love.

PASSION'S CHILD — September

Years ago, Nick Browning nearly destroyed Amy's life, but now that the child of his passion—the child of her heart—was in danger, Nick was the only one she could trust....

DESTINY'S CHILD — October

Cattle baron Jeb Jackson thought he owned everything and everyone on his ranch, but fiery Megan MacKay's destiny was to prove him wrong!

NIGHT CHILD — November

When little Julia Jackson was kidnapped, young Kirk MacKay blamed himself. Twenty years later, he found her... and discovered that love could shine through even the darkest of nights.

Don't miss PASSION'S CHILD, DESTINY'S CHILD and NIGHT CHILD, three thrilling Silhouette Desires designed to heat up chilly autumn nights!

Silhouette Special Edition

THE O'HURLEYS! — CHANTEL'S STORY

from
Nora Roberts

Skin Deep

Available September 1988

The third in an exciting new series about the lives and loves of triplet sisters—

In May's *The Last Honest Woman* (SE #451), Abby finally met a man she could trust . . . then tried to deceive him to protect her sons.

In July's *Dance to the Piper* (SE #463), it took some very fancy footwork to get reserved recording mogul Reed Valentine dancing to effervescent Maddy's tune. . . .

In *Skin Deep* (SE #475), find out what kind of heat it takes to melt the glamorous Chantel's icy heart. Available in September.

Silhouette Intimate Moments

COMING
NEXT MONTH

#257 BUT THAT WAS YESTERDAY—Kathleen Eagle

Sage Parker had a busy life on the reservation, rebuilding his ranch and struggling to teach his people the value of the old tribal ways. Then Megan McBride became his boss and turned his familiar world upside down. She was everything a woman could be, and before Sage could back away, he realized she was also the only thing he needed.

#258 CODY DANIELS' RETURN—Marilyn Pappano

Border Patrol agent Cody Daniels had never wanted to see Mariah Butler again, but when she became a suspect in his latest investigation, all his old feelings for her resurfaced. His sense of duty wouldn't let him clear her without question, but his heart wouldn't let him betray the woman he was beginning to love all over again.

#259 DANGEROUS CHOICES—Jeanne Stephens

Abby Hogan had believed for years that Jason Cutter was a cold, uncaring man—until her job as an insurance investigator brought them together again. Abby soon discovered that she was interested in Jason, but old habits die hard, and only a dangerous confrontation with some real villains made her realize that what she felt was love.

#260 THIS ROUGH MAGIC—Heather Graham Pozzessere

Wolves were howling and the Halloween moon was full when Carly Kiernan came to the castle and met the count, a fascinating man who dressed in black and disappeared at will. Carly knew that everything would seem different in the light of day, but the morning only brought another question: why was she falling in love with a man whose very name was a mystery?